WHAT BECOMES US

MICAH PERKS

Outpost19 | San Francisco
outpost19.com

Perks, Micah
        What Becomes Us / Micah Perks
        ISBN 9781937402983 (pbk)

Library of Congress Control Number: 2016912997

This is a work of fiction. Names, characters, places and
incidents are either the product of the author's imagination
or are used fictitiously. The character of Joan is not meant as
a depiction of any of the actual "Saint Patrick's Four," except
that the author deeply admires Joan's courage and conviction
in the way she deeply admires the courage and conviction
of "The Saint Patrick's Four." The conscious fetuses are an
imaginative conceit and are not meant as a commentary on
the abortion debate.

An adaption of a scene from *What Becomes Us* won The 2015
New Guard Machigonne Fiction Contest, and appeared in
New Guard, volume IV. An adaptation of another scene was
published in *From The Finger Lakes: A Prose Anthology*, edited
by Rhian Ellis (Cayuga Lake Books, 2015). An excerpt was
published in *Red Wheelbarrow*, Volume 11, 2010. Some of
the material in "Quiero Bailar Slowly With You Tonight,"
(Zyzzyva, Spring, 2004) was later used in *What Becomes Us.*

OUTPOST19

ORIGINAL
PROVOCATIVE
READING

Also by
Micah Perks

We Are Gathered Here
Pagan Time
Alone In The Woods: Cheryl Strayed, My Daughter and Me

WHAT BECOMES US

For Juan

"I was fain to go and look after something
to satisfy my hunger."
Mary Rowlandson

"Not to be devoured
is the secret objective of a whole existence."
Clarice Lispector

CHAPTER ONE

Our parents had failed five months in a row to make a baby, and Father was growing frustrated. He couldn't figure out what our mother was doing wrong. For his Christmas/Chanukah present she gave him a skiing vacation in Steam Boat Springs, Colorado. She secretly thought it would give her a break from him, but he insisted she join him, so he could continue his spermatozoon campaign.

At first, it was tranquil. They stayed in a cabin in front of a hot springs. Father, the chef-owner of a health food restaurant in Santa Cruz, California, made whole-wheat chapattis on a camping stove the night they arrived. Mother, an elementary school teacher, suggested they take turns describing the highlights and lowlights of their day. The next morning they awoke and went down to the hot springs, where the old man who ran the place floated naked in an inner tube, wielding a ski pole to spear any debris that had fallen into the springs the day before. Our father thought the steaming water might damage his potency, so he did his 250 push-ups on the edge while our mother slipped in. Mother saw a mountain goat scrambling along the cliff above the pool.

But that was the end of the tranquil part of the vacation. Father was an experienced backcountry skier, and Mother began disappointing him on their first day out. He tried to help her. He told her she was leaning too far forward, locking her knees, raising her heels too high, holding her poles too far out.

The conditions were icy, and she fell and skidded on the crusty snow while he made perfect, whirling turns down every slope, then called up complicated directions through clenched teeth.

Have we mentioned what they look like? He: blond curly hair, a gladiator face, Roman nose and cleft chin, and then a wrestler's body, no neck, all chest, bandy legs. Our mother is skinny, long neck, long arms and fingers, wide flat hips. She's like a curvaceous paper doll—the curves all on the edges.

Because she was ovulating, at night they continued their sexual exertions. She lay there while he performed his quick, efficient operation. She felt like she was the mortar and he the pestle.

On the fourth day, they woke in the morning to a pretty blanket of powder over everything. Our father was elated. The old man floating in the tube said the new conditions were dangerous, but father said the old geezer didn't know his ass from a hole in the ground.

In early afternoon they came to a slope that was more like a cliff. She was exhausted, on the verge of tears, her face cold and wind burned. Her legs were shaking and her arms ached. She said she'd wait at the top for him.

Father said, "You're hysterical. Irrational. Just follow my directions." He told her she needed to grow a spine. "Man up," he said. He continued his pep talk.

Finally, she said, "Okay, fine, I'll do it."

He wiped her nose with his sleeve and tapped his fingers twice on her forehead. "Think, buddy, think," he said. "Keep those knobby knees tucked, pivot on the pole."

She looked down the smooth white drop. She allowed herself to slip over the edge. She fell head first on her second turn, her poles clattered away, one ski came off. Her left cheek was scraped raw from going through the ice just underneath the snow.

She sat up.

She could hear Father yelling down at her.

There was a kind of whump sound, big and hollow, like a bass drum that reverberated uncomfortably in her heart. She looked for Father, but he was skiing into the line of trees. Then the upper slope detached itself and began to slide towards her. The snow turned liquid. She tried to swim with it, like he'd instructed, but it poured over her. She couldn't keep her head free.

She woke curled in a cold fist. The snow was heavy, dense, pressed on top of her and packed inside her nose and ears and mouth. It was so dark she didn't know if her eyes were open or closed. There were tiny sparks and frissons of dizzying light. She thought she might faint. She spit snow out and heard whimpering, little mews. She realized it was coming from her.

She waited for Father to rescue her. She counted to a hundred, six times. It felt as if her lungs were shrinking, her throat squeezing closed. Please, she thought. She couldn't remember what number she was on.

Finally, she thought, I'll just go to sleep. Her tears made two warm roads down her face. She exhaled, readied herself to give way for the final time.

But then she remembered that there might be life inside her. She pictured a tiny mouth opening in her pelvis. She was sure it was there, starving for air, desperate for breathing room.

She moved one finger. The middle one. Then she moved her shoulders. As soon as she began to try to escape, that pelvic need sizzled through her, shocked her awake. She began to roil. She bucked and shook her head and arched and reared up into blue sky, gasping and crying, covered in powder.

And not alone. Because that is the moment we came to consciousness in an explosion of bright, bright blue. Not one, but two mouths opening in perfect synchronicity. Twins startled into being, we immediately knew every thought our mother ever had, her past, her present, everything that is, except our future.

CHAPTER TWO

The morning after we return from Colorado, Mother tells Father she needs to talk. A healthful breakfast is in process, tempeh scramble and a spinach-kale smoothie. His broad back to her, he's in a Kelly green t-shirt, and he's busy chopping, stirring and whirring.

"I've made a decision," she says, hovering in the kitchen doorway in her long nightgown, hands tearing at a tissue.

His slicing skills are extraordinary—notice the almost transparent petals of garlic flowering from the knife. "I've got this," he says. "I need to get you off dairy and wheat and get you in for some acupuncture. That should kick start those droopy eggs."

"Not about the pregnancy. I don't want, I mean," she croaks, "I want to live without you."

He doesn't turn around. "Don't blame me. Your fall triggered the avalanche, buddy. If you had listened to me that never would have happened."

"That's not true," she says.

He pulses the blender, creating a small green tornado in there.

She throws the shredded tissue at his back. It floats on the forced air, rocks gently to the floor.

He fires up the gas under the wok.

She goes into the bedroom and opens her suitcase on the bed. Dumps her underwear drawer in it and the black velvet case with her antique heirloom comb falls in, too.

And then he's there, his face so close to hers. That face! The gold curls jostling on his high forehead, the very light blue eyes and blond lashes, the cleft chin. He says, "If you fold your clothes correctly you could fit twice as much into that suitcase." He says, "You're hysterical. You need to calm down. We'll talk later." He leaves, closes the bedroom door. She hears him wedge a chair under the door handle from the outside.

She pushes at the door, rattles the knob, keeps her voice calm, calls, "Open this. Please. Open this right now." He doesn't answer. The knife work starts back up in the kitchen.

She paces a little, sings one of the songs from fourth grade circle time, *Simple Gifts*, to calm herself. She picks up the phone by the bed. It's beeping. She feels the air thickening, her throat closing. She thinks she hears that whump sound again. It startles her heart. There's not enough air in here. She unlatches the window and pulls it up. Cool, late January ocean air washes over her. She hears a seal bark. She's on the second floor. Beneath her—the side of the house with the garbage and recycling bins up against the neighbor's privacy fence. The last owners used it as a dog run. It's just packed dirt. She dumps more clothes into her suitcase, zips it up, mumbling, *'tis a gift to be simple, 'tis a gift to be free, 'tis a gift,* heaves the suitcase over the window and drops it. It falls hard, skids in the dirt, one of the wheels chips off. *'Tis a gift to come down where you ought to be.* She laces on her sneakers, hikes up her nightgown with the little blue flowers and the ruffled yoke. She straddles the sill. Her face is flushed and hot and her vision is doing that sparky-fizzy thing again. She drops her legs over, her second half still inside the room. She starts to lower herself down along the side the house.

She thinks then, finally, of us. Not exactly us, because she doesn't know we're both here, doesn't even know for sure there's anyone else here at all, except she has a feeling. She thinks: what if the fall jostles the baby? Undecided, she hangs there by her burning fingers, but she doesn't have upper body strength and the indecision only lasts a groaning moment before she drops. She does remember to bend her knees and tuck, and she rolls into the dirt, her shoulder nudging the suitcase. As she yanks her nightgown down over her scraped knees, she thinks, Why didn't I change into pants?

Then she gallops down the dog yard, her suitcase rolling bumpily behind her on its one good wheel. She unlatches the gate, drags her rollie through the early morning streets. How wondrous it feels to be running, the rollie bouncing and scraping, her heart yelling freedom. She runs all the way across town to her cousin Molly's house.

Molly makes her breathe into a paper bag while she stands over Mother, clenching-unclenching her hands and cursing Father. Molly is a vivified version of our mother, rich, chestnut hair instead of light brown, bright green eyes instead of grey, buff and busty instead of skinny.

Father arrives about twenty minutes later, knocking on the front door over and over like he's hammering in a nail. Mother and Molly stare at each other across the paper bag. They watch the knob turn. Neither of them remembers if the door is locked. The door holds. He seems to be gone, but then he's on the back porch looking at them through the sliding glass door.

Molly goes right up to the glass. "I'm calling the police." Her hot breath steams a tiny curtain between them.

Mother starts to wheeze again.

Molly picks up the phone, stabs 911.

Father looks over Molly's shoulder to give Mother the eye. He growls, "You need a therapist," or maybe "You're a terrorist," it's hard to hear through the glass. He taps the glass twice with his finger, as if he were tapping mother's forehead. He says, and this time she's sure he says it because he's yelling now, "You're not quitting. Not happening, not happening, not happening. Get it?"

Ten days later, first week of February, and Mother is taking a home pregnancy test in Molly's bathroom. Still sitting on the toilet, Mother grips the stick and watches the red plus sign appear. She imagines the red plus sign turning into a row of red plus signs, like a yellow brick road only red, until she reaches a picket fence made of red plus signs around a red farmhouse hidden in the woods where Father will never find us. She can see the baby's bedroom painted the color of sunshine and the blue morning glories growing up a trellis by the red door, and she can smell reddish cinnamon wafting from the pie in the open kitchen window with the curtains decorated in red pluses.

She decides right then to move as far across the continent from Father as she can get.

Our father withdrew all the money from their joint bank account, but she and Molly each have a mutual fund given to them by their late grandfather: seven thousand dollars. She calls to cash it in right now, the hand holding the pee stick with the red plus sign shaking, the red plus sign yelling, Go, go, go.

She doesn't tell Father about us, doesn't go back to her job as a fourth grade classroom teacher. She sleeps on Molly's couch, looks for work on the east coast, even though it is the middle of the year and she has California certification.

Mother quickly lands two offers for long-term emergency substitutions. One is a derelict New York City school district teaching sixth grade, the other a derelict town in western New York teaching tenth grade American History. New York City, she thinks, has just had a giant hole blown out of its middle this past September. Dangerous, she thinks, to be at the center of the world. She has an MA in Early American History, and she's always wanted to live in New England, the place where it all began. Western New York—New England, she reasons, same thing, right?

And then, there is the house. She sees an ad on-line: furnished three bedroom two hundred year old farmhouse, grape arbor and private pond. Three hundred a month. She checks the address, and it is only a few miles from the high school. She rents it over the phone.

Seven weeks after the avalanche, nine weeks pregnant, end of February, our mother waits on the sidewalk in the gloaming, all her worldly belongings either in Molly's garage or in the two new suitcases beside her. Above her, the high Santa Cruz sky is morning glory blue streaked with pink. She smells the eucalyptus trees and the brine of the ocean six blocks away. Pregnancy has intensified her sense of smell, so that it's as if she's coated in Tiger Balm and wearing a necklace of seaweed.

What Mother actually wears is a paper bead necklace made by one of her students, a light blue cardigan, and a stretchy long beige skirt. There's a zip lock of saltines in one pocket of her newly purchased used wool coat, a paper bag filled with papaya pills in the other, and on her thin wrist she wears a knobby bracelet that claims to massage her pressure points, proven to cure morning sickness, which Mother has all day.

We're still too feathery for her to feel us, although now she knows we're both here. She saw us on the ultra sound, a pulsing yin yang. Each an inch long, we are see-through things, our skin as thin as paper. We're the liquor we swim in, and the liquor passes through us. We twirl and twine and double somersault in love-drunk motion, no telling where one of us ends and the other begins. How much did Scheherazade love the Sultan? Or Joseph love Pharaoh? Or Huck and Jim love their raft? How can we pry apart love and need? Three minutes without her and our hearts would stop.

Mother is an agnostic, but we know the three of us are not alone. We don't have delusions of grandeur, we don't expect God, if there is a God, to intervene in our tiny drama, but still, we know someone is out there, listening, perhaps deciding our fate. We feel a watchful eye over our miraculous transformation, our cells furious division. We pledge to bare witness from the womb. We will sing the song of our mother, which is also the song of ourselves.

So, to return: when the airport shuttle turns the corner and trundles towards her, Mother grabs Molly's hand. "Don't tell anyone where I am. Anyone. I'm having the lawyer send the divorce papers to your address."

"Not to freak you out, but I don't think Steve's going to be that easy to get rid of. But, whatever, focus on your move to freezing hicklandia. Or focus on those gremlins." She pokes Mother's belly. "Everyone needs a couple of monsters inside.

Especially you. Especially you without me. Remember in sixth grade when I slapped that kid who kept bullying you in the lunch line? He just stood there breathing on your neck and whispering your name over and over. Evie, Evie, Evie. His lips were so close to your neck it was disgusting. It was like you had to wipe your neck to get his hot skanken' breath off it. And you just stood there in Evie La La Land."

"I think he had special needs."

"He had the need to be an asshole. Like Steve."

The shuttle driver pulls over beside them, rolls down the window.

"I'm a pioneer woman now," Mother says to Molly. "A pilgrim."

The shuttle driver climbs down and grabs a suitcase. "It's the beginning of a great adventure," he says.

The shuttle drops us at SFO, where mother throws up in the airport bathroom. She plods through the new security lines, boards a plane, flies through the night to JFK, dreaming of being eaten alive by a two-headed slug.

We confess that when mother first saw us on the ultrasound she was a little taken aback. The midwife pointed us out, her finger tracing our double pulsing lima bean shapes, explaining brightly that this is why Mother's morning sickness was so intense. She went on to describe "What multiples mean for mom": higher weight gain, more frequent check-ups, risk of high blood pressure, possible bed rest, premature birth, C-section. Mother hissed, "Steve." She told the nurse that Father had a twin sister who ran an eco-tourism company in Costa Rica. The nurse tried to explain to Mother that twins weren't passed down from the father, but Mother wasn't really listening. She was remembering the Alien movies, the milky creature uncoiling out of a burst stomach. Then she imagined her breasts attacked by two giant-headed babies, mouths like suction cups. The nurse asked her if she was feeling faint and brought her some orange juice in a paper cup. Mother took a sip, imagining the bigheaded babies turning up to look at her, and they were two redheaded and freckled Lindsay Lohans from *The Parent Trap*. She even fleetingly imagined giving one of us to our father, just dropping the extra baby off in a basket with an explanatory note. But then the sugar from the juice began to rally her. She told the technician who hovered over her that she was surprised, but fine, totally fine, shazam—instant family. A gang, a frat, a cult. She even said, "Yay," and shook her fist in the air.

At JFK she switches to a propeller plane, where she throws up in the small white bag provided, lands in Syracuse at seven am, rents a car, heaving those two suitcases into the trunk herself, and drives an hour south, the directions propped above the radio, the way the Japanese pilots navigated towards Pearl Harbor.

The February sky looks bruised. She had imagined there would be a pretty blanket of snow, but everything is out in the open, eaten away, skeletal. A few pruned leaves wisp across the ground. She passes a leafless birch tree, a barking dog, a field of papery corn stalks. She thinks of Ichabod Crane, all elbows and knees and ravenous mouth. She has the feeling she is being swallowed by a wilderness of closed down factories, fallow fields and little towns with boarded up main streets. On the county road there are hand painted signs: *Nuke Bin Laden, Nuke Iraq, Nuke The Terrorists*, and a huge wooden cross spray painted with the words *Going Up?* American flags everywhere too, wilting on front lawns, plastered on gas station windows, yellow ribbon decals on every pick-up truck.

It's a little harsh, she thinks. But I only need to brighten up my tiny part of it. To keep her spirits up, she sings, *Fifty nifty United States with the thirteen original colonies! Each individual state contributes a quality that is great...*

She pulls over to dry heave, then turns left on another county road, drives steeply up a hill covered in trailers and dogs on chains. She takes a final left at the hand painted sign that reads

10

Lonely Rincon Road right under the official sign that says, *Dead End*. She passes a prefabricated house with a large American flag sagging over the door, parks in front of Lonely Rincon Volvo where she is to pick up the key to the house. As the car door opens, a crow squawks, a sound like scraping a tin pot.

The garage is in a pine forest, sided in unvarnished boards. They have both garage doors open, one Volvo on the ground, one up on hydraulics, ten more parked haphazardly in the dirt. It smells like Christmas and like gasoline. She feels her gag reflex kicking in, tries to breathe through her mouth.

There are a few middle-aged mechanics there, gringos and Latinos, all in grey coveralls, some wearing wool hats or leather gloves, their body-heated breath smoking in the cold. While they work they talk steadily in a mixture of Spanish and English. She catches a few words, enough to understand they are teasing each other about women in between talking about an engine. She feels dumb, a civilian. She waits for someone to help her, but no one does.

Finally, she notices a bald Latino mechanic sitting on three tires in the corner by the big space heater reading a book. She feels the orangey warmth of the heater on her thighs as she walks towards him.

"Pardon," she says softly in her halting elementary school teacher Spanish. He looks up, his eyes blurry behind his glasses. She continues, "Estoy mirando por el jefe, el hombre con la casa viejo."

The mechanic places a bookmark on his page, closes the book, crouches down beside a brown Volvo sedan, fishes underneath it, and rolls out a man by his ankles. The reader points his chin from the prone man to her, but before he returns to his book, he takes his glasses off, and then, as if she is finally in focus, he smiles.

It's the kind with a wall of perfect, white teeth. That smile illuminates his face—gold-flecked green eyes half-curtained by dark lashes, bushy black eyebrows, flared nose, dimple on the left cheek. The viscous emotions—exhaustion, nausea, hope—that have been clogging her head fall away for a moment. It's as if she's just eaten a teaspoon of Wasabi, it burns straight up her nostrils, clears her brain. It's as if she's bitten an electric cord, the way the shock leaps across synapses, re-arranging molecules, changing the charges on atoms, so that his smile feels both completely new and like déjà vu.

The mechanic sits back on the tires and opens his book. She glances down at the name on the man's coverall. Everett. Everett is a weird name for a Latino guy, she thinks. Thinks, I'm over-tired. Temporarily off balance. Thinks, Let it go.

Meanwhile, the owner, Michael, his name is embroidered in red over his grey covered heart, wipes his hands on a rag and looks her over. You can tell right away he's an alcoholic, charming in a beaten up, beaten down sort of way, a man who likes women.

Our mother is a woman, but she's not beautiful in the ordinary ways, even we can see that. The morning sickness has given her an even more fragile look, her lips dry, her eyes hollowed out. A generous man, one who reads Tennessee Williams or fixes broken things, might like her. And Michael, though we doubt he reads Tennessee Williams, is probably patient with old cars.

"I'm Evie Rosen, the one who rented your house," she says, not looking at the man on the tires. "We talked briefly on the phone?"

"Jeez, you're the substitute."

"I'm starting in three days, tenth grade at the high school."

"So you're alone," Michael glances around as if for a family ambush.

She nods, her hand hiding her still flat belly.

"My son's in your class. River. Keep an eye on him." He propels her by the small of her back out onto the road, away from that smile. "Where'd you say you hail from again?"

"California, Santa Cruz—"

"I'm not even gonna ask why you left Shangri La to come here, not even gonna ask—I'm on a need to know basis—that goes for everything around here." He jerks his chin at a trailer opposite the garage. The trailer has a perfectly manicured, dead brown lawn without a leaf or a stray stick on it. A neatly lettered sign reads, Give Peace A Chance. A three-legged dog is tied beside a doghouse. The skinny mutt looks at us askance and hops for shelter. A large woman in a sari sits in the kitchen window. She waves, smiles, and uncranks the window. "Are you renting the house, Miss?" she calls in a precise, upward-sweeping Indian accent.

"I got a time line here, Neela," Michael yells, and pushes Mother along. Mother waves. "That's Neela, a do-gooder friend of my Ma's. She's from India by way of Binghamton. She lives with a woman who used to work with us over to the garage. Sondra still comes by to check up on us, and the Indian lady, Neela, real helpful, whether you need it or not. I got a full-time mechanic lives in that prefab just as you come onto Lonely Rincon. He was an illegal, used to work for the farmer who owned this whole road, ended up marrying the farmer's daughter. Got a son and daughter, the son's still at home. They're Evangelicals, which means they don't drink and they're what you'd call over the top, religiously speaking. Lately his better half has gone a little off her rocker, or a little more off her rocker. Long, sad story. Whoopsy daisy, you're not evangelical, are you?"

She shakes her head. "Jewish."

"Ah. Like my brother-in-law." He throws his hand towards a driveway right after the garage. "He lives there with my sister and their kid. I built the house for my sister so's my ma would have some peace, before I knew Ma was gonna join the nuns over to Rochester. I myself live above the garage, by the by. Sister's husband works at the garage, sister makes a hot lunch for us every day. Terrible cook, God awful. You're better off with them stale crackers you're nibbling on. Refuses to use a cookbook, claims she has natural ability. The guys complain, but

13

there you have it. That's my sister. Joanie. I call her Saint Joan of Rincon, not to her face of course.

"She spent two years in jail. Maximum security, on account of she did some damage to a nuclear submarine with a crowbar. Tossed her blood about, icing on the cake so to speak. Lost the government close to a million dollars. She's cost me a pretty penny, too. I been telling her, keep your head down, Joanie-girl, terrorists aren't popular right now. But she don't listen to me.

"I guess someone has to be the practical one. There's the practical ones in this world, and the dreamers. Which are you?"

"Practical," Mother says, thinking, Starting now.

"You look kind of blurry around the edges, but I'll take your word for it. My ex was a dreamer, now she lives in a rental in town with our two boys, hellions, well, the younger one, Oshun, kind of a whiner, sensitive we call him. I already warned you about River, he's the older one. Moves through men like water, my ex that is, probably I should have grabbed a clue when she named our boys River and Oshun. But we get along, me, her, the kids, all the boyfriends. I don't believe in the opposites attract theory, though. I think we should marry our likes. Hardly ever happens, which is the reason for the high divorce rate. Wait for your like, that's my advice." He winks.

"Down the road there we got a kind of swamp, or private pond you might call it, if you was advertising." Another wink. "My ex skinny-dips in it with her boyfriends. I wouldn't. Slimy, snapping turtle type place. You might come outta there missing some essentials. Up to you, but since you're the practical type I'm betting you'll give it a miss."

A hail of burrs flies out of the woods. They put their hands up to shield themselves, but they're both hit. Mother pulls two burs off the arm of her new used beige wool coat.

"Jeez Louise." Michael grabs up a frozen dirt clod and heaves it into the woods. "She's a walking advertisement for the dangers of homeschooling. Joanie's kid. Inez. Can't do nothing with her. Don't ask me what she knows. A little auto mechanics,

14

a little liberation theology mixed up with Catholic S and M from Joanie, some Jewish hoo-ha from her Dad. She speaks a messed-up Spanglish no one can understand, just to annoy people. She can read, and I mean big chapter books, in both languages. She's six years old and just stopped drinking from a bottle, did I mention that already? She's going to have to spend the rest of her life on this road, if Joanie don't civilize her soon."

The dirt clod comes sailing back at them, ricochets off the gravel and hits Michael on the calf. "Hey, you girl, go home and learn something. It's school hours, for Christ's sakes. I swear to God, I'm calling the truant officer." He kicks the clod, which collapses.

"Okay, so here we got your rental."

The lawn, front to back, is ringed in purple blackberry brambles, beyond that the ground inclines steeply into a narrow gorge. We can just hear the heckling from the stream below. There is an umbilical looking grape vine. The barn's caved in on one side. In its doorless doorway Mother can make out a plow becoming a lace of rust. A cellular phone tower blinks its red light in an empty field, about three hundred yards away. "The electromagnetic waves won't hurt you, safe distance," Michael says. "There's radon in the cellar—level five—borderline," Michael adds. "Keep the basement door closed," he says. "Let's see, truth in advertising," Michael continues. "I got a call last week from some rangers—wanted me to know they were dropping radioactive fat from helicopters so they could trace rabid raccoons in the area."

But Mother only has eyes for the house. It's small and white with faded red trim, and it has a red door with a heart-shaped window in it, as if the red plus signs had led her right here, she thinks. The bottom panes of all the other windows are stained glass, alternating blue moons with yellow backgrounds and yellow suns with blue backgrounds. She imagines the brambles plump with blackberries. A trellis of morning glories. She imagines us, her gender-neutral children with bowl cuts, dressed in linen, filling baskets of berries and grapes from the vine. The smell of cinnamon wafting out the windows.

"Can we go in, please?" she asks. Michael brings out a heavily loaded key ring. She glances down at a cat door with a rubber flap by her feet.

"Hasn't been a cat in here for years." He begins trying keys.

She mumble-sings *Dinosaurs, Dinosaurs, they are no more* to calm herself.

"This is the original farmhouse," he says. "Though there hasn't been a genuine farmer living here since 1960. I'm always thinking of selling, but it's the house we grew up in, you know how it is. Dad died of drink in here, Ma brought us up, steady as she goes, I take after her that way. She's practical."

Aren't you glad that there are no more dinosaurs, Mother mumble hums.

"Ma joined the nuns over there to Rochester when she hit sixty-three. Before that she spent most of her time down there to Latin America. She tried to provide the basics. That was her hobby, mopping up after the U.S. government. The CIA installs a dictator, the people try to overthrow him, and she hands out sweaters and toilet paper and Tylenol. She was in Chile way back there during the coup, then again during the protests in the 80's, brought back a boy to live with us, kind of a foster brother, best buddy type guy, my sister's husband, Mateo."

"Do you want me to try the lock?" she asks. She begins nibbling a cracker she's pulled from her pocket.

"Nah, I got it." He hits the door a couple of times. "And Ma brought us Sondra of the lesbian persuasion, got jumped right here in town one night when she was just a young butch. Sondra has a new job over to Montour Falls, but Mateo still works at the garage with a Mexican buddy, used to be illegal, now he's married to the neighbor girl, Ma fixed that up, too, but she's lost some of her marbles recently, the neighbor." He looks up from the keys and the lock: "I told you all that, already, now didn't I?

16

"I'll be honest with you, Evie. We're a little worse for wear, the bunch of us. This used to be a Queen bee type place—all of us buzzing around my ma, so to speak. But we lost our queen bee when Ma joined the nuns. Now we just kind of buzz around. We got a soccer team though, everyone plays. We got a monthly Friday night potluck, everyone goes to that, too. The ladies'll pound down your door if you try to avoid it."

He turns the rattley black doorknob. "Hah. Wasn't even locked, doorknob's a little broken is all. I had Hector come over and get the heat going this morning."

They stand in the warm kitchen, the windows steamed over. It smells mildly moldy, with an after-whiff of rodent. There are peeling white cupboards with angels carved into them, wide board wooden floors, a round oak table, and a blue woodstove. Our mother imagines doing a back flip though she's never even been able to do a somersault. "Wow."

"People here before you were punk rock hippies, they had a band. They wouldn't kill a living thing, so the place got a little run down." Michael unlatches the door of the stove and opens it. "I think bats are living in the woodstove, to tell the God's honest truth, but I'll get 'em for you. No problemo. Meanwhile, you can use the oil heat. Heat included by the way.

"Don't worry over loneliness. The women will take an interest, God help you. We have free bootlegged DSL—don't ask. The phone works, still in my Ma's name. One of the wives is an Avon rep, in case you get a sudden urge for apricot facial scrub, and I have a reliable car at a decent price for you, any trouble with it, come on over to the garage, we'll fix you up. You just pay for the parts. Everything you need is pretty much right here. We got our own little dead end republic."

"It's perf—"

"—I almost forgot to tell you. You already got a package. Hector brought it over." Michael picks a manila envelope up off the counter and hands it to her.

"Thanks."

"Aren't you going to open it?"

"It's from the school." She rips off the flap, slides out a small, wilted beige book. *Narrative of the Captivity and Restoration of Mrs. Mary Rowlandson.* The blurry woodcut on the cover shows a woman in a long dress with a gun protecting her house from a line of men with hatchets and muskets.

"Don't get me started on that book," Michael says. "That's got some history to it. You'll find out soon enough."

"I read an excerpt of it in graduate school. I don't remember it very well."

"You're not getting cold feet are you? Don't worry about the book. Ignore it. Are we all good?"

Our mother holds the book to her chest. "Perfect."

CHAPTER THREE

First night in her new home, Mother lies alone in the upstairs front bedroom. There are no curtains on the windows. There are country sounds, which are stranger than city sounds, being inhuman. There are shadows of trees, and the dark trees themselves, and a raw sliver of moonlight on her face.

She hums a little of *This Land Is My Land*, then trails off. Pats the frayed silky edge of the pale blue wool blanket against her chest. "I'm home," she tries telling herself. "Hi, I'm Evie Rosen. This is my farm. I grow things. Farm things, actually. Bake bread. Weave. Weave from yarn made from my own sheeps. Yes, these are my twins, they work right alongside me. No, they don't bite—"

She hears something downstairs.

She remembers that the lock on the front door doesn't work.

She sits up.

Fingers scratching? Something trying to get in or out.

She looks at the other side of the bed where no one lies. Father always leapt up like a guard dog at the slightest noise and grabbed the bat he kept under the bed. Mother looks at the side table where there is no phone. Looks out the window at the empty moonlit dirt road lined with trees.

The scrabbling sounds frantic.

What can she do but climb out of bed into her blue fuzzy slippers, search for a weapon. She has put her antique folding comb inside the drawer of the bedside table. Now she takes it out of its black velvet case. She unfolds the steel comb from its whalebone sheath and holds it awkwardly in her fist up by her head, shuffles across the creaky wood floor of her bedroom, down the hall, to the top of the stairwell. "Hello?"

It's coming from the woodstove. Banging around in there.

19

Of course, Michael said bats live in the stove. She breathes again, lets the fist with the comb drop down by her leg. She'll ask him to get the bats out, however one does that, and she'll ask him to fix the lock on the front door, tomorrow. "Hicklandia," she shrugs exaggeratedly, rolls her eyes, as if Molly were here, and goes back to bed. She thinks since she's awake she might as well get started reading the Mary Rowlandson book, but she falls asleep and begins the dream that keeps recurring since the accident. Not the slug dream, that was just the once. This one is not even a dream, just a feeling, just the slow cinching closed of her throat, until she startles awake, gasping, not remembering what woke her.

Next morning, 8 a.m., Mother already dressed for her meeting with the principal in one of her favorite outfits—a brown shirtwaist and navy blue clogs, plus new brown tights for the cold—when the phone rings.

"Miss Rosen, this is the principal's assistant Mrs. Joyce Little. The principle needs to cancel his appointment with you today. He'll try to visit you during your break on Monday. Good?"

"Oh, okay, thanks," Mother says. "But, I don't even know my schedule. And you can call me Evie."

"Come into the office early, 7:30 a.m. on Monday and I'll give you a copy of your schedule, and you'll sign papers if I have the time."

"Okay, thanks Joyce. But sorry to bother you, would you mind telling me what my schedule is now?"

A heavy sigh. Some shuffling of papers. "You've got it easy, Miss Rosen. First a study hall, then lunch, then two American History classes, same prep, hour and a half each. We're on the semester system and we just started the spring semester this week. You'll be teaching out of a textbook, *Discovering Ourselves*, we've used it since the late 80's. History doesn't change, right? The students already have it. They've had a sub all this week, just been silent reading —anyway, ask them what page they're up to—some decent girls in tenth grade, they'll tell you. What page. Okay, all set, see you Monday. Good."

"Thanks, but what about the book you sent me?"

"We didn't send you a book. You can pick up *Discovering Ourselves* on Monday."

"Are you sure? It's *The Captivity and Restoration of Mrs. Mary Rowlandson*."

Huff of outraged breath. "Probably one of the parents from the church sent you that, or someone who thinks they're real funny."

"But the return address was the school."

"Miss Rosen, I can assure you that book was not sent in any official capacity. However, it is possible that Mr. Lassiter or a supporter of Mr. Lassiter's may have sent it from these premises."

"I'm sorry Joyce, who is Mr. Lassiter?"

"Everyone calls me Mrs. L. Mr. Lassiter was the history teacher hounded out by the left wing radicals on your road. We had a controversy last semester, and we don't like controversies. Enough said. I recommend you teach from the textbook."

"Was the controversy over the Mary Rowlandson book?"

Another sigh. "If you want to teach that book, Miss Rosen, by all means, teach it. But just don't go connecting it to God or terrorism or anything. We have a lot of religious conservatives in this county and we have some loudmouth radicals on your road, and we don't want to stir things up. So nothing controversial. The student copies are in the storeroom. See you Monday."

Mother looks around the kitchen for the book. What did she do with it? She can't remember, but it will turn up.

She calls Molly: "I'm here, about to start homesteading. Where are you? Oh, shoot, forgot the time difference. Sorry, sorry, go back to sleep, I'll call again later. Yeah, I know, Evie La La Land."

She returns to the garage (no sign of Everett) and writes the rent plus deposit check and another check for a 1989 brown

Volvo sedan. Michael promises to return the rental car.

As she pulls out of the garage she begins to dry heave, remembers the need to eat. She meanders around the county until she stumbles on a supermarket, then meanders around the grocery store. It's the first time she's shopped for herself in two years. She wheels her cart past the few bins of limp vegetables and iceberg lettuces. When alone she has always reverted to bagels and yogurt. She's one of those people who forgets to eat, and now that she's nauseous all the time, eating is even less compelling.

She buys several packages of pale, salty crackers. Then, thinking vaguely of nutrition, she picks out a steak, milk, assorted canned soups, a bag of mixed frozen vegetables, and then the staples—a dozen coffee yogurts, frozen plain bagels, tea and sugar. Finally, she grabs some duct tape—Father used it for everything. The cashier rings up her items efficiently but never returns her smile or asks her how her day is going so far. She wonders if this is what they mean by Yankee stoicism.

Back at the house, Mother unpacks the groceries, eats a yogurt and half a sleeve of crackers standing up, then takes a broom and inventories the house. She hasn't done any of her own cleaning in years either. If she even picked up a wet rag to wipe down the counter, Father would say, I'll do that. To be fair, Mother didn't protest.

Besides the master bedroom where she slept, there are two tiny empty bedrooms upstairs. This one closest to hers will be the babies' room she decides, using the broom to reach cobwebs in the highest corners. "Sorry, Charlotte," she says aloud, regretfully smacking at an escaping spider with her broom. It scuttles out from under the bristles, so she lets it go. When she finishes vigorously sweeping the floor, the dustpan holds a tangle of honey-colored hair, and she can see long pale strands drifting in the dusty sunlight coming through the double windows that face the back yard. She pictures a beautiful Rapunzel punk rock hippy brushing out her long hair. On the floor of the closet she finds a big rock with a frayed bit of rope tied around it. Strange, she thinks, looking at the window, wondering if someone might have tossed it through. She carries the rock out under her arm.

The third bedroom is empty except for three ancient looking rum bottles and a dusty fedora. She takes those, too, closes the door.

Because the windows face the woods crowded with evergreen trees, the light in the living room has a dim, greenish, underwater quality. It contains a grey futon couch, a rocking chair with a frayed rattan seat, a standing lamp and a full-length oval mirror with a chipped and peeling antique gold frame leaning against the far wall. The mirror is speckled and dim with age. On the mantel sits a baby doll with a single tuft of hair and a half burnt face. One blue eye is open.

Creepy, she thinks, closing the doll's eye. Then she loads the baby doll, the rock, the bottles and the fedora into a cardboard box and carts it all to the basement door. The light switch doesn't work, and it is, of course, filled with radon down there. She drops the box just inside the door, imagining the radon waves pulsing into her stomach. We imagine it, too.

She shuts the door and examines it, no lock, loose in its frame. She rests her hand on the crack between the door and the wall and feels that cool, moist, radon-breath on her palm. This basement is the only part of the house she dislikes. Californians don't have basements. She doesn't like the idea of the ground underneath a house hollowed out, destabilizing the whole structure. She duct tapes stiff old sponges she finds under the sink across the crack between the basement door and the floor in hopes of sopping up the radon before it enters the house. Then she pulls a strip of the duct tape across the door to the wall.

She throws up a little in the bathroom, then changes into her granny nightgown and begins organizing the kitchen, avoiding drinking the large glass of milk she has poured herself. She thinks she'll figure out how to make that steak for dinner.

She checks her email. There are five from Father. The subject of the first is "This is not happening." Then "Re: This is not happening," "Re: Re: This is not happening," and so on. She deletes the emails without reading them, and then decides to delete her whole email account. Gone.

Through the kitchen window over the sink she sees a rusted blue Volvo station wagon driving down the road in the twilight. Lonely Rincon describes a U around the farmhouse, so that the garage can't be seen from the far side of her yard. The Volvo pulls off there at that hidden end. She spies on it through the stained glass. Everett the mechanic climbs out.

Mother presses both fists over her heart.

He glances at the house. Without meaning to, she raises her hand in a little half wave over the stained-glass moon. He doesn't respond. He walks around the hood. He opens the passenger side door, sits down with his feet flat on the cold ground. He takes out his glasses, pushes them up the bridge of his nose. He takes a little bottle from his front pocket, and she thinks, Oh, no, a drinker. But then he pulls out a rag from his back pocket, unscrews the jar, holds the rag to the mouth of the bottle and shakes the liquid onto the cloth. He cleans his hands with the rag, rubbing methodically, paying special attention to the thumb and forefinger. He puts the bottle and the rag back in his pockets, reaches behind him for a book, which he holds above his knees. He begins to read.

No wonder she is protecting her heart, because it is as if he has lain his turpentined finger there. She can feel the organ shuddering with the sting of it.

The racket in the woodstove starts up again. Bat wings against tin, tiny claws scraping. In the country there's too much of the outside inside, Mother thinks. She calls the garage.

Everett puts his book aside.

The bats keep up their clatter.

Mother waits for someone to pick up.

Everett digs into his pocket.

"Lonely Rincon Volvo." Accented English, Latin American, with some slight British formality to it. "Hola? Hello?"

She crouches down below the window. "Is Michael there?"

"No, he is not available. I am able to take a message."

"No problem, I'll call back."

"Who is this please?"

"Nobody." He'll recognize her voice. "I mean, of course, somebody. This is Evie, his new renter. It's just that there are these bats in the woodstove. Michael told me he would get them out."

"I am able to fix that."

"You are?"

"Yes. Chao."

She is still crouching in her nightgown beside the kitchen counter. There's a knock on the door, a cheerful one-two.

She stands.

Everett's face peers into the heart-shaped window. He knocks again, one-two, one-two.

She takes a long swig of milk for courage, then fluffs over in her slippers and turns the knob. She jiggles it. "I can't get the door open," she calls. "It doesn't even lock. It worked earlier today."

He puts his shoulder to it, bursts into the room. There he is, so close up in his grey uniform, smelling faintly of rubbing alcohol. "I'll fix that door for you. First the door, then the woodstove."

"Thank you." She doesn't know where to look, so many places to avoid—the eyes, hair on chest at the top of the long zipper, that smile, the whole lower area. She thinks, Why is he standing so close, why is he smiling so big, he's ridiculous.

"You have milk on your moustache."

Mother wipes with the back of her hand. "Would you like some tea?"

"Yes, please." While Everett brings in his toolbox and works on the knob, she makes tea.

He groans a little as he straightens up. "So, problem two—bats are in your belfry." He laughs big and open. "That's what one says? It means one is crazy, correct? What is a belfry in any case?"

"I think it's a bell tower." She hands him his tea, looks at his shoes, sports sneakers with stripes. "I heard the bats last night, and just a minute ago. Maybe they were flying out to hunt."

"It's very rare, because they are sleeping in winter. In winter there is nothing to hunt." He knocks on the stovepipe. The bats don't respond. "Sometimes the how do you call it—black chingity bongity—breaks off and falls. Maybe this is what you hear."

"I don't think so. It definitely sounded like something alive in there."

He goes to her cupboard and pulls out a big pot. "I cooked in this," he says. "When I lived here."

"You did?" She pictures him helping the princess punk rock hippy let down her golden hair, then pushes that thought away.

"Please open the stove door, and I will cover the opening with this pan."

"Ready?" she asks. He nods. She unlatches the stove and creaks it open. He holds the pot up to the opening. They wait. Nothing. He puts the pot on the floor. Sticks his whole bald head in there. Mother winces and steps back, imagining the tiny claws on his face. His neck looks soft. It has three dark freckles on it that makes her think of the handle of the Big Dipper. He pulls his head out and bangs on the inside of the pipe with his hammer. Some creosote falls down.

"There is nobody home. I'm going to put a screen over the stovepipe up on the roof. They wont be able to get back in, just en caso." That grin again, and he stands there bouncing a little in those silly sneakers. "I see you have decided to punish the poor, mischievous book."

"What?"

"I understand you don't want trouble, but it hurts me a little to see a book treated like this, that's my opinion."

"Do you mean the Mary Rowlandson book?"

"How are you?"

"What?" It's hard not to constantly smile big back.

"How are you in this place? Are you fine?"

"Fine, thanks."

"You are a woman of mystery, no?"

"What? No," she laughs. "I'm just a substitute teacher."

"I will drink your tea another time."

"Okay," she says.

"Okay," he smiles. "Welcome." Finally he stops smiling and leaves. That was awkward, Mother thinks, still smiling. She watches him bring out a ladder from the barn. She tries out his accent so she can repeat it for Molly: "I will drink your tea another time." She hears him walking on her roof. Then she thinks, What did he mean about the book anyway? She goes to the stove and opens it, winces, then forces herself to lean down and peer in. She reaches her long, thin arm into the dark and pulls out *The Captivity and Restoration of Mary Rowlandson*. Here it is, smeared in soot. She brushes it off, goes for a paper towel, realizes she forgot to buy any and wipes it off with her belled nightgown sleeve. Weird, she thinks. Michael wouldn't have thrown it in there, would he? He did tell me to forget about it, maybe he did, or maybe it fell in somehow.

After dinner, a yogurt and a dry bagel because she forgot to buy butter, Mother grabs a pen and that sooty book and moves to the living room. She sits in the rocking chair next to the futon couch. She turns the standing lamp on, thumbs through *The Captivity and Restoration of Mrs. Mary Rowlandson*. There's a brief introduction with a time-line and the basic facts. Mother takes notes on the inside front cover:

first book of prose by a woman published in the Americas

Mary Rowlandson, thirty-nine years old, wife of the Reverend Rowlandson

*garrison in Lancaster, Massachusetts attacked during King Philip's
war 1676*

*Mary and five year old daughter shot with the same bullet, Mary
through her side and her daughter through her stomach and hand*

captured

daughter dies nine days later

*Rowlandson lives with the Wampanoag as the servant of the warrior
queen Weetamoo for eleven weeks and five days*

ransomed

The narrative is organized in Removes instead of Chapters,
each section removing Rowlandson further into the wilderness.
There's a map at the beginning, too, showing each remove,
from Lancaster, Massachusetts up into Vermont, all through a
northeastern winter. The editor writes that the narrative is taken
up with "Rowlandson's near starving condition and obsession
with food as well as her determination to see her captivity in a
religious context."

Mother thinks, Mary Rowlandson had her daughter when
she was 34, three years older than I am. She starts reading a few
pages from the beginning: "Now is that dreadful hour come,
that I have often heard of (in time of War, as it was the case
of others) but now mine eyes see it. Some in our house were
fighting for their lives, others wallowing in their blood, the House
on fire over our head, and the bloody Heathen ready to knock
us on the head, if we stirred out. Now might we hear Mothers
and Children crying out for themselves, and one another, Lord,
What shall we do?"

Mother remembers the weight of the snow, how heavy it
was, pressed around her, pressing the air out of her, squeezing
her throat closed. The way she bucked and tore so she could
breathe again. She touches her throat.

"Then I took my children (and one of my sister's hers) to
go forth and leave the house: but as soon as we came to the
door and appeared, the Indians shot so thick that the bullets
rattled against the house, as if one had taken a handful of stones

and threw them…but out we must go, the fire increasing and coming along behind us, roaring, and the Indians gaping before us with their guns."

She goes back to the beginning: "On the tenth of February, 1675 came the Indians in great numbers upon Lancaster. Their first coming was about sun-rising."

Mary Rowlandson is separated from her son, and away she and her daughter must go "with these barbarous creatures" into the "vast and desolate wilderness." She writes, "the first week of my being among them, I hardly ate anything; the second week, I found my stomach grow very faint for want of something; and yet it was very hard to get down their filthy trash: but the third week…" Her master, Quinnipin, is "her best friend," but she hates Quinnipin's wife, her mistress, "the proud dame" Weetamoo. After her daughter dies, Mary survives by haunting the camp, entering wetu after wetu, scrounging and begging for groundnuts and acorns and chestnuts or the broth from a horse hoof, until she begins knitting in trade for food. She is given a bible, and reads it often. She believes God is testing her, but that he is always with her. She believes she is not alone. *When though passeth through the waters I will be with thee* she quotes, then writes, "But to return," and resumes the descriptions of her search for food.

An hour later Mother looks up, her finger on the sentence she has just read. She reads it again. "As we went along, they killed a Deer, with a young one in her, they gave me a piece of the Fawn, and it was so young and tender that one might eat the bones as well as the flesh, and yet I thought it very good."

Mother is taken over by this sentence. Her cheeks burn. She reads it again. And again.

Why does she keep reading that sentence?

Maybe it's like us, floating blind inside our jellyfish sacs through warm water, and then we slide against each other. It startles us sometimes. Like that.

Mother glances up dreamily from the book and glimpses

something in the old, wavy mirror against the wall. A woman sitting in the rocker. Dark leather shoes, blue dress, ragged apron. Her head is past the frame of the mirror, but we can see the ends of her long, matted brown hair. There is a rusty stain on the right side of her blue dress, under her breast. It looks like dried blood.

She's sitting in the rocker, but Mother is sitting in the rocker, so where is our mother?

Then the woman is gone.

It's just Mother in the rocker now, her finger still pressed on the sentence. For some reason Mother thinks of that boy whispering into her neck in the lunch line, *Evie, Evie, Evie*. She even reaches up and touches the warm back of her neck under her hair. Her breath is quick and shallow. She gets up and looks closely in the mirror. She sees only herself. She turns the mirror the other way, so that it faces the wall. It's heavy and dusty.

She thinks to call Molly, but Molly always heads to the gym after work. She shakes her head vigorously. Evie La La Land, she shrugs to herself. She snaps the book closed as if to clear her vision and goes to finish her glass of milk.

FOURTH REMOVE

Mother wakes up hungry the next morning for the first time in weeks. The sun shines on the bare trees in front. As she gets out of bed she sees a deer in the backyard. These white-tailed Eastern deer are so much prettier than the mule deer in Santa Cruz, she thinks. Mule deer are grey, squat and barrel-chested, but this one is reddish, long and slim, dancer-like. She notices that its stomach is swollen and its hide ragged. The doe mouths the barren grape vine, noses the bare ground. She might be pregnant.

Mother thinks cheerily that the deer is a good luck sign. She thinks it must mean she's landed in the right place. Mother doesn't think of eating the fetal fawn, which is a good luck sign for us.

She sets out to drive all the way to the nearest box stores in Syracuse. On the way she stops at a diner decked out to look like a log cabin, with log wallpaper, red gingham curtains and a carved bear in the corner. Mother orders The Hungry Man Special, pancakes, sausage, bacon and two poached eggs. She hums a little while she eats more than half of it, dipping everything into the yellow yolk.

After eating The Hungry Man, she heads for the mall and purchases white sheets with beige borders, beige towels, and a navy handmade-looking quilt. Even though, or maybe because her parents were new-age Jewish hippies, she has always liked muted colors and antiques when she can afford them. Heading towards the Volvo with her new linens, she passes a paint store, runs in on impulse. She gets so carried away she has to make three trips to the car with all her purchases. Then she pulls into a large supermarket and fills her cart. She lets the sullen bagger help her load up the bags into the Volvo's bottomless trunk.

On the way back to the house she sips an apple juice box

through a straw and tosses cheddar goldfish into her mouth from the bag on her lap. About ten miles before Lonely Rincon, she passes a little library she hadn't noticed. She wrenches the wheel into a U-turn, pulls into the three car parking lot next to the two other Volvos.

The library is an old one room building on a corner of a crossroads opposite a two bay firehouse, otherwise surrounded by frozen fields. White with a little peaked roof at the entranceway, dim inside, crowded with shelves, smelling of old books. A green leather armchair slouches by one of the windows and a long, scratched wooden table with benches takes up the middle of the room. And there at the library desk in the corner sits Neela, the woman from the trailer on Lonely Rincon, wearing a green and gold sari with a big flowered cardigan over it and thick Ben Franklin glasses that make her eyes huge.

"Miss Evie Rosen. How delightful to see you here. I'm so sorry I haven't stopped by yet, but I was hoping to have a good long heart to heart at the potluck this Friday."

"This is the most charming miniature library I've ever seen," Mother says. "When I was a kid I would have wanted to set up a secret hiding place under that table and live here forever."

"Ah, a book lover. What were your favorite books as a child?"

"I was a book worm. Probably *Little House On The Prairie, Wind In the Willows*, The Narnia books—I read those over and over. I read them every year to my students even now."

"How lovely. I'm working on a little children's book project of my own. May I show it to you sometime?"

"Oh, sure," Mother says.

"But now you are busy preparing for your new classes, am I right? What are you looking for? I am at your service."

"I just wanted to check out the library, but since I'm here I'd love to see any books about the Algonquin, the Wampanoag, King Philip's war, captivity narratives. Anything related to those topics."

Neela blinks her magnified eyes. "Perhaps you should talk to Joan before you begin teaching that Mary Rowlandson book. She has very strong feelings about it."

"I'm not planning on teaching it. I'm just curious. For personal reasons."

"Ah."

"Really," Mother says.

"Of course," Neela says. She stands and goes to a shelf behind the desk. She hauls out a stack of books. "Here you are."

"Just like that?"

"Mr. Lassiter dropped them off before he left town on Friday."

Mother takes the books to the long table and sits down. The top one is *A Key Into the Language of America* by Roger Williams, "an help to the language of the natives in the part of America called New England. Originally published in 1643." The next is *Edible Plants Of The Great North Woods*. Then there is *Domestic Life of The Puritans*; *The Wampanoag and Their Ways*; *A History of King Philip's War*. The last one is bright yellow and glossy: *Wolves At The Door: A True History of Left Wing Terror in America*.

Neela, at her desk five feet from the table, whispers loudly, open hand to mouth, "Have you found anything personally interesting yet?"

"It all looks really interesting."

She opens the book about left wing terror. A picture of Emma Goldman with the caption, "Red Emma Goldman, that venomous snake, plotted to overthrow the government."

"Are you hungry?" Neela whispers.

"No, thanks."

"I have homemade nan in a Tupperware. I could microwave it."

A phone rings in the stacks. "Lonely Rincon Volvo."

For some reason Mother puts her forearm over the book to hide what she's reading.

"Por supuesto. We'll have it ready for you by Friday morning.

Chao." Everett appears with three books and a big smile. "I have betrayed myself."

"Have you been here this whole time?"

"I didn't want to bother you. Pues, really I was hiding from you." He laughs. "Since I am supposed to be working not reading, I hide in the stacks when someone comes to the library. Have you discovered something exciting?"

"Maybe." Her arm still over the book.

"Que maravilla."

She loves the way that sounds. "Not really a marvel."

"Now our new neighbor knows you are a book lover more than a car lover," Neela says. "May I introduce—?"

"We know each other," he says. "I removed the bats from her belfry." A giant smile. He really seems to think that's funny. He puts his books on Neela's desk. "Can you check these out for me?"

"Will you check out my books, too?" Mother says. "I just remembered I have groceries in the car."

While Neela stamps books, he sits down on the bench opposite Mother, his back to Neela. He whispers, "You have discovered my secret. Only you and Neela know. I am sometimes with the library when I am supposed to be with the garage."

"But it's Saturday."

"I am doing the accounts on Saturday and answering the phone."

"I wont tell. About the library."

"Mil gracias."

There they are, sitting with just a few inches between them, nothing to do with their hands. "I have a question for you," she whispers. "Why did Mr. Lassiter get fired?"

"Ah, now you want to know the whole story, but before you throw Mrs. Rowlandson into the stove. You are a woman of mystery."

"I didn't throw that book in the stove. It must have fallen in."

He grins.

"Really. I just read it last night."

"But you are out of steps. We are now just getting over this captive woman." His cell phone rings.

"Your books are all checked out, both of you," Neela says.

"Lonely Rincon Volvo." Everett nods, mouths "Gracias" to Neela and heads out with his books under his arm, but before he leaves he shoulders the phone and says to Mother, "You must come to the potluck on Friday and try my rosquitas. Leave Señora Rowlandson at home."

Mother pulls back up to the farmhouse, edges out of the car carrying the pile of books she belted into the passenger seat for the ride from the library, and teeters up to the house with them. She is trying to balance the books in one arm while she reaches in her pocket for the key when something crawls out of the cat door.

Mother yelps. The books topple over, skid and flap across the gravel.

It's a little girl crouched on all fours by Mother's leg. She wears a down vest, a mud-smeared maroon velvet dress, and rubber boots. Around her neck is Mother's paper bead necklace. With her long dark brown hair and her round face and the velvet, she looks a little like an 18th century portrait painting, except her face has an ironic, eyebrow arching 21st century quality to it. They stare at each other.

"You have beautiful hair," Mother offers.

"Tu hair just kind of blah blahs."

Mother smoothes back the feature she's always considered her best quality.

"What did you do with all my mother's treasures? Did you steal them?" the little girl who must be Inez says.

"Actually, I think it's you—" Mother reaches down for her necklace.

"Get off me." Inez takes off down the driveway, galumphing

in her rubber boots across the road, through some poplar saplings and into the woods.

Mother gathers up the books, unlocks the door, drops the pile on the table next to a wicker basket. Her heart flickers—where did this basket come from? She thinks of Little Red Riding Hood. There's a note attached to the basket that starts "Welcome!" in a hurried scrawl and is signed "Joan." Eyeing the basket and the cat door, Mother estimates Inez could have just about squeezed it through. The basket contains a loaf of tin-foiled bread. Mother unwraps it and chips off a piece. It tastes of molasses. She has read about a biscuit called hardtack that the pilgrims took on their voyages because it lasted for months. Hardtack is a good name for this bread. She chokes the piece down. She picks up the note: "Welcome! Some black strap molasses bread, a known cure for cancer, anxiety, joint pain and can give limp hair body." Mother pats her head again. "IMPORTANT: There are these in the house, a doll, a rock, three empty rum bottles and a hat. DO NOT MOVE THEM. I look forward to finally meeting you at the potluck. Joan."

Mother crosses her arms and rereads the note. She checks the message machine. Molly: "It's me, calling you at a decent hour, you know actually calculating the time difference. Where are you? How are the monsters? Meet any hot guys yet? And speaking of men that are not in any way hot, your ex has called me three times demanding that I tell him where you are. Call me."

Mother looks back at the table. She calls Molly: "You need a cell phone. I know, I need one, too. Come on, pick up. Do not under any circumstances tell Steve anything. I know you wont. This house is beautiful and perfect except it's a little porous or something. Things keep getting in. Like I just got home and—anyway, it's too complicated. Call me." Mother starts to click off, then says, "I did meet a man. Maybe."

She watches the note on the table. "This is ridiculous," she mumbles. "I'm not doing it." She goes back to the car and makes four trips in, carrying groceries to the kitchen, paint materials to our baby room, and bedding to her room. During each trip she eyes the words, DO NOT MOVE THEM. She maneuvers the crate of logs so it blocks the cat door. She glances at the note again. She thinks, She can't tell me where to put things in my own house. True, it's not really my house, but I'm renting it. On the other hand, why shouldn't I do what she wants? And it's really important to her for personal reasons. And what about when I meet her and she asks me if I touched her things?

Mother goes to the basement door, picks at the duct tape. Puts her hand on the crack in the door and feels that radon-filled air licking her palm.

"Who gives a care," she says and turns away.

After she makes her bed with the new pretty sheets and quilt, she goes into our room. She should really ask, she thinks, before she starts painting the walls. She looks at the exciting strips of sample colors fanned out on top of one of the many cans. "Who gives a care," she says again, and this time she even grins at how wild and willful she's becoming.

Three hours later, the drop cloth on the floor, the sills covered with tape, she's put down the first coat of yellow paint. She had wanted a canary color, the color of our room in her red plus sign vision, of Toad's gypsy caravan in *Wind in The Willows*, the color of the suns and moons in the stained glass windows, but now she thinks maybe she likes this milder color, like pale northeastern winter sunshine.

She eats some dinner, forces herself to finish a big glass of milk. Thinks about drinking another full glass of milk and gives up, pours it back into the carton, trying not to imagine our bird bones softening. She plans the first day of classes. She wonders where Everett lives, not on Lonely Rincon or Michael would have pointed it out on his tour. She pictures him in a small room in a leather armchair surrounded by books. She pictures him, then, here in the backyard. It's spring, everything absurdly green, like in Oz, and he is holding one of us up to reach grapes high on the vine. Mother holds the other one of us. All the bright *Wizard of Oz* light is coming from his smile.

She starts reading her library book about King Philip's War. The windows darken to black, no cars pass. She can see the lights on in Neela's trailer and through the trees, a glow from Joan's house and Michael's light up top of the garage. Neela's dog barks.

Then, maybe she falls asleep in the rocker or maybe something different is happening, but she hears a sound like stones thrown against the house.

She's in a smoky log cabin trying to breathe. Smoke stings her eyes into slits and pinches her throat closed. She is pressed everywhere by people and dogs and smoke and the smell of urine and sweat. The pressing, the choking, it's familiar in a terrible way and she puts her hand to her throat. Everyone else is coughing and gagging too, arguing about whether they should make a run for it, arguing whether 'tis better to die by an Indian club or from smoke or immolation. Mother's sister is crying out to herself or to God. The seven long-legged dogs pace and cower and whine, ears flattened, tails down.

Mother thinks, Fuck it.

She lifts her blue skirt to move over to where her thirteen-year-old son Joseph crouches with a gun before a tiny window. Do you have anything in there? she asks him. He shakes his head. She goes to a cupboard, reaches way in the back where she keeps her dessert forks in a wooden box covered with a cloth, the ones her mother brought from England. She and Joseph crush them in their fists and tamp them down the barrel of the gun.

She pulls the thin rug up, heaves open the root cellar door underneath. The faces of the five children inside look up at her, round and white as china plates. It smells putrid, of rotting potatoes. Mother reaches down, and her daughter Sarah climbs up the wooden ladder. All will be well, Mother says to her. Mind me. Then she heaves Sarah onto her hip. Sarah buries her face into Mother's neck, rests her lips there. Sarah is solid, and as soon as Mother picks her up she can feel the burden of her like a sack of corn meal, how she has grown almost too big to carry. Mother begins to untie her pocket, an embroidered apron that holds her sewing things inside, but then she changes her mind.

Her chest is thrumming with anxiety, but she tells her son calmly, We will make a run for it. She puts him in the lead with the gun, pushes him in front of her as if he is already a man, to give him courage. The low door opens up into the chaos of grey February sky, no walls anywhere. She stands before the doorway in the rush of cold air, thinking, Perhaps not, but Abraham, her sister's boy, desperate for clean air, pushes from behind, and they stumble out into the open. Abraham runs, bent over, heading down hill towards the stream. He is shot. They'd been teasing him lately, because since he'd turned fourteen a sparse moustache had come in, and without realizing it he is always worrying it, smoothing it like a beaver pelt. He falls. He screams out, My leg. One of them jogs over and clubs him on the head, twice, passionless, like splitting wood. Mother's son, Joseph, just in front of her, stares at where his cousin lies. She grabs him behind the neck, it's wet there. Joseph, towards the bridge, she says.

Then an Indian stands in front of them. Joseph raises his gun, but it won't fire. Joseph begins to cry and fiddle with the flintlock. The Indian holds his hand out for the gun. Joseph gives it to him. They watch the Indian check the barrel, empty out the forks onto the dirty snow, fluidly reload with a lead ball. Then he aims at Mother.

Joseph knocks the gun with the side of his arm as it goes off.

Sarah screams. She screams, Mama, it burns! and like an echo, Mother feels burning in her own side. No, Mother says sharply, and instinctively puts her hand over Sarah's hand, which is over Sarah's stomach. Mother's legs begin to shake, but she doesn't drop her baby. The screaming and smoke and noise move into the distance. Up close there is only an intense heat, boiling between herself and her little girl. Sarah pulls her hand away from Mother's side. The plump hand cups blood, and there is blood spreading through Sarah's apron, over her round stomach, blood wet and warm between them. Mother thinks, Please, Lord, mend this. Mother turns to go back inside the house. Her sister blocks the door, smoke roiling out of the garrison and around her as if it were coming out of her head. She stares at Mother. Mother says to her, or thinks to say to her, Sister, He can mend this, let's go back inside. But Mother's sister doesn't hear, or doesn't agree—perhaps because her son lies shot and beaten to death on the ground.

Mother thinks to say to her sister: The hem of the world has ripped open. The seam has broken and things I cannot fathom have fallen through. But with His help, we can still sew it back up, please Sister, please help me, we can fix this together. I have my needle and thread in my pocket. It's not too late.

Her sister says, Lord, let me die too. As if in answer, a lead ball enters her sister's head just above the ear, the force banging her head against the doorjamb. She slides to the ground and sits there, not moving.

One of the painted ones grabs Mother's arm. His face all red but not with blood, with a cape fashioned from raccoon pelts around his neck, their ringed tails swaying when he moves, and black tattoos all over his naked chest and things hanging from his neck, little bags and animal teeth, and smelling of rancid animal grease, and shiny from the grease, and carrying a club rounded and polished, the size of a baby's head at the top, smeared with blood and blond hair, and with one half of his head shaved and one half long and loose, as if he didn't understand simple symmetry, everything about him seems to tell her that he is closer to an animal, a bear, a lion, than to her, this monster has his fingers around her forearm. Now, she thinks, her throat squeezing and squeezing. She turns Sarah's wet face into her armpit. Now.

Parlez=vous francais? he says, and when she doesn't answer, he tries again in hesitant English, his voice so low and reasonable it could have been her own: Come, go along with us. I am Quinnipin. I am yours.

Mother wakes the next morning in her bed at sunrise to the sound of freezing rain pelting the windows like stones thrown against the house. Her first thought: The hem of the world has ripped open. The seam has broken and things I cannot fathom have fallen through. She thinks, That's from my dream. In the rocking chair before I stumbled off to bed. It was something about Mary Rowlandson, she thinks.

Her nightgown is twisted around her, the part of it under her breast is warm and wet. A thrill of fear for us, her babies. She cradles her belly. What is it? This seems connected but she can't connect it.

She realizes she's peed herself. Thinks, Maybe it's a pregnancy thing.

Then she remembers, It's my first day of work.

As she rinses out her nightgown and new bottom sheet in the kitchen sink, Mother looks out the window several times, watching for Everett, but he does not drive by or stop, and why would he, in the freezing rain at six am? After her shower, back in her bedroom, she pulls on her new black wool tights, a long grey wool skirt, blue turtleneck and her blue cardigan, gathers her hair into a loose bun, then hangs little books from her ears.

When she opens the front door sleet smacks her in the face. She squints into the ice beating at her, sticking in her eyelashes, making her nose run. She returns to get a hat, remembers she didn't bring one, and picks up an umbrella instead. As she runs to the car she thinks of telling Molly: Now I understand why Easterners need their stoicism.

When she enters the chaos of the high school hallway in her unfamiliar damp, itchy wool clothes, kids snicker at her umbrella. The violent slamming of a locker startles her. She smells cow manure.

She signs the papers in the office in front of the unsmiling secretary. Mrs. L looks over her form, taps the place where Mother has written her home address with her long maroon nail. "I don't know why you didn't consult us about where to live, Miss Rosen. One of your neighbors is a convicted terrorist. And then there's the drunks and deviants up there to Lonely Rincon. Check the Penny Saver for rooms for rent before it's too late, that's my advice."

As Mother turns into her classroom she slips on the dirty sleet melting and dripping and smearing over the floors.

She prepares for her classes, monitors a restless study hall, then at 10:45 the lunch bell rings. She puts her soup into the microwave for three minutes in the teacher's lounge and goes to the bathroom. She returns to find her food has been tossed out of the microwave, the Styrofoam container on its side next to the sink, half the chicken noodle soup spilled on the counter.

As she eats saltines and what is left of the soup, she thinks of her California elementary school covered in ocean murals with smiling dolphins and dancing octopi, where the kids lunch at picnic tables and wear flip flops all year, and the principal, a yo-yo champ, puts up a new encouraging note at the entrance each morning, like, There Are Alternatives to Plastic! Or, Skill of the day: Sharing.

In her first real class after lunch, Mother writes: "Rules: 1. Respect" on the board, then four more numbers with blanks next to them. She plans for everyone to create the rules of the class together. She turns to face them.

There's something grotesque about fifteen year olds. Some of the boys are six feet tall with full beards, some are four feet with high voices. And the girls have no idea what to do with their breasts or with the lack of them. They either stick them out absurdly or hunch over them, arms crossed. It's a freak show, a hormone experiment gone wrong. And their clothes. Rural white boys dressed like rappers on MTV, jeans sagging, baseball caps backwards, gold chains, sunglasses in February, rural white girls dressed like back-up dancers on MTV, tiny T's and tight jeans. Mother's heart fills with pity.

One of them yells out, "The first rule is there are no rules." Screams of laughter. A girl shrieks: "Rule number three, Bling bling." "Yeah," a boy says, suddenly standing on his seat and pumping his arm. "Yeah!"

Her usual tricks, flicking the light switch or ringing her blue glass bell for quiet, are not successful.

"Okay, rules later." She has to yell, but tries to make it sound cheerful. "Why don't you tell me what you did in class last week? Did you read out of the textbook?"

A boy calls out, "I think that's my textbook hanging from your ear," and the entire class collapses into hilarity.

"I've heard you've been reading *The Captivity and Restoration of Mary Rowlandson*."

"No way!"

"Wicked boring."

"It's all about God."

"It's about this crazy lady who eats trash."

"Mr. Lassiter got fired for teaching it."

"He got fired for saying God sent the Islamo terrorists to attack us because we let homos be homos."

"He got fired for punching a student." Sly sideways looks and snickers follow this declaration.

A boy raises his hand.

"Yes?"

"Bathroom."

"Okay go. So, no Mary Rowlandson. Did you learn in your textbook that in the Massachusetts Bay Colony children had to stand at the supper table and the whole family drank beer every night?"

Some possibly interested laughter.

"Did you know that the pilgrims loved bright colors and spicy food?"

But she's lost them again. They are twisting away from her in their seats, jeering, pointing out the window. Mother goes over to look. The student who supposedly had to use the bathroom is now in the middle of the highway, dancing right along the double yellow line. He wears a big black sweatshirt, hood thrown back. He pulls up his sagging camouflage pants, dances now like a mime or a robot, slides on his feet like Michael Jackson, then drops right down on the wet road and begins spinning on his shoulders like a turtle in its shell. "What's his name?" she asks.

"Fred," someone offers.

Mother uncranks the window, feels a shock of cold, wet air, calls "Fred!" which makes everyone laugh. A truck flies by him spraying what must be icy water, horn flat out and angry. The boy does not even flinch, does not deign to look at the truck.

Mother hands out markers and sheets of stickers to decorate their safety-pinned nametags. She pulls on her coat, takes her umbrella, leaves the room. Outside of the building she calls from under the eaves: "Fred, please come over here!" Nothing but dancing. She checks the road twice and hurries out into the middle. Her umbrella immediately turns inside out and breaks. She lets it go, and it skitters down the road. "Please return to school property," she says, ignoring the umbrella wheeling away. This is a skinny boy with a big head. He has a square chin on which he must have been trying to grow a beard because there are some dark hairs wisping on it. He turns away and she sees his thin neck, wet with sweat or rain. It looks weirdly familiar, and she ignores the urge to touch him there, guide him by the neck in front of her to safety.

"Hey," she whispers, this time right in the kid's dripping face. The kid gives her an empty look, really eerie, almost like he can't hear. She notices the white wires snaking out of his ears and into his sweatshirt. She pulls on a wire until an earphone pops out. They stare at each other, their rain soaked faces still close.

"You're a good dancer," she says in a normal voice. "Do you take classes?"

"Nah, that's for ho's." But he smiles with a mouth full of crooked teeth.

"Go back to the classroom, please."

He shrugs a shoulder, swaggers across the road to the school.

Back inside, Mother tells them charming and interesting facts about the pilgrims while they decorate nametags. The simple art project seems to have temporarily soothed their raging hormones. Mother glances over at the street dancer. He has stuck his nametag through his eyebrow. A tiny trickle of blood has hardened over his eyelid and cheek. The nametag is decorated with glittery palm tree stickers and reads, "River."

Michael's son.

"Excuse me, River, can you—"

The bell rings. Her students join the chaos in the hallway. New students start squeezing into her room for her next class. One of them says, "Mrs. Sub, you got books in your ears." Everyone cracks up.

She erases "Rules: 1. Respect" from the board.

Five days later, six pm, sky already dark, cold with heavy clouds, first Friday in March, ten weeks pregnant, Mother walks down Lonely Rincon carrying a Saran Wrapped plate of ruggelah she's baked for the potluck that night. She has a bounce in her walk. She doesn't have to go back to that extremely challenging school for two days, and she will see Everett tonight. She will try his rosquitas, and she imagines Everett tasting her raspberry jam filled cookies, his eyes closed in bliss, his gorgeous smile rising. Que maravilla, he will say.

A boy of seven or eight with Michael's stick-up hair and crooked teeth bursts out of the woods and throws himself behind her, standing too close, panting on her shoulder. "He said he's going to kill me, and he IS going to kill me! He already squeezed my face like it was a potato!" The boy is giddy with fear, and when Mother puts her arm around him she can feel the frenzy of his heart through his skinny chest.

River lopes out of the woods. He jerks his chin at the boy cowering behind Mother. "That's my brother Oshun. I'm supposed to be watching him." They face off, Mother between them, two lollipop boys with skinny bodies and big heads, the older one dressed like a gangsta, the younger one, maybe seven or eight, in tight, high-water jeans.

Mother says, "Do you guys want to try a Jewish cookie?"

River shrugs, paces around a little. Mother lifts up the plastic and brings out a ruggelah. The younger boy nibbles on his. "Yum," he says noncommittally. She holds one out for River. He takes it and tosses it whole into his mouth, turns towards Joan's driveway. "Let's go, Ms. R," he says with his mouth full. "You're late."

As she hurries down the dark driveway following River, Oshun walks so close to her that he keeps stepping on the heel of her boot. The driveway opens up into a small soccer field with two goals made from tail pipes and held up by old tires filled with cement. The floodlights mounted on poles give everything a mall-like glow. There are dark hulks of cars strewn about the woods. The spectators sit on more piles of old tires. Mother can't tell much about the house, but it has a barn-like shape.

The players stand in a clump, finishing an argument. The whole neighborhood seems to be playing, even Michael with a cigarette in his mouth, who winks at her, even River has jogged out onto the field, earphones in, doing some shoulder shrugging and other little gestures towards dance. Oshun joins Inez on defense. Everyone's skin looks yellowish in the floodlights. Everett is setting up for a penalty kick.

The plate of ruggelah trembles.

Everyone else on the field wears jeans or sweats or leggings and sweaters or coats or sweatshirts, but Everett wears a bright, red silky shirt and blue silky shorts, red socks to his knees. His legs are hairy and muscular. He shouts, "Para the team, para Chile y para mi mama!" He kicks the ball into the corner, the potbellied goalie dives for it and misses, landing on the frozen ground with a middle-aged "Oof." Everett jumps in the air, twists, that alarmingly bright smile shines yellow under the floodlights.

Radiant, Mother thinks.

There is high-fiving and complaining, the game seems to be breaking up, everyone jostles up the wooden steps into the warmer light of the wood-shingled house. Mother follows. Joan's downstairs is dim, packed. A log garrison crowded and filled with smoke comes into Mother's head, and she puts her hand to her throat. She shakes the image away. It actually reminds me of the beaver's lodge in Narnia, she thinks instead, snug like that— two tweed couches, two pleather armchairs, a velour lazy boy recliner. The crowded dining/living room is lined in homemade bookshelves—they've been ingeniously built on every available wall space, over doorways, under windowsills, jammed with books. There are framed photos of the Dali Lama, Gandhi and Emma Goldman propped on the shelves. That venomous snake, Mother smiles.

On the dining room table—an open bag of potato chips, a plate of corn dogs stuck on popsicle sticks, a bowl of tubular carrots, a store bought cake in its white box, two six packs of beer and one bottle of New York State wine. Mother puts her cookies down and takes off the plastic. Only the children seem to be eating. Everyone else drinks beer from cans or wine from paper cups. Mother looks at the food, super concentrated on the task of choosing just the right potato chip or perhaps a corn dog, so she doesn't appear lost and alone.

"Welcome, neighbor!" The woman before her is as brightly colored as an Easter egg—yellow leggings and green sweatshirt, shiny bottle-blond hair, pink lipsticked smile—only her skin seems powdery and forlorn.

Mother says, "Hi, I'm—"

"—I know all about you, Evie Rosen! I was hoping you'd be here. I'm Margaret Langley Gonzales. I've brought you a complimentary Welcome To The Neighborhood bath set."

The Evangelical daughter of the last farmer, married to one of the Mexican-American men who work at the garage, Mother remembers.

Margaret hands her a small plastic zippered pouch containing miniature blue-themed bottles. "I'm an Avon representative by trade, but a community builder by vocation. Now, I'll tell you right up front that we pulled our son Christian out of the high school when we heard you were coming. No offense!" She sticks out her bright pink lower lip and sags her eyes to mime sadness and pats Mother's arm. "Graham Lassiter, the teacher whose job you took, was a deacon in our church, and we were just so heartbroken when they fired him! The man was trying to teach history—that was his job for pity's sake. Isn't 9/11 part of history?"

"Maybe more of a current event," Mother says.

"I felt very close to his teachings. Because of our loss."

"Oh, no. What happened?" Mother asks.

"Our daughter Deandra died in the twin towers."

Mother squeezes her own hands together. "That's awful. Terrible. I'm so sorry."

"I'm still trying to identify her. Graham was helping me." Margaret continues to smile, perhaps bravely.

"How awful," Mother says.

"I was cleaning when I heard," Margaret says. "They interrupted a sermon on the radio to report it. I fell to my knees. I thought, It's come, Judgment Day. The wolves are at the door, just as Graham predicted, and they've taken my baby—"

Mother reaches her hand out towards Margaret, but Margaret plows on, smiling or grimacing—"Of course, it was someone who shall remain nameless in our neighborhood who had it in for Graham. I'll just say her name rhymes with groan. Ha, ha. Oh, well, we all agree to disagree on Lonely Rincon. But I can tell just from looking at you that you're as mild as milk!"

Everett's right there, across the table, recently showered in jeans and a button down shirt. Mother can see a wedge of the dark hair on his chest.

"Yes," Mother says, dropping her own hands to her sides.

Everett puts a bowl of small fried donuts dusted in powdered sugar and orange zest on the table.

"So you hail from California," Margaret says.

Everett smiles at Mother. Walks away.

"So what brings you to our neck of the woods?" Margaret asks.

Mother thinks to follow him.

"So what brings you—"

Neela bustles through the front door in a whoosh of cold air, down coat, the gold and green sari. A wide-shouldered, handsome woman behind her, must be her roommate or maybe partner, Sondra. Both have flaming cheeks, from the oven or the weather, both loaded down with food. Sondra sweeps the junky food and the ruggelah to the sides of the table and begins unloading steaming clay pots and silver trays of food. The house fills with the smell of curry and ghee. One of the kids yells, "Nan!" The children push in, grabbing the hot bread. The adults crowd behind them, filling their plates.

Mother is stuck near but not at the table, surrounded, and then suddenly Neela is next to her with a full plate of jewel-colored food, two steaming nan riding on top. She hands it over to Mother. "Go, go, sit," Neela says. "Eat and relax after your first week of work. You are teaching our children, and we are so grateful."

Mother squeezes through the crowd. She doesn't see Everett. She doesn't even see Michael, but there's Inez sliding off the lap of a woman in a giant velour armchair in the corner.

The woman is obviously Michael's sister Joan—even the same haircut as Michael—short, thick dark hair sticking up every which way. She has the same long, narrow hipped body, too. She's striking in a ravaged, aging rock star, Patty Smith kind of way. She wears faded jeans and a white t-shirt and black rubber boots. Copper bracelets run up both her arms. Mother brings her plate over and sits down in a metal folding chair near Joan's armchair. Joan is drinking wine from a real wine glass.

"Aren't you going to get some food?" Mother smiles.

"I love Indian food, but I can't eat it, too spicy—I have a nervous stomach. I'm Joan, by the way."

"I'm Evie Rosen. Thank you for the molasses bread. It was so substantial."

"Inez told me you moved my memorials." Joan raises one thin eyebrow and doesn't smile.

"Your memorials?" Mother says.

"I told you not to move them in the note."

"After I got your note I put them back," Mother says, thinking, I will when I get home.

Joan smiles, crooked teeth, all delighted. "Ha. I knew you'd put them back. I just had a feeling about you. I like your name. It sounds like a garden." Joan reaches behind her chair, pulls out a bottle of wine. "I just quit smoking so I have to drink to distract myself." She tips it towards Mother, Mother shakes her head. Joan puts the bottle back, toasts Mother. "Here's to you and not Lassiter."

"What's the story with him anyway? Mr. Lassiter?"

Joan gives Mother a little nudge with her leg. "That neo-fascist born again asshole? He shirted all the girls in his class. He kept all these giant t-shirts in a milk crate at the door and the girls had to put them on as they walked into his classroom every day. I wrote the letter to the paper that helped get him fired. And I made everyone on Lonely Rincon sign it, or everyone who's not insane. Of course, then he attacked my nephew River. So that was the end of that."

"He attacked River?"

"He threw his ruler at him. It hit him right in the eye. The whole eyeball turned bright red. Even after that Old Lassy thought firing him was a conspiracy to suppress the truth."

"So you're the left wing terrorist I've been hearing so much about."

Again the delighted face. "Yup. Supposedly, Lassy wrote some letter to this new Department of Homeland Security accusing us on Lonely Rincon of who knows what—unpatriotic, godless acts." Mother notices that Joan's arms are stained green from the copper in the bracelets that line both her arms. She wonders if this could be healthy. Joan's eyes pop and spark. "So, tell me about you, Evie. Are you one of those Bay area summer of love hot tub types?"

"My parents were. I grew up in a geodesic dome in the redwoods. My father was a professor, then he had a midlife crisis and now he lives in an ashram in India."

"And your mother?"

"My mother quit her pottery business and went into real estate in the early nineties. She rode the real estate boom right into early retirement and now she is celebrating in Amalfi, Italy, for who knows how long, reinventing herself as a collage artist and a sipper of lemon drinks."

"And you turned out just like them. Striking out on your own."

"No, not at all. I used to hide in my room reading and drawing while they had wild red wine and marijuana parties, but you know though—that striking out on your own—I am kind of trying to do that. I want to stop settling and become a settler."

"A pioneer. Except west to east."

"Exactly!"

Joan laughs, knocks her knee companionably against Mother's knee again. Mother thinks, I haven't felt this making a new friend rush of happiness in a long time. It's like entering a British children's book. You're Rat and Mole punting down a

51

river, you're walking through a snowy wood and at a lamp post you meet a fawn who invites you to tea. "Your turn," Mother says. "Tell me what it was like in jail."

Joan rolls her eyes. "Did you read about that in Margaret's blog?"

"No, I didn't even know she had one."

"You're going to show up in the next entry," Joan grins.

"She told me about her daughter. That's awful."

Joan rolls her eyes again. "Deandra waitresses in New York City. Margaret can't stand the fact that her daughter snorts coke and doesn't go to Church and fornicates outside of wedlock and never calls her, so she killed her off in the twin towers."

"Seriously?"

"Yeah, and Lassy got Margaret these photos of people jumping from the towers—she scours them with a magnifying glass looking for Deandra. It's so sick."

"Yikes. I thought there was something odd in the way she talked about it. She kept smiling."

"Margaret never stops smiling." Joan sips her wine.

"So, what was it like? Jail."

Joan sighs, waves her arm dismissively, spills some wine on her wrist and sucks it up. "I was in a maximum security federal prison for three years. Felony charges. That's it."

"What did you do in prison?"

"I read about the Saints. I took up knitting. That's where I learned to cook, in the prison cafeteria."

"I admire you. I can't imagine the courage it took to do that. To risk everything."

"Risking everything is easy. Daily life takes guts."

"Tell me about your interest in the Saints."

"Saint Agatha kept her virginity even though her breasts were cut off and shown to her on a plate, even though she was rolled naked over hot coals and splinters of glass." Joan puts her empty wine glass on the floor where it falls on its side and rolls under her chair. "And Saint Mary of Egypt lived for 47 years in the desert on three loaves of bread and found it pleasant. They made themselves into arrows. A straight shot from belief to action. They said no. They refused."

"That's exactly what I find so fascinating about Mary Rowlandson." Mother says, bending down to retrieve Joan's glass. "She refused to give up."

Joan's smile curdles. "What."

"I think Mr. Lassiter sent me a copy of her book. I'm sure he taught it in an awful way, but it's really important. We can't let Mr. Lassiter determine how we read it. She's the first woman to write a book in the Americas. She's our founding mother."

"Founding mother?" Joan's voice rises. "That book made me ashamed, once again, of our racist, colonial history. The moment when the starving little girl is sucking on a horse hoof and your pilgrim lady literally grabs it out of her mouth and eats it herself. That's the American way, right? I threw that shitty little book across the room when I read that. You should refuse to teach it!" Joan's eyes are bulging and sparking and she's staring at Mother.

"I'm not teach—"

And there is Everett, with his own plate of food, lowering himself onto the floor beside Joan's chair.

Rescued, Mother thinks.

"Hello," he smiles at her.

"Hello yourself," Mother smiles back big.

Joan tips her head towards Everett. "You've already met my husband, Mateo."

Mother grips her plate so it doesn't tip. "But, I thought— Everett."

Joan and the man formerly known as Everett both laugh merrily. In fact, Joan's outrage seems to have disappeared. "Pay no attention to the nametags," Joan says. "Michael bought those uniforms used, except his own of course—they all have random names on them. They've been wearing them for years."

Mother takes a huge forkful of food. She imagines the spice

steaming "Everett" out of her brain. She can see that smile out of the corner of her eye, the same as before, signifying neighborly good will, nothing more. Just let it go, Mother tells herself. You haven't lost anything. There is no Everett. She takes another huge bite. She can't taste anything but heat.

"Jeez, you must be starving," Joan says.

FIFTH REMOVE

She carries her wounded daughter Sarah, following the others away and away and away into the winter woods.

It's happening again. A dream-vision Mother will later forget.

Sarah grows heavier with each step. Perhaps she is soaking up moisture from the air or collecting grief. Mother matches her pace to the rhythm of her daughter's moans, the pulsing pains in her side, her back, her arms, her neck, the sound of the crunching snow under her shoes, the occasional crack of sticks as she trods on them, the moan, the pain, the crunch, the crack a kind of frozen hymn.

As she walks she thinks about her husband, the Reverend Joseph Rowlandson. Built like a wrestler, with the regal nose and wavy blond hair of a Roman charioteer. It is his job to correct Mother.

Mother heaves Sarah and herself over a log. Her face is wind burned, her nose runs. She doesn't drop Sarah, but she shifts her painfully onto her other hip.

Buddy, do not forget to thank God for this great sack of turnips, only a very few wormy and rotten. God will forsake us if we consume without giving Him, our tenderest friend, the glory of our blessings.

Sarah moans, It burns. Mother whispers Sha, sha sha into Sarah's ear and kisses her forehead. Sarah's skin is dry, burning. The snow crunches each time she steps, again and again and again. Her right leg cramps.

Buddy, I fear your greatest sin is your horrid pride in your daughter, a pride that is almost idolatrous, which is spiritual adultery. You dress Sarah as if she were in Boston supping with the Governor. All are plagued with lice, but for Sarah you spend hours combing the nits out of her hair and douse her with lamp oil each night to smother the vermin. You curl her hair in rags. You coddle her excessively.

Mother skids a little on an icy patch, her ankle twists painfully in her boot.

She doesn't drop Sarah.

Buddy, look at your countenance! When I remind you of your failings your face is harder than a rock. You look as if you will choke on your own rage. Take care, Buddy, for if we puff up, God will empty us. He taps her forehead with his finger. Think, think, he says.

Now she is dragging herself and Sarah into the Nipmuc village of Wenimessit. Here she discovers she is not Quinnipin's and he is not hers. He presents her as a gift to his wife, the Warrior Queen Weetamoo, head sachem of the Wampanoag. Face painted black, in a British Kersey coat, girdled with wampum, with white stockings and white shoes and powdered hair, and a necklace of jangling British buttons, with both arms covered in bracelets made from English forks and spoons wrapped from the elbows to the wrists, as if she had eaten the English owners of the silverware. Her arms are stained green under the bracelets.

Weetamoo has a toddler at her breast. His nose is caked with dried snot, and every time he tries to suck he chokes. He has a wheezy cough, and his cry is thin as a thread.

The two women face each other. Mother and her wounded daughter have not eaten in days, Weetamoo and her sick baby both wasted. The children cry and moan for more, the women jiggle and soothe because there is nothing more to give.

They hate each other on sight.

The morning after the potluck, Saturday, Mother looks up from reading her library books at the kitchen table. The early morning world is rimed in hoar frost, the sky clear and blue, and someone dressed in green is slinking out of the frozen garden. Welcome to my world, Mother plans to tell Molly. She walks out on the porch in her slippers. There is a light, cold wind whispering through the trees, scaring up the back of Mother's neck. Everything, the trees, the grape vine, the blackberry bushes, wears a thin jacket of ice. She crosses her arms over her baby blue fleece pullover, calls: "Hello?"

The Peter Pan woman waves and glides over. She wears green corduroys, a brown vest tight over the curves of her breasts, a green scarf knotted at her neck. Golden hair and goldbrown cat eyes with laugh lines radiating like sunshine on a child's drawing, a friendly, vague, heart-shaped face. She looks like a stewardess from Air Sweden or a retired Playboy bunny dressed as a leprechaun.

"I'm Juniper. I spent a lot of time in this house." She comes right up onto the porch and perches herself on the railing. She points to a frosted spider's web stretched from the rain gutter to the top of the back door. "Nature."

Ah, Mother thinks, the golden-haired punk rock hippie who wouldn't kill a living thing. "It's so cold out here, you're not even wearing a jacket. Would you like to come in?"

Juniper shakes her head. "Just passing through. These grapes grow sour, but you can make jelly when they ripen in the fall. It's a sweet garden, if you give it some love."

"I'm not much of a gardener." Mother smiles apologetically, thinking, I live on a farm with my twins. We make jelly.

"So is that your sister who lives with you?" Juniper asks.

"My sister?"

"The one in the long dress."

"What?"

Juniper swings her green corduroy legs back and forth. "I was on a moonlit stroll last night, and I saw her walking out from behind Joan and Mateo's. Long blue or white dress, long hair in her face. She was plodding through the woods, real heavy tread. Burdened. I saw her coming up these porch steps and going into the farmhouse. Then I saw her in the basement window, dropping that sack or whatever it was."

"I don't understand. What?"

"I think she stole something from Joan's house. She was

carrying something heavy, she kept shifting it from hip to hip."

"Into this house?"

"Anyways, no offense, but I had a hunch she might not be all there, am I right?"

Mother's arms are crossed over her own chest like a breastplate, hands squeezing her own shoulders. "I don't have a sister. I have no idea what you're talking about."

"Weird." Juniper swings her legs.

"Are you sure you saw a woman come in here?"

"Yep, up these stairs and then a minute later in the basement. It could have been a ghost, I guess. Wouldn't be the first time I've seen one. Crazy, though, right?" Juniper gestures towards the delicately rimed web above the door. "That's a black widow by the way." She wanders down the stairs, turns back. "You could get a ladder and find the egg sack and move it somewhere else before they hatch. The egg sacks contain like 900 little spiders."

As Mother watches Juniper wander away, she thinks, That woman is totally crazy. I'm not paying attention to any of that. She walks inside, ducking down low under the sparkling black widow web, goes to her laptop, opens it up to check her email, remembers she deleted it, than searches for Margaret's Blog.

City On A Hill:
The Community Building Web Log
For Lonely Rincon Road
By Margaret Langley Gonzales

Number of hits last month: 97!!

Spring's a'coming, folks, and this green thumbed gardener's got her trowel ready. When I'm done with my yard I'll move ever outward until all of Lonely Rincon is a bower of flowers! Love hath no boundaries.

March's potluck last Friday—what a treat! Thanks to all who contributed, especially Neela, with her monthly mysterious bubbling pots of who knows what, but for those brave souls who dip in, they're in for a difference! Yellow, orange and green, with spices that will blow your head off! And for those of us whose stomachs aren't steel plated, the so-called "nan" is just like normal bread! And there's always corndogs. Three cheers for diversity!

In Other News:
1) Our local Avon representative, yours truly, announces that Almond Serenity and Rejuvenating Vanilla body wash are on sale the whole month. When you call, just mention the blog to receive your discount or click the contact button to place your order.

2) I've had a letter from Deacon Lassiter. If anyone wants to donate to a fund to help him get back up on his feet after his unjust and devilish dismissal, press the donate button at the bottom of the page. He assures me his spirits are high. With the Lord's help he will continue to work with The Department of Homeland Security to unmask the evildoers who have tried to silence him. We all know that there are a lot of wolves in sheep's clothing out there.

3) On a lighter note, we have a new resident on Lonely Rincon!!! Meet Evy Rosen, who has relocated all the way from California, all by her lonesome to boot!! Teaching history at the high school, Evy is of the Jewish faith. I've heard through the grapevine that she hasn't quite gotten her sea legs in the classroom, so if you have teaching experience, some advice might surely be welcome (Help, Mr. Lassiter! ha ha). Evy made her debut at our last pot luck, where she fearlessly (or politely—she's very soft spoken, which may be part of the problem in the classroom)

sampled Indian fare (Evy was very pale. I had a sense she might be anemic, so neighborly gifts of iron rich food could be in order). Joan and Mateo have clearly reached out a warm hand of friendship to her already, and hopefully next potluck they will give the rest of us a chance to get to know our new neighbor. ☺ I hope everyone will make a point of welcoming the newest addition to our own little city on a hill! Welcome Evy!! God bless!

Mother closes the laptop. She stares at the frozen back garden. Then she goes to the basement door. The duct tape hangs down in grey ribbons. Pulled off the door. Mother's vision shimmers. Her throat starts to close. She shakes her head to clear it. Coughs open her throat. The tape must have fallen down, she tells herself.

She puts a hand on the black doorknob, turns it and pulls. The sponges duct taped to the bottom scrape against the floor. Underground air washes over her. Dark down there, just a gash of weak sun on the dirt floor. And of course the grimy light switch still doesn't work. All Mother can see are bulky shadows.

She climbs halfway down the stairs, past the box of Joan's things she left on the landing. She holds tight to the rickety railing. She can see now that the basement is crowded with wilted boxes. And a broken rake, a toilet, a child's plastic toy stove on its side. One of the windows just has a screen, no glass, which must be why it's freezing down here. She forces herself to walk down the rest of the way.

At the far end of the basement there is a hole in the cement wall, crudely hollowed out.

Mother takes a few steps along the side of the stairs towards the small cave, running her hand on the wooden steps to steady herself.

She stops. The hollowed out place goes back several feet into the dirt. She thinks she can see something hunched in there.

"What are you doing?"

Mother yelps, jerks around.

Inez stands behind her wearing a multi-colored wool hat and scarf. She holds a heavy black flashlight with two hands. She pushes past Mother and shines the light into the hole. "Mi mama says the farmer who lived here before mi abuela built this as a shelter to save him from the A-bomb. That's the biggest bomb in the alphabet."

"How did you get in here, Sweetie?"

"I opened the door."

"Where'd you get that flashlight?"

"Under the sink." She hands Mother the heavy flashlight.

"Don't go—" but Inez has already climbed into the hole. Mother shines the light in. Inez backs out clutching a bundle. It's about a foot long, wrapped in a flowered shirt, the sleeves used to bind it. "This is my shirt!" Inez says, outraged.

"Let's take it upstairs," Mother says. She follows Inez back up, suddenly recalling the radon and imagining how much of it has just snuck into her belly, imagining us beginning to glow. We imagine this, too. She leaves the flashlight at the top of the stairs next to Joan's box. Inez puts the bundle on the kitchen table and begins untying the sleeves of her shirt.

"Wait!"

Inez cuts her eyes at her. "It's my shirt. What did you hide in here?"

"Not me," Mother says. "I don't know what's in there, but we can find out. It's like buried treasure. But you have to wash your hands first."

"The shirt's already all dirty."

"Don't you want to find out what the treasure is? I'll count to see how long it takes you!" She begins, "One, Two," pretending to look at her watch, and finally Inez whirls off towards the bathroom. Mother hears the faucet turn on. She unties the sleeves, slips the shirt off. "Use soap!" she calls. Inside are two more bundles, one very small, both wrapped in more children's shirts. She hears the faucet turn off.

61

Mother snatches the larger package and shoves it into the cupboard above the stove. In the process she knocks over a jar of cinnamon with a loose top.

"You opened it without me!" Inez says. "Unfair!"

Mother closes the cupboard. Wipes cinnamon off on her sweatpants. Thinks, What am I doing?

"I just took off the first layer so you can get at it better. The knot was hard to undo," Mother says. "Look." She pushes the little bundle on the table towards Inez. Mother squeezes her hands together while Inez unwraps it.

Inside is a woman made of red clay, about the size of Inez's hand. She has two long dark braids and a long blue dress covered in white flowers. And the clay woman has been given an abundance of clay children—tiny ones sitting on her lap, on her shoulders, holding onto her braid, even one on her head. The mother's mouth is an open O, maybe surprised at all she has been given, or maybe calling for even more of her brood to come to her, or maybe, as Mother thinks, shouting Help! I'm being attacked by a plague of children.

Inez hugs the little mother to her coat. "Is she magic?" Inez asks.

"I don't know," Mother says, ignoring her impulse to snatch the clay mother away from Inez, to save her from Inez or maybe to pick all the clay children off her. "It looks very delicate. You can bring it to your mom, just be gentle. I'll go with you." Mother puts on her new gloves and scarf and walks Inez home over the frozen road. Inez carries the little mother against her chest.

When Joan opens her door, Inez holds the figure out cupped in her hands.

"That's mine," Joan says sharply, as if she's been cut. She plucks the child-covered clay woman up. Her cheeks simmer. "My mother brought her home when I was a kid," she says. "For me."

"It's buried treasure," Inez says. "We found it in the fall out shelter!"

"Michael." Joan smiles, but it is a bitter affair. "He was always spitting on my toothbrush, breaking my things, reading my diary. Putting stuff in my hair when I was asleep, peanut butter. He painted my face with mustard and stuffed Frosted Flakes in my mouth while I slept. I could have choked. He melted my doll's face on the stove. Once he rigged up a rock in a tree and got me to pull on the rope, and the rock came crashing down an inch from my head. If he wasn't such a fuck-up I'd be dead right now."

Inez says, "Expliqueme how he did that. With the rock."

"I don't think it was Michael," Mother begins tentatively. "You know that woman, Juniper? She came by this morning—"

"Juniper?" Joan seems disgusted. "Why would she hide my clay mother?"

"I don't know. She seemed a little crazy—"

"—An airhead who follows her own bliss, yes. Thief, no. She's Michael's ex-wife you know. She's River and Oshun's mother."

So River is Juniper's son, Mother thinks.

"And before that Juniper was Mateo's girlfriend."

Mateo and the crazy punk rock princess. Mother reminds herself that she doesn't care.

"Juniper came by just now to break the news she's going to Kauai with some guy she met at a rainbow gathering," Joan continues. "Michael's going to have the boys living with him now, for the spring at least, for who knows how long. Living with us half the time, more like."

"Michael mentioned her to me once—he called her a dreamer."

"Dreamer is a nice word for selfish. Which reminds me, she left something for you." Joan hands Mother a small tan leather pouch stuffed with dried herbs on a leather strap. It smells like bay leaves, like rosemary and pine. "You're supposed to wear it around your neck to ward off bad karma or dark spirits or something. She says it's a Native American thing. It has a name.

Can't remember, but you could probably roast a chicken with it." Joan laughs.

"You love Aunt Juniper, Mama," Inez says. "She's your best friend. And she's a real witch."

Joan rolls her eyes. "My best friend." The fierceness is down to embers, but Mother can still see it in the twist of her mouth. "It's true though, she says she's a Wiccan."

"Juniper didn't say anything about a woman she supposedly saw, did she? We had a weird conversation."

"Pay no attention," Joan says. "I have to get these chickpea patties to the garage, but let's have tea soon."

Mother glances at the pile of dried-out, blackened discs on the platter. Joan turns away from her and places the clay mother on a shelf on top of some books, out of Inez's reach. The clay mother's round little mouth seems to be calling to Mother: Don't leave me.

"Hey," Inez grits her teeth. "I found it."

Mother stuffs the leather pouch into the pocket of her coat as she walks away. Wet snow has begun to drift down. The frozen fairy world is dripping away. She looks at her watch—already noon. She stands still then, right in the middle of the snowy road. What just happened? she thinks. She feels pushed and pulled by strange emotions, unsettled. She thinks, Who put those bundles in my basement? And when? Inez? Juniper? It couldn't have been Michael long ago because they were wrapped in Inez's shirts. I have to get that front door lock working. And put glass over that basement screen. And why did I steal that bundle from Joan and Inez? I have everything I need, a house in the woods, a job, twins. More than I need. I am perfectly content. She thinks then that pregnancy is like being taken over by a poltergeist, by two poltergeists, the way her hormones compel her in odd directions.

In our own defense, we only ride inside, passengers without a steering wheel.

Back inside she pulls off her winter things. She goes to the

64

kitchen counter, still dusted with cinnamon, Inez's filthy shirts tangled on the table.

There's a knock on the door. "Evie?"

It's Neela.

"I just saw you come in," she calls. The knob jiggles. "Hello?" The door opens. Neela stands on the top step in a blue sari, snow boots and a down parka. "I've brought you lamb curry Korma, for iron, as I read in Margaret's blog!"

Mother moves quickly to block Neela's view of the kitchen table. "Thank you so much!" She takes the little cast iron pot. "I read her blog, too."

"I mentioned to you that I need your advice. You see, I've written a children's story."

"I'm not a professional judge of children's books. I was actually—"

"—I think you'll enjoy it." Snow drifts onto Neela's head. "And you are a teacher!"

"Of course, I'd love to see it. Maybe you could leave it with me and—"

"—Oh, no, I don't want you to worry over it—just take a look while I heat up your dinner." Neela has wet snow on her hair and flyaway eyebrows now.

"You don't have to do that," Mother says, but her body has already turned sideways, and Neela takes back the pot and bustles in, headed towards the stove. "Great," Mother says, not glancing at the table. "Would you like some help?"

"Oh, no, I've used this kitchen many times."

Mother picks up the package and the shirts. "I'll be right back, I just need to—"

"What's that you have there?"

"I love your sari."

"Thank you very much. It's from New York, where my daughter lives. It's very difficult being away from one's family."

Mother slides the package and the shirts onto one of the kitchen chairs and quickly pushes the chair in with her hip.

"That's why it's so nice that we have a close community," Neela goes on. "It smells lovely in here. Cinnamon."

"Would you share the curry with me?" Mother asks.

"No, no, it's for you. I will eat later, with Sondra."

Mother rinses her hands at the sink. Neela unties the string on her manila envelope. The smell of ginger and garlic begins to overpower the cinnamon.

Neela hands her the manuscript. Mother does not sit down. Stick figure drawings of different colored people: yellow, beige, black and brown on printer paper.

Mother tries to concentrate on the book, which has been hand sewn at the edge with red and yellow yarn. Neela watches her. It's about a potluck. Everybody brings ethnic food. The Jewish people, colored beige, bring bagels, the yellow-colored Chinese family brings yellow rice, the beige Indian family brings beige nan, the black-colored black family brings black-eyed peas and the brown Mexican family brings brown tortillas. They all try each other's foods and find everything delicious. There are words like, Delicioso! Swadista, ruchir! Shalom! And, Let's share!

The tea kettle whistles, and Mother smiles at Neela. She puts the book on the table, notices dark roads of cinnamon still in the creases of her palm, half-moons of cinnamon under her nails. She wipes her hands again on her sweatpants. She turns off the kettle but doesn't pour the tea. "This is a charming story," she says firmly, still standing.

"Thank you so much. I chose very safe food, you know, so that the different items wouldn't scare the little children." Neela brings the whole pot of curry to the table, places a fork next to it, and pulls out the chair with the package on it.

"Let me get that," Mother says, but Neela just moves the bundle back to the table and sits down in the chair.

"All different kinds of bread, except for the Chinese, because they don't really eat bread, and the blacks have black-eyed peas. Speaking of which, I take my tea black, with sugar."

Mother brings the flowered cups over with tea balls inside

and the blue sugar bowl. "Very charming," Mother repeats.

"Eat, eat," Neela says, her elbow right next to Inez's bulging shirt covered in cinnamon and dirt.

Mother decides she will eat a little and save the rest for dinner. She takes the iron lid off the pot. The curry is golden yellow. Her first bite is creamy, everything melting together. Then comes an explosion of spice—cardamom, cloves, the garlic and ginger. Her eyes immediately water. She gulps some tea.

"So, you must help me. What should I change?"

"It's great." Mother continues to eat, continues to weep. "Are their nuts in it?"

"Pistachios."

"How do you get it so creamy?"

"That's my grandmother's extra touch. Along with the yogurt we use heavy cream, white wine, and shallots. But there must be some advice you can give me."

She is beginning to sweat as well as cry. Her tongue feels thick. It's like she's in a sauna, which has always felt great and unbearable at the same time. The curry has opened all her pores. "Do you want to share with me?" Mother asks.

"I will need to go back to have lunch with Sondra in a moment. But what about the story? Any notes, as a professional?"

"The only thing is," Mother says reluctantly, "I think stories are supposed to have a conflict."

Neela sips tea. "A conflict you say. How so?"

"I mean, there's always a problem." Her mouth is full again, but she keeps talking anyway. "Some writer said that all stories are two dogs fighting over a bone. Like Little Red Riding Hood," she says. "The wolf wants to eat Little Red and Little Red needs to get to her grandmother's house to feed her grandmother."

"What is the bone in that case?" Neela asks.

"I'm not sure, actually. Maybe Little Red Riding Hood?"

"In any case, I don't want to scare the children with wolves, or bones for that matter. I couldn't put a wolf in, not even an unruly dog. The potluck is in a city park and there are leash laws."

Mother drinks the last of her tea. "Even with a problem, it can still turn out happily ever after in the end. You know, like the wolf is killed and Little Red and the grandmother pop out of his stomach. A rebirth. This curry is fantastic. It's nothing like curries in restaurants."

"That's not a very happy ending for the wolf." Neela spoons more sugar into her tea. "I'll probably just send it like it is to my grandchildren. I don't want to create more problems. There's so many as it is, you know."

"I'm sure they'll love it."

"Any other suggestions?"

"Just one thing. Jewish people don't usually say shalom after they eat something good. That's more hello, good-bye, peace. They might say geshmak—that means delicious. Like this curry."

"You see, I knew you would be helpful. Thank you so much. I find the Jewish people to be such great dancers. That Horah dance! The lovely kicking." Neela glances at the empty pot, puts her soft, soft hand over Mother's hand—the first person to touch her since she arrived. "My, you must be very anemic," she says.

Mother puts her other hand over Neela's—Neela's skin is so suede-like Mother strokes it. "I'm pregnant."

Neela's whole face sparkles up. She gives Mother's hands a big squeeze. "Pregnant! How wonderful and how strange. I love nice surprises. Not very far along, though. Don't worry, I'll feed you. Everything is coming together so beautifully, as it so often does."

"You're right. I don't know why I didn't tell anyone before."

"And Sondra is a midwife, you know."

"Seriously? Your partner?"

"Sondra is the love of my life. Joan's mother introduced us. She's a younger woman, so it's scandalous. When I met Sondra, she was a mechanic at the garage, but with a little encouragement, she followed her dream. Now she is a midwife at the birthing center. You must go see her. She has wonderful hands."

"I will. I really loved the curry." Mother imagines herself hooked up to a curry korma I.V., chili and cardamom coursing through her veins until even the tips of her fingers tingle with spice.

Neela gently loosens her hand, pats Mother's hand, rises. "Speaking of Sondra, she'll need her lunch." Neela scrubs out the pot and heads for the door. She shrugs on her coat. "Sondra likes Indian food very, very much. Like you. Even when she worked at the garage, she was the only one who came home for lunch. To tell the truth, Sondra doesn't care for Joan's cooking. Many people have speculated why Joan's food is not quite as delicious as it could be. I believe it's because she overcooks everything a bit. Muy seco, as they say in Spanish. Perhaps she's punishing everyone a little, for needing to eat."

Neela pats Mother's cheek. "Take good care of yourself now. How exciting."

"Thanks again. Shalom."

"I get it," Neela laughs. "A Jewish joke. Next time you'll dance for me."

Mother touches her cheek where Neela touched it. She already misses the curry. Then she slowly untangles the shirt and the package. A small black bible, wooden knitting needles and brown yarn. Mother pretends to herself she is not sorely disappointed, had not longed for that little mother covered in children or something just as antic instead. She decides that it must be Juniper who took these things. Why? Because she's mentally ill. And then Juniper made up or actually believed the story of the woman in the long dress stealing them. Mother thinks she will have to talk to Joan or Michael about Juniper, because Juniper needs help, obviously. Except she's leaving for Hawaii, Mother remembers, so perhaps it's best to just find a way to get the stolen things back to Joan without making an issue of it.

She opens the first page of the bible. It's inscribed in a pretty, curving script—*Para ti, mi querido Mateo, en tu octavo cumpleaños. Tu mamita.* Mateo's bible, given him by his mother when he was eight years old. How strange to have something so personal of his right here in her hands, she thinks. Perhaps Juniper still secretly has a thing for Mateo, and that's why she stole it. She smells it. It smells like an old book. I'm being creepy, she thinks. She gathers up the bible, knitting needles and dirty children's shirts and hides them in a kitchen drawer under some dusty placemats.

Now Mother gets busy. She wedges a chair under the front door knob, then goes to the entrance to the basement, contemplates descending into that dank-aired dark again and nailing a board over the window. Instead, she drags the rocker over and wedges it under the basement door handle.

Then mother heads up to our room to continue painting. She looks at the pale yellow walls, wondering, what next? She decides to make a record of her journey. To represent the avalanche, she chooses snowflakes. And then after that she will paint red plus signs, no, red hearts, all around the baseboard, and a grape vine along the top of the walls. And on this left sidewall, a table with a feast. She makes a snowflake stencil out of cardboard, draws the outlines in pencil so they are all the same shape and size. As she paints a gathering of blue snowflakes on the yellow wall, she sings, *Bye Baby Bunting, Daddy's Gone A' Hunting*, her back to the door, peaceful, not alert for intrusions, as if wedging a chair against a doorknob could keep anyone in or out.

Monday morning before work, cloudy day threatening rain but not snow, finally a little warmth. Dressed in a beige cable knit pullover and brown velvet elastic waist pants, Mother backs out of the driveway on her way to work. She sees Mateo walking to the garage. Her heart jolts. She hasn't seen him since the potluck. He's hustling, a bouncy little half jog. She stops and rolls down the window.

He leans in. "Ah, teacher," he smiles, he smiles so close to her that her foot eases off the brake, the car jerks forward, and he knocks his head on the side of the car.

"I'm so sorry," she says. "I don't know how—"

He holds the side of his head, not smiling so much anymore.

"Can I see? Is it bleeding?"

He leans in again. There's no mark, the top of his head is reddish colored with a dark half moon of stubble along the sides. She wonders what that feels like, that carpet of tiny hairs. She very lightly touches him above his plump ear. It feels like a cat's tongue. "Does that hurt?" she asks.

He is smiling again, ducks his head out of the car, says, "I'll sue you." Laughs big. "Listen, teacher, I found some books for you, for your colonial teaching."

"I have a book for you, too," she says, deciding right then to just straight-out return his bible to him.

"Perfecto, let's exchange books!"

"At the potluck?" Mother asks.

"No, no, that is too far away. I think you will like these books for your classes. Why not Thursday? Meet me at the library at three-thirty, on your way back from school, yes? It will only take one moment."

"Okay, it's a date. I mean," she stares out the windshield, "that's a good date for me."

Driving away, hardly noticing where she's going, she imagines she is the one who has hurt her head. Mateo has to drive her to the hospital. They're in the waiting room, he's holding a bandage to her forehead, his hot breath is on her neck. He begins to kiss her. We shouldn't, she says, but she's so dizzy from the wound she can't think clearly.

She finds herself pulling into a parking space at the high school. She's running a little late now, bustles into her classroom, drops her coat on her desk, needs to set up the overhead projector to show images from Plimouth Plantation where they have a reconstructed Wampanoag village from before the arrival of Europeans. She plans to show the students photo transparencies of the neat rows of corn with beans twisting up the stalks and the squash growing below, the wooden platforms in the middle of the field where the children sit to scare away the crows. The half globe wetus with their pretty reed mats, the native volunteers dressed in loincloths or short deerskin shifts, digging out a canoe, baking corn pancakes, sitting on logs and talking to tourists. She pulls open the top drawer of her desk looking for the projector cord.

On top of her attendance book is an oily, magenta-colored slab of organ meat. There is a torn piece of notebook paper stuck into it with a pencil. A quote from Mary Rowlandson's book written in capital block letters in pencil: *WHAT SAYS HE, CAN YOU EAT HORSE-LIVER? I ATE IT AS IT WAS, WITH THE BLOOD ABOUT MY MOUTH.* Watery pink blood has leaked off onto a pile of corrected papers.

She closes the drawer and looks around the room. Nothing else seems vandalized, stolen, out of place. Her face flushes. This raw meat shames her, as if it has fallen out of her own body. Instead of calling a custodian or alerting the principal, she covers her hand in a plastic bag and disposes of it.

She shows the students the Plimouth pictures and later makes them color in two maps, one of the Wampanoag lands and population density pre-1600 and one in 1620: ten thousand Wampanoag in 1600, then epidemics brought by whaling ships plus harassment by neighboring tribes, and only a thousand Wampanoag left by the time the Pilgrims landed at Plimouth. The room smells slightly of the disinfectant she has sprayed. She resolutely refuses to glance at the wastebasket, where underneath a pile of paper the liver is hidden in a tightly knotted plastic bag. She also refuses to look at River, but she is fairly sure he's smirking at her with Michael's ironic mouth, watching her with Juniper's leprechaun eyes. And she swears underneath the disinfectant she can smell rotten meat.

After school and after grocery shopping, Mother pulls up in front of the house and there is River, sitting on the doorstep, hunched in his huge black sweatshirt with the hood up so she can't see his face.

"Hi, River," she says in what she hopes is a friendly, confident manner.

"Wassup, Ms. R."

She goes around to the trunk, opens it, reaches inside for one of the two paper bags.

River reaches in for the other.

"Thanks."

He follows her into the house, drops the bag on the counter. He just stands in her kitchen, so she starts to put groceries away. He makes small karate-like hand gestures, maybe part of his dance routine. "I want to talk to you about, whatever."

"Okay." She continues with the groceries. She has bought two of everything.

"It's, whatever, nothing, I took care of business. Handled it. It wasn't even a real horse liver. It was just a cow liver, hella scary." He smirks.

"How did you know about the liver?" She tries for a neutral tone.

"Everyone knows about the liver. But don't sweat it. I got your back, home girl."

"Thanks."

River picks up the box of Cheerios she has just unpacked. "I love this shit."

"Oh. Do you want some?"

"Sure. I'm always hungry. My dad says I have a hollow leg."

"I'm eating a lot lately, too."

"You? Seriously?" He executes a little foot shuffle dance. "We both need to bulk up, am I right?" He takes a body builder's stance, drops it. "Cereal's good. I'll show you a hella cool way to eat it." He takes out a switchblade from his jeans. Mother flinches. He slits the box open, a big square out of one of the sides, does the same for the wax paper bag inside. Then he says, "Got milk? Ha ha." He slides over to the refrigerator and pulls out the milk, pours about half the carton into the box. "Do you have another one?"

"Another cereal?"

"Dude, what are you going to eat?"

She hesitates, then takes out the other box of cereal from the bag. He performs the same surgery on this one. Carries both boxes carefully to the table. Opens a drawer. "Hold up, you don't keep the silverware where it's supposed to go." He opens the drawer where the stolen cache is hidden under the placemats, but he just closes it again. From the third drawer he retrieves two tablespoons.

They dig in, slurping milk, crunching cereal.

"If I'd been smart I would have cooked up that liver on a hot plate and made everyone eat it," Mother says.

"Oh, snap! You should have made us eat it raw with the blood all over our faces! Or put it in our stinkin' pockets for about a week and then made us eat it, Mary Rowlandson style." He cracks himself up.

"So, why do you hate Mary Rowlandson's book so much?"

He shrugs a shoulder. "Mary's a fruit loop." A little milk leaks down his chin. "These Indians are so mean," his voice high and whiney, "let me just munch on a horse hoof, wah, wah, wah."

"Except Mary was really radical for her time. It was taboo for a woman to author her own book. Monstrous. That's why Increase Mather wrote that whole preface apologizing for Mary, explaining that she didn't want to write it, but her friends made her."

"Whatever. I'm all about Weetamoo, Mary's owner. F'n Weetamoo. How cool is she? She's like Angelina Jolie."

"I agree, she's amazing," Mother says. "Isn't it interesting that there's all these stories about Sacagawea and Pocahontas, both of whom helped white people, but Weetamoo is completely erased from history—and she was a leader of the biggest native offensive of all—she almost succeeded in pushing the colonists out of New England."

"So why don't you teach the book then?" River says.

"I thought you hated it."

"Nah. That book is so dope. They should make a videogame out of it."

"Do you think that's why someone put the liver in my drawer? To get me to teach the book?"

"Kids just do shit," River shrugs, keeps eating.

"But—didn't Mr. Lassiter teach it already?"

"He was just getting started."

"But, don't you hate Mr. Lassiter?"

The milk is still on his chin. River stands. "Gots to go. My dad's taking us out to the diner when he gets off work. You should come, you and my dad should hang sometime."

Flustered, Mother says, "But you just ate an entire box of cereal."

"I'm in a growth spurt, Ms. R. I'm as tall as you, I bet, getting taller everyday." He pulls his hood over his head. "Maybe you should take out the garbage Ms. R, something smells bad in here." And he is gone, the door still open.

Mother closes the door, throws out his empty cereal box. Sniffs around the kitchen. It's that smell from the classroom, rotting meat, but she can't tell where it's coming from. Then, instead of finishing putting away the groceries or cleaning, she goes upstairs and begins to paint the feast table on the left wall over the row of red hearts.

When Mother returns from school the next day the message machine is blinking. Molly: "So, not sure what you were rambling about the other night. Just life in La La land? You should call me every day to check in so I know you are still on the same astral plane as the rest of us. Meanwhile, Steve is being his usual assholy self. Called last night, said there was some important matter about his trust fund, said it would be very good for you, but he needs to work it out with you personally. Did you know he had a trust fund? He really wants your contact info, bad. When I wouldn't give it to him I swear I could hear steam whistling out his nostrils. Okay, so all that babbling sounded like you were happy, but I need details. How's the guy? How's your little monsters? How's the horrible weather? Tell me what you want to do about your ex-asshole. Call me."

Mother calls back, gets the machine: "Pick up. Okay. Yes, I knew about the trust fund. The restaurant barely breaks even. Tell him I don't want his money. I'll sign anything to release him from any obligation. Do not give him any info. And there's no guy. I mean, there's a guy, but he's taken, which is totally fine, we're just friends. Neighbors. Monsters are not making me sick anymore. Maybe we're getting used to each other. There's some weird things happening here, though. Call me."

Everyone is asleep inside their wetus, except Mother and Sarah, who lie outside on the frost hard ground because Weetamoo is tired of Sarah's moaning. They've gone nine days and nights without food.

A slice of moon bright behind dark clouds.

Sarah's hot feet boiling in the folds of Mother's blue skirt. Mother chafes a fevered hand. The other hand is large and swollen, as if Sarah is wearing a mitten. Her daughter's breathing is shocking, rude and loud, like a drunken man's snore. Over the sound of the clogged breathing, Mother prays, but quietly so as not to call dangerous attention.

God, wonderful and good

God, do not take away this dear Child

And then Mother chokes and has to stop. After that she begins to whisper Sarah's name, first to try and rouse her from that snore, and when that fails, Mother continues to breath out the word—Sarah—marveling at the hiss of the S and the hard R surrounded by the ahs, yet every time she says the word it sounds more strange to her, until she can no longer remember what the sound refers to, and frightened, she tries to remember the names of other things—andiron, trencher, lug pole, and they all sound like nonsense.

Then she dreams that she is rushing through the winter woods, calling Sarah's name until that one, the one who traded a gun for her, Quinnipin, tells her: Your babe has been buried in an avalanche.

No, Mother says as calmly as she can, so he won't be afraid or disgusted, so he will help her.

Are you sure? she says. Because I unburied us, I'm sure of it. But they bring her Sarah, cold and hard and lay her in her arms, and Mother keeps repeating, Are you sure? Are you sure? And the grief squeezes her throat like a noose.

Mother's eyes open, her stomach hurts, and at first she thinks she is in her bed on Lonely Rincon but she's not. She is sitting on the cold ground holding her snoring daughter.

By and by there are long pauses between Sarah's clogged breaths and then there is only the space between breaths, and Mother lies by her side, clutching a fold of her daughter's dress and smelling her, smelling the yeasty back of her neck as the cold pulls all the smell out of her, until finally Sarah smells like nothing, or only faintly of cold, like a stone.

Then it's grey morning, and Sarah has disappeared.

Mother rises up. She feels light, light in her body, light-headed, achingly stiff and run-through with panic. She rushes hither and thither, asking everyone what have they done with her child, her papoose, Sarah, her baby? She rocks her arms to show who she means.

Finally, someone points to the ridge above the village and Mother climbs up there and finds the grave. She places her hands on the fresh dirt. She thinks, Don't leave me here alone. She will dig Sarah up, and she even pulls up a fistful of dirt to begin, but then she stops.

When Mother rises this time she is a hollow thing, a ghost

thing, a thing filled with air. She can imagine herself a dandelion gone to fluff, blown by her little girl's last breath, dissolving into a thousand separate seeds each with its own wing to fly off the ridge and away.

She waits for this to happen, but instead, something else happens. She is not coming apart, but concentrating, her whole self gathering into a fist in her belly. She realizes she is ravenous.

When Mother goes to wash up in the morning, standing in front of the sink, she notices that there is dirt packed under her nails, dirt smeared on the back of one of her hands. She looks in the mirror. What is that at the edge of her mouth, something pale and cakey? She doesn't remember digging in dirt, and she thought she cleaned her face the night before. She washes her hands and face for a long time, trying to remember something she can almost remember, something just out of reach. Then she shrugs, thinks pregnancy hormones, doubled.

When she's about to leave and goes to retrieve the knitting needles and bible from under the placemats, they are gone. Did she move them and forget where she put them? She feels a sharp slice of fear for a minute, but then she covers it with a decision to look up memory loss during pregnancy.

4:15 pm, rushing up the stairs to the library late, Mother encounters a charming scene: Neela in her glasses in a rocking chair reading to a group of small children. Neela gives her a delighted smile but keeps on reading—it is her own book about the potluck. The children appear captivated, despite the lack of conflict.

And there is Mateo, sitting in the slouchy armchair. When he sees her he gathers up his books, bounces up. She stands in front of him, doesn't sit down or take off her winter things. "I'm sorry, I'm late, I had to pick some things up—"

"No te preocupes, what a job you have. We all admire you."

Mother has already determined to be business-like, neighborly but business-like. "So, what do you have for me?"

"Ah, you have no time to sit down—"

"It's just, I have another appointment, so—"

"I understand. I will go quickly. We can talk more later. When Mr. Lassiter first began teaching this Mary Rowlandson, I looked into it, this King Philip's War, this captivity narrative. Fascinating. It was such a tangled world, no?"

"Yes." She stares at her shoes, determined not to make eye contact. Then at his shoes—white jogging sneakers with mud caked on the bottoms.

"Have you seen this incredible letter by Quinnipin, Mary's captor, to Reverend Rowlandson?" She looks up—Mateo is opening a book at a place marked by a yellow sticky: "'Mr. Rowlandson your wife and all your child is well but one dye. This writing by your enemies.' Why are you smiling? Are you laughing with me?"

She looks at his shoulders, broad, in a beige grandfatherly type overcoat. "No, not at all. Your enthusiasm is great. Did you always want to be a mechanic? Because it seems like you're really into books and studying."

"Ah, when I was a boy I had a dream that when I grow up I would be the, what's the word, manager, of a tall building, and I would have a room in the basement where I will live rent free and study all day, when I am not fixing things."

"So you're already living your dream come true." She's looking at his reddish neck now, curly dark hair up to the clavicle.

"Ah, we all have unfulfilled dreams."

His eyes. "Something weird happened that I need to tell you about," she says.

"Welcome to Lonely Rincon, we specialize in the weird, no?"

"So, okay, here's the thing. It's going to sound strange, but I found a pair of knitting needles and a bible in my basement, all wrapped up in Inez's shirt. The bible was yours, the one your mother gave you."

"That's strange."

"I know, right?"

"It's strange because this morning when I came downstairs my bible was sitting on the table, and knitting needles also."

"Are you kidding?"

"Yes, and also a milk carton was out on the table and some leftover roast chicken bitten. I think there is a trickster sneaking about."

Mother moves closer, uses a low voice, "Do you think it's possible that Juniper might do something like that?" She blushes because Juniper was Mateo's girlfriend.

"She's a vegan—she will never bite chicken. En todo caso, she is in Hawaii. Pero, don't be frightened, I will not be surprised if this is the boys. It seems Michael's boys would enjoy to do something like this."

"So, you think it's River?"

"Very possible."

"You know what? I just thought of something. River is really interested in Mary Rowlandson's book. Oh my gosh." Goosebumps thrill up and down mother's arms. "This makes so much sense. The only things Mary had with her were a bible and knitting needles. And she was always scavenging for food." Mother grips Mateo's arm. "River must be reenacting Mary Rowlandson. But why would he do that?"

"What is this smell? Do you smell this? Something spoiled, no?"

"You smell something rotten? Right now?"

"Yes, don't you?"

Mother does smell it. "I think that's another one of River's tricks."

"You think River brings a bad smell to the library?" Mateo is looking at her like she's crazy, or maybe as if he knows there's something rotten inside her. Her face burns with generalized shame. "You know what? I'm super late. I have to go. Let me know if you find out what's going on."

Seated in the car, hot air blowing onto her face, the rotten smell fills the car. Then she remembers Juniper's pouch. She reaches into her pocket, pulls it out. Sniffs it. It smells of herbs. Just in case, she opens the car door and dumps the contents of the pouch onto the snow. Just crumbly dried herbs. Mother reaches into her other coat pocket. There's something moist in there. She pulls out a green chunk of moldy meat. It reeks. She throws it onto the heap of herbs, climbs out of the car and washes her hands in snow. Mother remembers River saying that someone should hide pieces of meat in all their pockets. The way Mary Rowlandson did, he said. River, she thinks, and she slides back into the car and slams the door with fat satisfaction, because she is not rotting from the inside out, and she's not haunted, because as River himself told her, Kids just do shit.

It doesn't snow for a week, the ground clears, some green grass comes up, and then today, the first Friday in April, what the local's claim is a rare late snowstorm covers everything. Spring seems to stutter and stall here, and we are grateful for our own steady unfurling safely inside.

Mother has made an appointment with Sondra, the midwife, and hopes all pregnancy mysteries will soon be explained. Mother has observed River carefully in class, but she doesn't want to talk to him in school about his bizarre behavior. Perhaps she can approach him at the potluck. Meanwhile, she wedges chairs under the front, back and basement doors at night.

There is a teachers' meeting after school, then a slow drive home through the storm. She still has to cook something for the potluck, so by the time she arrives the game is over, the front yard empty. She can see the crowd through the windows. She stands there, feeling like the little match girl, warming her hands on the pot of packaged neon orange macaroni and cheese she's brought. She suddenly wishes to go home and eat the whole pot of macaroni and cheese by herself, sitting in bed reading her library books. Instead, she climbs the steps, hesitates about knocking, knocks, waits, then opens the door to the loud crowd.

The table is covered in Indian food, the pot stickers and crackers pushed to the side. She slides her macaroni and cheese onto the edge, thinking everyone secretly loves packaged macaroni and cheese. She pushes her scarf and hat into her coat sleeve and lays her coat on the chair with all the other ones. She takes off her boots, steps forward. Her socks immediately soak up water from the melting snow on the floor. She looks around—everyone else is still in boots.

She sees River in a corner, looking at a book. When she catches his eye, he smirks, lifts his chin and holds up *The Captivity and Restoration of Mrs. Mary Rowlandson.* He makes the book do a little dance for her. She's about to walk over to him, about to say, But why? when River is off up the stairs.

Joan, Mateo, and Michael are in Joan's corner, Joan in the recliner, dressed in her jeans and t-shirt, smoking and drinking red wine. Mateo is holding a huge glass of orange juice. He is also in a t-shirt with that tuft of chest hair showing at the top. He is wearing his jeans cuffed. He is slouching just a—

"—Here you are!" Neela says. "It is my pleasure to introduce you to Sondra." Sondra—tall and broad shouldered with a blonde crew cut. Small silver hoops line both ears. In a work shirt and jeans. "I hear you're going to pay me a visit."

Mother loves her deep, calm voice immediately. "Definitely."

"Excellent."

"I made you something special," Neela says.

"Evy Rosen!" Margaret bustles up. "Welcome! You're not going to believe this! I don't know if you've read my web blog yet? Anyhoo, you'll remember that in my last web blog I observed that you seemed anemic, and now I hear through the grapevine that you're in a family way! Can I spot it or can I spot it? But you know what I can't spot? The husband! But honestly, we're all family here, and in fact, River has been telling my son Christian that you are planning to teach Mary Rowlandson. Bravo!"

"Oh, no, I mean, I'd be happy to talk to your son about the book, but I'm not—" Mother looks over at the little group around the recliner. She thinks Joan sees her so she waves, but she must have been wrong because Joan turns away.

"Have you met my husband Hector? Hector!" Hector removes himself from a conversation with two other men. He is short and plump, clean shaven and clean-looking in general in an ironed flannel shirt and khakis. "Hector, this is Evy, the one you've heard so much about."

"So nice to meet you. My wife likes the book you are teaching." Hector has a quiet voice, a slight accent.

"Actually, I'm not teaching—"

Neela is pressing her cast iron pot into Mother's hands. "I made you your very own lamb again, just for you, because you loved the other one so." The pot is still warm. "And here's a lassi I made you, it's a yogurt drink, very good for you." The liquid is pale yellow, like the walls of our room.

"Thank you so much," Mother says. "I guess I should sit down and eat all this."

"Of course you should sit down! Margaret, Hector, let the poor girl alone, her ankles will swell."

Mother smiles at Hector and Margaret. She carries her pot and drink towards the recliner. Joan is smoking. Mateo and Michael each have huge paper plates of Indian food.

"You're all going to be so jealous." Mother jiggles her pot.

Mateo smiles at her. Mother tips her lassi onto the floor. Mateo wipes it up with a napkin. Mother glances down at his shining head, remembering how it felt surprisingly rough. Michael jumps up and offers his folding chair, drags over another one.

Joan inhales, taps her cigarette.

Mother sits down and opens her pot. "Look what I've got—my own lamb curry. It's incredible. Want to try?"

Joan exhales smoke out of the side of her mouth. "Eating lamb is like eating baby Jesus."

Mother laughs and begins, is taken over by a sense of well-being all over again.

"River tells us you're planning on teaching Mary Rowlandson. Following in Deacon Lassiter's footsteps. Because that went so well," Joan says.

"Oh, no way. I was just explaining—"

"I tried to read it," Michael says. "I gave it my best shot, swear to God. I liked the map at the beginning showing where she went. It's a frickin' incredible journey, but I couldn't wade through all that bible stuff. River gets caught up though. Two years ago he read *Call of the Wild*, said he was going to live by himself in the woods over to the swamp. He came back by dinner though."

"Does being kidnapped by natives turn you on? Mateo says gringas like the idea of being tied up by dark savages." Joan glances at Mateo, snorts, inhales the smoke she has just exhaled.

"You are the one who says this," Mateo smiles.

Mother's face heats up. She doesn't look at Mateo. "That's ridiculous," she says. "There's nothing sexual in Mary Rowlandson. As a matter of fact, there is no known case of a white captive being raped or sexually abused by Algonquian natives. That wasn't part of their culture." Mother keeps her eyes on her food.

"It is her hunger that one notices," Mateo says. "When Elie Wiesel wrote about his concentration camp experience, he said, 'From time to time I would dream, but only about soup.'"

"Exactly," Mother says. "She just wants to be fed." She swears she can smell his aftershave from two chairs down, woodsy, with a faint trail of jasmine that reminds her of home. "I know the book's not pretty and it's really religious and she is prejudiced," Mother says, "but think about it, the first woman to publish her story in the new world, and the first thing she describes is being trapped in a burning house with no escape, and for the rest of the book she's scrounging for food to survive."

"Perhaps the first whole book by a woman, but Sor Juana writes in New Spain in nearly the same time," Mateo said. "It's funny how the United States must insist on its Puritan roots. What about the Spanish missions in California?" His eyebrows are like dark wings.

"It's just a little racist and justifies genocide," Joan says in a mock girly-girl voice, "but it's so interesting because it's a lady who is doing it."

Mother glares at the curry, "I'm teaching them about the colonial period. It's a social studies class, not an ethics class. I'm not emotionally involved, the way you seem to be. I don't feel the need to judge her."

"Why shouldn't I judge her?"

Mother squints her eyes at Joan. "Because you have no idea how you would have acted in her situation. You have no idea what it would feel like to be starving and captured like that."

Joan exhales smoke. "I know what it's like to be captured."

"I'm sorry," Mother says quickly. "Of course you know."

"You're not arguing logically because of all those hormones raging through your system." Joan rolls her eyes. "Which reminds me, no second hand smoke for unwed mothers. I'll take it outside." Joan shoves off through the crowd.

Michael drops into the green recliner Joan has just vacated. "Saint Joan of Rincon strikes again. Joanie never stays friends with anyone for long. She's broken off with all her activist pals, but I can't say that she's ever dropped a friend this fast."

"She is unhappy because you never tell her you are pregnant," Mateo says. "She hears it from Margaret."

"Margaret!" Mother says.

"Joan likes you very much. Maybe you can talk with her." Mateo smiles at close range.

Mother smiles back, then recollects herself, grips her pot of food and rises. "I'll go talk to her."

She makes her way through the crowd, nodding and greeting, opens the front door. Joan is stretched out on a chaise lounge in the middle of the whirling snow.

"Joan, come in!" Mother calls. Joan doesn't respond. Mother

pulls on her boots, coat, scarf, hat and gloves and trudges out to the chaise. She looks down at Joan in her t-shirt. Joan's face has taken on a bluish, skim milk sheen.

"I'm sorry I didn't tell you that I was pregnant. I wasn't ready to tell anyone. I'm just in my fourth month. Neela came over the other day and fed me curry, and somehow she got it out of me. It was the curry." Mother is still holding the pot. She can feel the last warmth through her mittens. Her toes are drearily wet and cold.

Joan takes a drag off her cigarette. "What about the baby's father? Does he know?"

Mother hesitates, but she can't risk it. "He's gone. There was an avalanche. In January."

Joan swings her legs off the chaise to make room for Mother. The anger in Joan's eyes has turned to fierce empathy of the same intensity. "I'm sorry."

Mother smiles, guilty but also relieved to be rid of Joan's Mr. Hyde. She sits down. They just sit there together in the cold for a little.

"And why are you still clinging to that damn curry?" Joan nudges her shoulder.

"So no one will steal it." Mother takes off her hat and pulls it onto Joan's head. She unrolls her scarf and wraps it around Joan's neck. "You know what? I think the doe in my backyard is pregnant, too. There's this deer that comes every day, searching for food. She's all skinny and bony but her stomach is bulging."

"It's the time of year," Joan says. "At Seneca Falls the deer that live inside the nuclear facility are all albino. I used to think it had to do with radiation, but they say it's because of inbreeding. They can't get out, generations of them. Fenced in. The albino genetic tendency has taken over. They've lost all their color. During our whole action those white deer stood absolutely still and watched us with their big, pink-rimmed blue eyes. Like ghost deer, or angel deer. I remember one was clearly pregnant."

"That's incredible," Mother says. "And so is the curry. You

have no idea."

Joan laughs. "You'd think you hadn't eaten in a week. When are you due?"

"Supposedly September 27th, but I think twins usually come early."

"Twins! Amazing. Can I be at your birth?"

"You mean during labor?"

"Everyone needs someone with them at their birth. I could be your person."

Mother thinks that Joan is annoyingly, sometimes scarily moody, but often they click so easily, and she is brave, and it is true that everyone needs someone at their birth. "Only if you promise to come inside," Mother says.

"Pregnant widows shouldn't be sitting in snowstorms." Joan stands, reaches her hand down. "I'll carry your pot."

"No way."

They walk back into the house. Mother pulls off her coat, but leaves on her boots. Joan barrels through the crowd, still wearing Mother's hat and scarf. Mother notices that no one has touched her macaroni and cheese, and thinks, Fine, all for me.

When they reach the green chair corner, Mateo jumps up. "You are both crazy, las dos!" He bustles over, throws blankets over both their shoulders. "You're shivering," he says generally.

Michael vacates the green throne for Mother. "You need a stiff drink," Michael says. "Got any rum?" he asks Joan.

"Jesus, Michael, she's pregnant."

Neela bustles over with a plate of steaming nan. She and Sondra hand it out to everyone.

Oshun and Inez charge over to grab some. Inez climbs onto Mother's lap, sits on her knees, eats nan. Oshun jumps on his father's lap.

Mother smiles and takes a bite of the warm bread. Everyone in the little crowd is looking at her, their eyes shining as if they've swallowed a love potion. She thinks about the feast she's painting on our wall, and as if by magic here are all the guests, her new people. It's more than I could ever ask for, she thinks, not looking at Mateo.

Mother's lying in the smoky wetu, but there's something moving in the shadows across the fire. Quinnipin on his back, Weetamoo on top of him, both naked. Weetamoo faces her, eyes closed, grimacing, her hands gripping Quinnipin's shoulders, bracelets jangling softly. Quinnipin's breath deep and even, like a runner. Mother can see the top of Quinnipin's half bald head.

Mother remembers Father gasping over her while she squeezed her muscles efficiently, like milking a cow, that's how it had usually seemed to her, an ordinary chore. But now, watching Quinnipin and Weetamoo, she thinks how strange is the act of fornication, the herky-jerky movements, the great waste of energy.

But the moaning rocking rhythm reminds Mother of something else. Quinnipin frying strips of venison. The sizzling and the smell. Quinnipin reaching in with two fingers to pull out a hot piece, offering it to her, Mother's mouth opening, the gamey flavor blossoming in her mouth. Mother is rocking back and forth, and then she realizes that Weetamoo has opened her eyes, is staring at her. Before Mother can look away Weetamoo snatches up ash from the fire and throws it in Mother's face. Mother closes her eyes against the burning, ashy tears running down her cheeks.

Mother is still rocking, her fists in her eyes, something in her mouth. She takes her fists away. She's been pressing so hard at her eyes that they ache. She unsquinches them, blinking. She's crouched in her nightgown on the wood floor in the kitchen on Lonely Rincon. Beside her is the pot of macaroni and cheese turned on its side, empty. It looks as if its been licked. Her hands are sticky and neon orange, and she can feel that her sticky lips must be orange, too. There's a package of raw steak on the floor by her foot, the plastic ripped open, her foot resting in a smear of blood. She pulls a raw, half-chewed chunk of meat from her mouth.

She sits on her calves and takes a shuddery breath. Wipes her orange mouth with the back of her orange hand. Then she remembers Weetamoo and Quinnipin moaning and huffing in the shadowy light from the fire. She remembers the wetu, the heat on her face, the choking smoke, the ash. For the first time, she remembers all of it. She rubs her eyes again, to clear them of the ash that isn't there.

That dream, she thinks, it was so—thick. The realest dream I've ever had. More than a dream.

Then: I was sleepwalking. Sleep eating.

And then: I'm the one who has been stealing from Mateo and Joan. Walking into their house in the middle of the night, wrapping their things up in Inez's shirts while they sleep all unknowing, trudging back through the woods, my hair wild, so wild and weary in my gait that Juniper didn't recognize me. Then returning the loot another night, drinking their milk, tearing into their roast chicken. This must have been going on for weeks, maybe since the first night I read the book, when I must have secreted a piece of my own raw steak into my coat pocket, where it slowly spoiled.

It was never River, she thinks. It's me, nightly slipping into Mary Rowlandson La La Land.

She looks closer at the package of raw steak now. Most of it is eaten away.

She gags. She runs to the bathroom, crouches by the toilet, her bony knees cold and painful against the hard floor, the gagging wrenching her stomach and soring her throat. But nothing comes back up.

THE SIXTH REMOVE

Two weeks later, third Saturday morning in April, Mother unties herself from the bedpost. She takes off her nightgown, notices her profile in the mirror on the back of the closed bedroom door. She examines the swell of her stomach, the light brown line just beginning to appear down the center of her belly. She turns and faces the mirror—her skin, usually sallow, has a creamy flushed color, her breasts are full, her nipples and the circle around them have become dusky and enormous. Her thighs and butt have taken on weight, even her hair is thicker and glossier.

She becomes aware of her heartbeat again, as she has lately whenever she stops moving. It seems to have grown slower and stronger, a great gong calling her. She's read that in pregnancy the blood doubles.

A car honks three times down below. Mother pulls on her new size C bra and a green smock dress, throws back the curtains. She can see the wind chiming the infant poplar leaves in the front yard. A fat robin hops with faux importance on the lawn. Snowbells bob on their thread-thin stalks. She lays her hand on the window, spreads her fingers. Cool water trails down the outside of the glass.

Three more beeps. Mother startles from her trance—got to get all this blood moving, she thinks. She pulls the chair from under the bedroom doorknob. She checks the line of salt she's poured across the doorway. Undisturbed. She steps over it.

Downstairs, she grabs four energy bars and puts them in her purse.

Joan's rattley, bumper sticker covered Volvo is pulled across the driveway, one of the wheels on the lawn. To seat herself, Mother has to wade into a slush of balled up papers, wrappers, a hairy brush and two umbrellas. Inez is in the back, munching on Cheerios out of a mug. Joan wears blue hospital scrubs with her rubber boots.

The Volvo pulls out, begins lurching over back roads, one turn and another. "Our first midwife appointment," Joan says. "Excited?"

"Yes, super excited."

Inez is kicking the back of Mother's seat, by mistake or maybe on purpose. Mother pulls out an energy bar. Offers one to Joan, who shakes her head, offers one to Inez who grabs it. Mother gets another and begins to eat.

"Before we get there I have something important to tell you." Joan looks over at Mother portentously. The car veers towards the ditch. Joan recollects herself and wrenches the wheel back.

"Conchetumadre," Inez says from the back seat.

Joan laughs. "That means literally, cunt of your mother."

"Nice," Mother says. "So what did you want to tell me? And keep your eyes on the road, okay?"

"I signed up for a doula class."

"A what class?"

"Doula is an ancient Greek word for slave or servant. It's an eight-week course to become a birth assistant. I've wanted to do this for ages. I just haven't gotten around to signing up, but since I'm going to be at your birth, I finally did it! There must be something useful I can do besides destroying government property."

We come out of the woods, down a hill towards a little bank with a big clock, the center of Montour Falls.

"So, the thing is…" Joan grabs Mother's wrist, the Volvo veers towards the bank.

Mother presses her foot to the floor as if she's pressing the break, grips the side of her seat.

Joan rights the car again. They barrel through the short main street. "The training is every Saturday for the next eight weeks. And Mateo works at the garage on Saturday, so I was wondering if you could watch Inez while I'm in class."

"No one needs to watch me." Inez kicks the back of

Mother's seat harder.

"Sure," Mother says, seeing eight Saturdays disappear.

We are driving steeply up a hill now.

"Mateo will drop her off on his way to work. He'll cook you and Inez breakfast."

"No," Mother says quickly. "I mean, thanks, but that's not necessary."

"He always cooks breakfast on weekends."

"That's silly. Mateo doesn't need to cook for me."

Joan stomps on the break. Mother's seatbelt constricts, yanking her in. "Don't be a curry snob. You need to let us do things for you, too."

"Holy mother of Christ, drive right, Mama!"

"So you'll let him cook for you?" Joan says.

"Sure, why not?" Mother picks up her energy bar from the floor where she's dropped it. "I'm starving all the time now."

Joan pulls into the birth center, a white Victorian next to the hospital overlooking the tiny town. "Everything is fitting into place," Joan says. "Like God's plan."

Joan and Mother sit in the waiting room on a hard chintz couch. Mother starts on her second energy bar while Inez surreptitiously rips out pages of *Highlights* magazine and stuffs them down her shirt. Joan says, "I've been doing a lot of research on twins. You have to prepare yourself for the fact that you might not even have twins anymore."

"What do you mean?" Mother stops eating her energy bar.

Joan turns towards her, their knees touch. "It's called vanishing twin syndrome. It's very common, like 20 or 30 percent they think. One twin is absorbed into the lining of the uterus and just disappears."

Not possible. We are always brushing against each other in the dark. And yet, how can we tell whether we are brushing against parts of the other or parts of the self?

"They say that a lot of left-handed people are actually

mirror images of a twin that disappeared in utero," Joan continues. "We just didn't know before because we didn't do ultrasounds so early. Or sometimes one twin absorbs the other into its body and the fetus becomes like a cyst, just like a ball of matted hair and bones in their back or something. Once in a while the fetal twin lives on inside its twin's body, attached to their bloodstream. There was this case in India where a grown man had his fetal twin living in his stomach until he was 37 years old. And then of course there's conjoined twins. Basically, what I'm saying is that once there's two in there, you have to be ready for anything."

Joan goes on, telling twin freak stories, but Mother stopped listening after, "vanishing twin" and "common." She thinks of the word reprieve. She can almost feel the relief, like the flicker of a fishtail before it disappears underwater.

Our mother has always been singular, she doesn't understand. Conjoin us, bury one of us inside the other, but do not halve us. Do not leave us alone.

"Evie, Joan, Inez." Sondra greets all three of them with the same deep, calm voice.

There is something comforting about Sondra—tall, with a swimmer's build, those silver hoops outlining her ears, each hoop slightly larger than the next in a pleasing, orderly arrangement from top to bottom.

She will confirm us, we think.

I could tell her anything, Mother thinks.

Sondra shows us the birthing room, which looks a lot like a budget motel, including the awful oil painting of an ocean sunset on the wall. Inez jumps on the thin pink bedspread. "What if it's a boy, do you put a blue cover on the bed? Sexist! Or if it's a monster, a red cover! Sexist against monsters!"

Then Sondra brings them into the medical room and helps Mother onto the table. Inez sits on the floor reading a fairy tale board book. Joan has brought a yellow pad and pencil.

Sondra measures Mother's uterus. Mother thinks, Neela is

right, Sondra has great hands, large, capable, Little House on the Prairie hands with blunt fingertips. Mother can imagine her delivering foals and calves, kneading bread.

"I'd say about four and a half months," Sondra smiles.

"But these estimates are often wrong," Joan says.

"So, twins," Sondra says.

"I was having twins when they did the ultrasound at ten weeks," Mother says, "but Joan tells me one often vanishes."

"Are you worried about that possibility?" Sondra wraps a blood pressure cuff around Mother's arm.

"I've already prepared her," Joan says.

"I'm fine either way," Mother says.

It's just not possible. We couldn't be I.

"Good," Sondra says. Sondra pumps and the cuff grows tighter. Mother's throat starts to close, as if the cuff is on her neck. Mother tells herself to breathe. "In any case, if one of the twins is no longer there," Sondra says, "it's early enough that it won't compromise the health of the remaining baby." The cuff deflates. Mother's chest eases.

"I already told her that," Joan says.

Sondra folds up the cuff and smiles at Mother. "So, do you have any particular concerns?"

"The father is deceased," Joan says.

"I'm so sorry, Evie."

Mother would like to tell Sondra the truth, but not in front of Joan. "It's okay."

"Many pregnant women benefit from counseling," Sondra says. "Perhaps with all the natural anxieties that come along with new motherhood and the loss of the baby's father? Living alone during a period of such enormous changes is challenging. Emotions often intensify. We have a resource list of counseling options." Sondra puts a thermometer in mother's mouth. "If it is twins you'll need to be seen by a physician regularly. Then we'll just watch how the pregnancy develops. If all goes well, you may be able to give birth right here at the birth center. We'll do everything we can to make that happen, although the health of the baby or babies comes first."

Joan asks Sondra, "Do you ever have to decide between the life of the mother and the life of the unborn children?"

"Joan, please," Sondra's voice goes even deeper.

"Sondra," Joan taps her pencil. "I'm finally going to train to be a doula. I need to prepare for worst case scenarios."

"I'll prepare you for one thing. Your bracelets are not going to work for a birth assistant. You need your arms free. What if you had to measure dilation with all those bracelets? I've wanted to tell you for a long time, but Neela didn't want me to upset you. There's a condition called copper toxicity—you can absorb copper through your skin. You should probably get tested—it's a simple test—it can be done with a hair sample."

"Are you a toxicity specialist now, along with being a therapist?" Joan purses her lips. "I need a cigarette." She flounces out of the room.

Mother smiles apologetically at Sondra. "She's intense."

"Copper toxicity is associated with personality change," Sondra says in a low voice, so Inez won't hear.

"Like what?"

"Joan's right, I'm not an expert, but irritability, mood swings, trouble concentrating. Joan's been wearing those bracelets for years. I've tried to tell Mateo and Michael, but everyone's too scared of Joan. She seems to listen to you."

"I'll try to talk to her."

"Thanks. Any other concerns before we do the ultrasound?"

"I've been sleepwalking," Mother says very quietly, close to a whisper. "I never did before. And I eat when I'm sleepwalking."

"Some women do experience sleepwalking during pregnancy. You need to limit stress, get enough sleep. Maybe do some meditation or relaxation exercises before bed. You should also keep a safe sleeping environment."

"I tie myself to the bed every night—I cut a pillowcase into strips—and I put a chair under the bedroom door knob, and I have a line of salt that I poured across the doorway, so if it's messed up I'll know I walked through it. It seems to be working."

"As long as those things don't inhibit your sleep."

"I think I sleepwalk when I dream about Mary Rowlandson. I'm trying not to dream about her, and I stopped reading the book."

"Vivid dreams are not unusual during pregnancy."

"I'm trying not to have anything to do with her anymore."

"Okay, well, I'm going to print out two copies of therapy resources in the area, one for you and one for Joan."

"Please don't tell anyone about the sleepwalking," Mother says.

"What sleepwalking?" Sondra smiles. "Now, do you want to see what you've got in there?" Sondra adjusts the monitor position. She turns some dials on the machine, spreads clear, cool gel around Mother's protruding belly button.

Sondra runs the wand slowly over her belly. There's the grey triangle surrounded by black. The grey staticky material roils, coagulates, dissipates.

Mother holds her breath.

So do we.

"There's one," Sondra says.

"Only one?"

Sondra doesn't answer.

She moves the wand.

She moves the wand.

"And there's the other. See?"

Both our hearts leap. We knew we were two. We are doubly grateful.

Sondra keeps adjusting the wand, moving it around for the best view.

Mother looks again, makes out an undulating line that must be an umbilical cord. "I can't really see."

"Each of your twins has their own placenta, so we can't really know yet if they are identical or fraternal. This is good news, Evie. There are less chances of complication if each baby has their own placenta."

Mother thinks she sees a blob that looks like a leering face, then it disappears. "There were these twins in my class a few years ago," she says. "They were always whispering and giving each other looks and secret hand signs. The other children felt excluded. I couldn't even tell them apart."

Sondra stops moving the wand. "So you're concerned about having twins."

"I just thought having a baby would mean coming as close as possible to another human being, but now it feels like I'm just a temporary incubator for a couple or something." She laughs in a wobbly way. "Plus I can't even see them on the ultrasound. Last time I could see them."

Sondra moves the wand through the gel again. "This is baby A over here, closer to the cervix, and this is baby B on this side."

Mother sees the shape of a baby. She sees one of our black hearts beating and then the clear profile of a face, the pug nose, the round stomach, the delicate fish spine. Then it's gone. "I saw one!" She sits up.

"I know it's hard, but try not to move."

Now Mother can see one of us winking in and out of the grey pulsing mess. "I don't like the way it disappears."

"It's not disappearing. Just moving. Or because I move the transducer. Here's the other one."

"I see it. Wow. I see it."

Joan pushes the door open with a bang. Her bracelets jangle a little as she grips Mother's hand. "Oh my god. There they are. It's incredible. Isn't it incredible, Evie?"

"Yes, it's incredible."

"They're right there." Joan starts to weep, and then Mother cries, too.

"Do you want to know their gender?"

"Wow," Mother says. "Yes."

Mother and Joan's hands squeeze together.

"Okay, so, see this knob here, Baby A is definitely a boy."

"A boy," Mother and Joan say, their voices all breathy with miracles.

We're boys? With knobs?

"And this one, let's see, I think it's a girl, but I can't be 100 percent sure."

That's a mistake. If we're one boy, we're two.

"So they're fraternal," Joan says.

"Possibly," Sondra says. She turns some dials. "Here's the heartbeat."

There is a swishing underwater sound, or a sound like a flock of birds rising into the air, and then—our heartbeat—emphatic, rushed.

"It sounds so fast, is it too fast?" Mother asks.

"Completely normal," Sondra says. "Here's the other one."

"What's that sound?" Inez says.

Mother startles. She'd forgotten all about her. "Do you want to hear the babies' heartbeats? It's very cool."

Inez stands on the step next to Joan and pokes her finger in the gel. She sniffs it. Sondra pushes the monitor around on Mother's belly until she finds our heartbeat again. "Can you hear that?" Sondra asks Inez.

Inez puts her mouth right above the wand and speaks into it: "Testing. Testing 1-2-3, can you read me in there? Can you hear me? Talk, Baby." Then she puts her ear up next to the stick. They all listen to our frenetic heartbeat and the seawater sound around it.

"She's talking," Inez says.

"There's two of them in here," Mother says. "Does it sound like talking to you?" They all listen to the hissy swishing sound underneath the heartbeat.

"It does sound a little like talking," Joan says.

"It is talking," Inez says.

"What do you think they're saying?" Mother asks.

Can Inez hear us? Inez, can you hear us?

Inez looks up from the wand to Mother. "They're saying, 'Little Pig, little pig, let me in or I'll huff and I'll puff and I'll blow your house in.'"

The next Saturday morning, 8:30 a.m., Inez bursts into the house, Oshun right behind her, and Mateo in the rear cradling an armful of cans. Mother has already eaten two bowls of oatmeal, draped a plastic tarp on the kitchen table, blown up a balloon, cut up strips of newspaper and set out a basin of tepid flour and water. She doesn't falter at the unexpected addition of Oshun, just divides the paste in two and gets out another balloon. She blushes at Mateo's delighted smile when he sees the piñata set-up.

"So this is what school is in the U.S.? Why is Joan so preferring home schooling?"

She crinkles her eyes at him while she finishes blowing up the balloon, ties it off, and hands it to Oshun.

"Congratulations! A boy and a girl! This is very special." And Mateo is leaning in as if he's going to kiss her cheeks, Latin American double-style. Instinctually her head rears back and he laughs and grabs her hand for a shake instead. "Are you happy with this boy-girl mixture?"

She nods, takes her hand away. "I can imagine them as two separate children, now. They might even be fraternal, they might not even look alike."

One of our knobs must have been hidden in the ultrasound, that's all. Please, help her accept our doubled selves.

"Have you had breakfast?" Mateo asks.

"Yes," she says, hoping she sounds firm but cheerful, "I am all set breakfast-wise."

"No more early eating, yes? The least I can do is to make breakfast for the pregnant flaquita who agrees to care for my daughter."

"Flaquita is skinny," Inez says, patting the white goop gently with her open palm. "But Evie's not skinny. She has giant boobies."

"Potty talk!" Oshun giggles.

Mateo laughs.

Mother crosses her arms over her chest.

Mateo unloads the cans on the counter. "I knew you might try to be stubborn, so I brought you dulce de leche." He pulls open a drawer. "Ah ha, you moved the silverware," pulls open another, takes out the can opener, grinds the top off the can, grabs a teaspoon. "Inez doesn't like it," he says. "It's incredible to me."

"I like it," Inez says.

"Here, have some." Mateo sticks the teaspoon of white, viscous stuff in Inez's face.

Inez purses her lips and nips the end of the spoon. Her face prunes. "It fills me up too much."

Mateo laughs and scrunches her hair. He shakes it in front of Oshun's face. "Aquí, sobrino, muy dulce."

"No way, Tio, it looks like snot!" Oshun and Inez crack up.

"Incredible!" He refills the spoon and brings it over to Mother.

He is standing way too close. That pine-jasmine aftershave prickles her nose. His thick neck is at eye level. He holds the spoon so the metal tip is just touching Mother's lips. She hesitates, then takes the spoon out of his hand, careful not to brush his skin, and puts it in her mouth. It is perhaps the sweetest thing she's ever eaten. Her back teeth ache. "Wow."

"It's good in tea," Mateo says.

"Would you like some tea with it?" Mother asks, her automatic manners getting the better of her resolve, as usual.

"I would love a tea," Mateo says. Mother puts the kettle on and explains to Inez and Oshun how to construct the piñata. Mateo tries to help Inez, but she isn't having it.

"Papi, es mio. You two go away y cuando haya terminado I'll surprise you. Right, Oshun?"

Oshun nods, caught up with the feeling of the paste as he

slides his long, skinny fingers down the newspaper strip.

They go sit on the top step of the back porch. The dew dampens Mother's butt through her maternity pants. The cool morning wind shakes the hard green beginnings of purple grapes on the vine. Mother thinks she can almost reach out and grab a fistful of perfect, puffy clouds. The garden is a scraggly mess. She imagines how it must have looked when Juniper took care of it. "I really need to work on that garden," she says.

"But your passion is history, not gardening," Mateo says. "So, tell me why you love history."

Mother blows on her tea. "It makes me feel grounded or connected or something. When I was eight years old my mother got me a Cabbage Patch doll." She notices his uncomprehending face. "Just this doll that was popular back then. Anyway, I returned it, took the money, and bought an antique comb. I pretended to myself that it had been handed down to me by my great-grandmother. It's from the late nineteenth century. The cover is carved ivory. We never had any heirlooms in my family. You know, the whole grandparents escaping from Europe thing and never wanting to talk about it, and then my parents are hippy baby boomers, always all about the next new thing."

"And why do you love this Mary Rowlandson? She is nothing like you," Mateo says. "She only cares for her own survival. But you're generous, maybe too generous, am I right?" He passes Mother a spoon of the dulce de leche. "Tell me, what do you have in common?"

"Nothing." Mother eats the spoonful of dulce de leche. The cool breeze and the dew on her jeans make Mother cradle her tea close to her face, for the steam. She passes the teaspoon back. It's embarrassing, she thinks, how happy she is. To make up for it, she refuses to look at him, or acknowledge that he is feeding her with the same spoon he's eating from.

"So, enough about Mary Rowlandson then," Mateo says. "What about you? What is the story of the captivity and restoration of Evie Rosen?"

Mother smiles. "Last year we did a honey bee unit in my forth grade class. When the bees want a new queen they feed the larvae royal jelly, the larvae are literally bathing in it, and this rich mixture transforms one of the larvae into a queen. I imagine royal jelly must taste something like this."

"So?" He refills her spoon and passes it back.

"You mean what happens next for the larvae?"

"No. I mean, so, your life story."

Mother waits for her throat to open after the third bite of dulce de leche. "Let's see, my amazing, exciting life. My parents divorced when I was thirteen. In college I majored in history and minored in art. Then an MA in early American history. My best friend's named Molly. She's also my cousin. We've been best friends basically since we were born. We've had a hard time keeping in touch, with the time difference." Mother begins to feel unmoored—she feels as if she's talking nonsense. "I have a photo of her." She jumps up, goes inside, the kids yell, "Don't look!" She puts her hand over her eyes, says, "I'm not looking," just stands there for a minute, takes a few gasping breaths, as if she's coming up for air.

She grabs her purse and goes back out. She fishes out a wallet-sized photo—it is one of her favorites, Mother laughing at something shocking Molly has just said.

Mateo puts on his reading glasses. Even his farsightedness seems charming to our Mother. He holds the photo carefully by the edges. "My God. Incredible. I see why you wanted me to look at this."

"You do?"

"Because you are twins."

"What are you talking about?" Mother takes the photo from him and examines it. "Maybe we look a little more alike now that I'm pregnant," she concedes. "Anyway, our personalities are nothing alike—she's super outgoing. Men are always falling in love with her, everywhere we go." Mother takes a sip of tea to shut herself up. She looks over towards the line of swaying pine trees at the right edge of the property. "I don't know why I'm going on and on about Molly's romantic life."

"And what about you? Tell me the story of your romantic life."

That floodlight smile. "That would be a very short story."

"Who was the first person you ever kissed?"

Mother feels dizzy. She thinks, this is a little horrifying, the way something inside of me, some secret wish has escaped my body and is manifesting out in the world. A little like the sleepwalking or like the liver appearing at school, also a little too sweet, like this dulce de leche I can't stop eating. Stop thinking about what it's a little like, she tells herself. You're freaking out. "Tell me about your first kiss," she says.

"Hmm... I have a terrible memory, my bad memory disgusts Joan, but..." he pushes his cheek out with his tongue. "I think the first girl I kissed was when I had eleven or twelve years." Mother notices that his earlobes are curved and meaty, like pirate ears. He has a freckle on one ear right where a piratical hoop might go. "We were going on a bus, for a what do you call it? Outing with the school."

"Field trip?"

"Yes, field trip. I sat next to a girl, and we kissed the length of the trip. What was her name? Carmen? Camilla? But that's not really a story, is it?" He sips his tea, refills the spoon for Mother. "Let me think of a better story.

"When I was sixteen, in Santiago de Chile, me y mi novia decided to make love. We were virgins, of course, and so we searched for a place to perform this passionate transaction. We rejected a park bench, an alley, then a bush, all too public or too dirty. It's completely crazy that I work in a garage and marry with Joan, because I always hated mess and dirt. So, it grew late, the curfew horn blew, but our passion over-ruled our sense.

"Finally, we climbed under a bridge. We were just on the, how do you call it, preliminaries, when a military police officer shone his flashlight in us. I must explain that this was during the dictatorship, and people our age were both blowing up bridges and disappearing for being in the wrong place on the wrong time.

"I told the officer that mi novia had lost her ring over the bridge, and that we were looking for it. She held up her naked finger to prove." Mateo holds up his own hand, which has a thick gold wedding band on it. His hands are much smaller than Mother has imagined—Teddy bear hands, clean and soft-looking, not like mechanic's hands at all.

"The officer, who was also young, trained his flashlight on her wrongly-buttoned blouse. We were quiet while he reached his decision. Finally, he waved us off, his gun still hidden."

Mateo laughs. "I think I should thank that officer, because if it wasn't for him, right now I might be living on a tenement with six children."

"What was the girl's name?"

He shook the spoon at her. "Now, no more about me. It's your turn."

"I think it's time to check on the kids." Mother pulls herself up, presses her lower back, sighs.

"What am I thinking, you are uncomfortable. And I must be getting to work. But you have been very tricky. Always the woman of mystery. You told me nothing. Now I am ashamed for revealing my childish story."

"I'll tell you a story next time."

"I don't believe you."

She squints through the glare of his smile, shrugs a shoulder, turns before he can see her smiling back.

When they walk back in, Inez says, "Hey! I'm not done!" Inez has created a devilish looking cat piñata, with cunning pointy ears and short whiskers.

"That's a great cat, Inez," Mother says.

"What is mine?" Oshun demands, holding up a lump.

Mother has no idea.

"It's a second cat. Precioso," Mateo says.

"My primo es muy estúpido, Papi, por que está copying me siempre?"

"Porque a él le gustan tus proyectos."

"What does that mean?" Mother asks.

"They're always talking about me in Spanish," Oshun says mournfully.

Mateo snaps his fingers.

Who snaps their fingers since The Rat Pack? Mother wonders.

"Inez, we have to teach Evie Spanish, yes? And Oshun, too. We'll start next time. Chau, gracias Evie."

Mother watches him hurry up the road towards the garage with that funny walk of his, as if he longed to run on those short, muscular legs, but forced himself to walk responsibly instead.

Come back, she thinks. Go away.

When Joan arrives to retrieve Inez and Oshun, they drag her over to the windowsill to admire their drying art objects.

In his excitement to show off his blob, Oshun knocks his head into Joan's braceleted arm. He squeals, holds his ear. Mother cups her hands over his ears, says over his head, "Joan, I'm really curious. There must be a story behind all those bracelets."

"Sondra," Joan says, her eyes slitting. "I can see a midwife worrying about the pregnant mother, maybe about malnutrition, smoking, drinking, carcinogens in the environment, but bracelets. Bracelets!"

"Mi Mama says when I'm twelve I can start wearing bracelets," Inez says primly. She steps on Oshun's foot.

Oshun wails and curls over the toes inside his trailing sock.

"I'm going to wear them on my legs, too," Inez says, "so I turn completely green."

Joan laughs, and the cords in her neck disappear. She runs her hand through her stick-up hair and sits in a chair, legs apart. Inez climbs on. "When I was about fifteen, my mother was away, as usual, helping others, and my Dad had gone carousing the night before and neglected to return. I had no idea if my father was dead in a ditch or what. I don't remember what Michael was doing, setting fires, playing hooky, the usual, and I was crying and wandering in the woods behind the house. I was scuffing my clogs through the leaves, and I unburied this." She jiggles the first bracelet on her right wrist, a simple flat band with little hands clasping. Inez strokes the brass hands. "It was a sign from God. I'm not a flake, I know these others aren't like the first, they're just to remind me of the miracle of God's presence, the way God keeps us company."

Mother flinches in expectation. "Would you consider getting tested for copper toxicity?"

Joan breathes through her nose. "Okay, let me try again. The bracelets are a sign of my relationship with God. If they've colored my skin, even entered my bloodstream, that's just another miracle. Okay?"

"It seems very old testament somehow," Mother says, thinking she'll bring the test up again another time. "Like all the things Jews wear to show their devotion to God, yarmulkes, tzitzit, or how God put the sign on the doors of the Jews in Egypt so they would be passed over."

"Passover!" Joan says, jumping up, Inez slipping off. "It's next week. I always do Passover. You're not Jewish are you? Who cares, come anyway. I'm not Jewish either. I always make tofu instead of lamb." Joan's hustling the kids into their outdoor clothes now.

Mother helps wrestle a sweatshirt over Oshun's big head, imagines the tofu alternative. "I am Jewish, actually, and you can come to my house. I mean, your house, you know, here."

Oshun and Inez rush out onto the muddy lawn. Joan is at the door. "Are you sure? We're a big group."

"Positive."

"Okay, actually thank God, I hate making Passover dinner, almost as bad as sitting through it—but, it's supposed to be like that, right? Isn't the interminable length of the Seder supposed to represent the Jews interminable slavery in Egypt?"

Sunday, Mother is just starting to chow down on a mixing bowl of pasta with butter and parmesan cheese when there is a knock on the door. The knob turns, falls off. An eye appears at the peep hole where the knob used to be. "S'up. My dad says I gots to clean the stovepipe."

She opens the door. River wears a grey jumpsuit rolled up at the cuffs and a bandana around his neck. He is carrying this charmingly old-fashioned long handled iron brush and a tin bucket. He reminds Mother of the chimney sweep in Mary Poppins. He even looks a little like Dick Van Dyke.

"Can't you just fix the door? The stove's fine. I don't even use it."

River picks up the pin and the knob, fits them together and pushes them back in the hole. He looks at the pasta. "Carbo load. You're a beast, Ms. R." He ties the red bandana around his nose and mouth. He sticks the wire brush on a long pole up the flue. The soot begins to crackle off in black flakes. A fine dust billows out of the mouth of the stove.

"River!"

"What?" he shouts through his bandana and the sound of his own scraping.

"You're making a—" River keeps scraping. Mother grabs the bowl of pasta, sets it on the kitchen counter and puts a pot lid over it. She throws some newspapers around the floor next to the stove. She opens the kitchen windows and the back door to the grey day. Cold air washes in.

Then she gets her bowl of pasta and takes it into the living room. She sits down on the futon couch and goes back to eating.

After a few minutes River comes in carrying an empty bowl. He sits down on the couch. She fills up his bowl from her bowl. For a while they just swirl and eat, swirl and eat.

"So, what?" River says.

"What do you mean, what?"

"You said you wanted to talk to me."

Mother shrugs, talks with her mouth full. "Oh, nothing. It was a mistake."

"Like what?"

"It's dumb," she sighs. "I thought you were impersonating Mary Rowlandson, like going into people's houses and stealing things and eating their food."

"You trippin'."

"I know, sorry." She puts her empty bowl on the floor by their feet.

"Dude, it's the ghost of Mary Rowlandson—that beeotch haunting up in here."

She looks at his face—he appears serious. "It's not a ghost, River."

"Yeah it is." He jumps up, stands in front of her. "It's logic. Everyone thinks it's me, but they're trippin', and no one else would do that crazy shit. I'm going to get Hector to bounce her back to Puritan times." He starts up his moonwalking.

"Hector?"

"Fo' sure. Exorcism is his thing."

"I can promise you it's not the ghost of Mary Rowlandson. Trust me."

"Oh, right. Like I trusted Mr. Lassiter." River smoothes his invisible moustache.

"You trusted him?"

"Hells yeah. He was the only one in that school who gave a shit about us. He was all like, 'Respect yourself.' Always up in our grills, know what I mean? Like an old timey preacher dude, like I will now give you the truth. Like, I love you, God loves you. His face would get all red and sweat poppin' and he shook his fist. He was like a straight up savior man. And he taught us survival skills. You know, for the coming apocalypse when the terrorists invade. Like what wild plants to eat and how to build a snare and how to make a fire with two sticks. He was so dope."

"But why did he throw a ruler at you?"

River shrugs. "Whatever." Starts doing a wave with his clasped hands. "Ms. R, what happened to Weetamoo?"

"Teachers don't throw rulers at students. That's terrible. That's just wrong."

"Okay, whatever, what happened to Weetamoo, after the war?"

"I'll tell you if you tell me why he threw the ruler at you."

"Jesus," River says, exasperated. "He was talking to us about how our bodies were temples and the temptations of drugs and weed and sex were like the terrorists trying to invade us from the inside. And I was feeling it. I stood up, and I was like, Yeah! and I started rapping back at him, just echoing the last words of his sentences, call and response time, tapping out a beat on the desk. But he thought I was straight up sassing him, everyone thought I was, because everyone was like ha ha ha, and then he was all, Infidel! and hit me in the eye with a ruler."

"That's awful."

"Did Weetamoo die in battle?"

"At the end of the war, when it was clear the colonists had won, she was leading a small group of Wampanoag women and children. They were headed home, back to the Wampanoag summer land on the coast. The British ambushed them, captured everyone, except at the last minute she slipped away. But sadly she drowned trying to swim across the Tauntuan River to escape." Mother leaves out the gruesome end.

"That story blows," River says, pulling his bandana back up over his face. "You can do better than that, Ms. R."

Message from Molly: "Okay, get this. I come home from work and someone's broken into my house. Smashed the back sliding glass door. They didn't take my computer, my television, nothing like that. The only thing missing is my address book. I told the cops I thought it was Steve, and they're going to question him. Oh, he checked my email, too. I'm glad you deleted your account. Don't worry, your address isn't in that book. It's up here, memorized. Ha. That mofo. I'm going to get an alarm system. I'm going to get a security camera and catch his ass with that baseball bat of his."

Mother's message back: "I can't believe it. What an asshole. I hate him. What are we going to do? We need Weetamoo. She's this warrior queen from the seventeenth century. Seriously, I wish so much Weetamoo would come back and wise Steve up. Actually, she'd probably wise us all up."

Mother walks along the aisles of her classroom, placing a small, wilted beige book on each desktop. Someone says, "Not again—no, Mary, no!" A boy bangs his head on the desk several times. She switches off the overhead lights, turns on the small lamp on her desk. A girl giggles, is hushed, there is an expectant quiet. Like when someone is about to tell a ghost story, Mother thinks. She opens a fatter book on her desk where she has placed a yellow sticky, reads aloud to the class:

Nummokokunitch—I am robbed

Manowesass—I feare none

Nickqueintonck-quock—I will make war against him

She closes the book and looks up at them. "History seems inevitable. We know the Native people lost their land to the Puritans. But during King Philip's war, they almost won. They could have won. The Algonquians were led by King Philip also known as Metacomet and the Wampanoag warrior queen Weetamoo." Mother opens up Mary Rowlandson and reads her description of Weetamoo: *She has a Kersey Coat, and covered with Girdles of Wampum from the Loins upward: her armes from her elbows to her hands were covered in Bracelets; there were handfuls of Neck-laces about her neck, and serverall sorts of Jewels in her ears. She had fine red Stockins, and white shoos, her hair powdered and face painted Red, that was always before Black.* Mother stares at her students. They stare back.

"Perhaps she has disappeared from history because she led her people against the people who wrote the history, hoping to drive them into the sea, hopefully in time for spring planting.

"A few days ago I told one of you that Weetamoo drowned trying to escape the British, but now I'm going to tell the whole story. It was August, 1676 and Weetamoo had been alone for three days. Three days earlier she had been making her way home to Mattapoisett, on Cape Cod, urging on almost thirty exhausted Pocasset Wampanoag women, children and old people, when they were surrounded by the British. She alone had run, a musket ball biting the tree near her shoulder as she escaped. Three days later and she still had a long way to go.

"For three days it had been muggy, threatening rain but no rain. She wore only her British kersey coat. The coat was heavy and made her sweat, but protected her from the mosquitoes. On the first day she ate blackberries near the edge of a meadow. On the second day she chewed on—River what did she chew on?"

"Cedar bark," River calls.

"Yeah, Cedar bark," another kid says. Others nod.

River begins beat boxing. Two girls crack up, lean against each other, someone else hushes them.

"So, that night Weetamoo sat in the smoke, chewing on Cedar bark. She thought, In a week I will be by the ocean, will be baking clams and raspberry bread.

"When she woke in the morning, she saw that she had fallen asleep and left her fire smoking through the night. She kicked dirt over it. She dug around for something to eat and found—what did she find?"

"A Lillyroot," someone calls.

"She ate that. Then she heard a crow. This was a warning to her, so she was not surprised to hear voices speaking in the ugly language of the British. They were very near, and they were not yelling like they usually did in the woods, which must mean they were tracking her.

"Run," someone yelled.

"She began to run towards the Great Taunton River. She heard them shouting behind her, and she thought she heard the squeal of iron as one loaded a musket."

The bell rings.

They all blink at each other. One of the students turns on the light. Mother laughs, smoothes her rounded tummy, pushes her hair back. "I'll finish the story another day." Several students groan.

River moonwalks by Mother's desk. "So, you know those words you were saying in Indian—I think Mr. Lassiter had that book."

"It's called *A Key Into The Language*. Roger Williams wrote it about 35 years before Mary Rowlandson's book came out. You can borrow it." She hands it to him.

He slips the book into his sweatshirt pocket. "You showed the class who's boss, Ms. R. You're like, Listen up 'cause here comes the truth motherfuckers."

A letter Mother sends Molly for Molly to mail in Santa Cruz to Steve: "Leave us alone. Our next step is to get a restraining order. You could lose everything. You're hysterical. You're irrational. Think, think."

Mother is getting ready for Passover. She brainstorms, makes to-do lists, shops, googles and researches, cuts and pastes. She enlists Oshun, Inez, River and his friend Christian, Margaret's son, in the accompanying theatrical production. The first Passover that she is the hostess. She can imagine the whole Seder—the taste of the sweet apple, nut and wine charoset with the pleasingly dry matzah and the bitter horseradish, eggs dipped in salt water. The lace tablecloth, maybe she could borrow one, the candle light, everyone singing together, maybe even holding hands, would that be too much?

On the night before the big day, Mother sets up card tables end to end in the living room and covers them with the long white tablecloth, only slightly stained, from Goodwill.

But that night Mother roams the Wampanoag village, trawling for something to eat. She finds an old dried corn and is going to take it back to her wetu and boil it, but her wetu explodes with wailing when she approaches. Mother turns away and finds another wetu in which to boil her corn. She hides it in her pocket, picking off one kernel at a time, then wanders back to her own wetu. They are laying out Weetamoo's dead baby, surrounded by three bowls of parched corn and a wampum belt. Mother stares at the bowls of corn.

Then she realizes Weetamoo is watching her. Weetamoo's face is terrible to behold, but strangely familiar. Mother wonders where she has seen that face before. Weetamoo gestures that she wants a piece of Mother's apron to wrap her papoose in, but Mother shakes her head. Another woman says in English, She will kill you if you don't give her the cloth. But Mother shakes her head. No.

A strangled sound comes out of Weetamoo's throat. She hefts a log over her head. Mother rips the bottom half of her apron off and throws it on the ground. She runs. The heavy log thuds next to her.

Crouched in the smoky shadows, Mother watches as they carry the dead baby into the woods. She reaches into her pocket for a kernel of corn, puts it in her mouth and begins to suck on it, so it will last longer. She thinks, At least there will be less noise, and that is a good thing. She pinches some hair at the nape of her neck, pulls it out and lets it go. She watches the hair, each strand on its own wing, separate and drift away.

Mother wakes to the sound of wind. It's a sullen morning. Through the window she can see wind ripping all the new leaves off the trees. She remembers the dream this time, how ugly it was. The patchy snow still on the ground. The weak cry of Weetamoo's baby—like an old record scratching, the tiny prick of pain when she pulled hair from the back of her neck.

Mother notices that the palms of her hands are smeared with blue paint. It's a periwinkle blue, almost a light purple. She had chosen the color thinking of morning glories on the walls of our room. The beige pillowcase strips that have tied her to the bed hang loose to the floor. The salt trail across the doorway is scattered. There is a blue handprint beside the door. She rushes down the stairs to check the front and back doors, but they are locked, the chair still wedged under the front door.

Mother's shoulders drop. So she has not stolen out to do damage to her neighbors. She looks at her blue palms again. Walks back up the stairs to our room.

It's ruined. There are smeary blue hand prints over the snowflakes. Slashes and strokes that look as if they were painted with a stick cover her red checked tablecloth, the half-painted lattice crust on the pie and the bowl of grapes. Wide swathes of thick, dripping paint over the table.

Mother feels a thrill of hatred for Mary Rowlandson. She hits her blue fist against the doorjamb. She starts to cry, then wipes her nose fiercely with her wrist. She pries open the red, grabs up a blue paint-stiffened brush and writes in big red capital letters across the right side wall: STAY OUT OF MY HEAD. She leaves the room.

Later, after she eats, Mother returns to look at her miniature disaster. The open periwinkle paint has grown a skin. She breaks through, mixes it. She opens a new roller and begins to paint over the pale yellow walls, over her red letters, her snowflakes, her red hearts, her feast table, covering everything in blue.

As soon as the adults are blown in on the wind for Passover, Mother can tell something is wrong. Joan and Michael, awkward and silent, hovering around the card tables in the living room, until Mateo sits himself in the middle chair, and then Joan and Michael arrange themselves on either side. Mother gives Joan a questioning look, and Joan rolls her eyes towards Michael and makes a choking gesture with her hands.

This performance will cheer us all up, Mother thinks, standing in front of the sheets strung on clothesline across the other half of the room, scrubbed hands clasped, just a few pale streaks of blue left on her fingers, hair braided down her back, cheeks pink, wearing her favorite shirtwaist dress, now strained at the middle. She says, "Instead of reading aloud the story of the Jews escape from Egypt, tonight we will watch an original play depicting the exodus."

She carefully slides back the sheets on either side to reveal Oshun, playing, appropriately enough, a big baby Moses crying in a wicker laundry basket, a towel diaper over his jeans. Inez, the princess, adorned in many scarves, skips on, and after a short and complicated scarf dance, she pulls Oshun out of the basket so roughly that the basket tips. Oshun squeals.

Mother closes the sheets, there is scrambling and urgent whispering behind it, and then the sheets open to reveal a grown-up Moses, played by Christian, Margaret's son. Christian is stocky, with John Denver glasses slipping down his nose. Dressed in a bathrobe, a towel turban on his head, he watches River, an Egyptian, beating Oshun, now a Jewish slave, with a ladle. Christian pulls River off of Oshun in slow motion, grabs the ladle and stabs River politely in the heart with it. River's agonizing death scene goes on so long that Mother is forced to close the sheets while he is still twitching.

When the curtains open again, Christian/Moses is mime walking through the desert. He looks shyly at the floor through his glasses with the thick lenses, and mumbles something. Behind him, River moonwalks onto the stage in a silver lame disco shirt, courtesy of The Goodwill. He carries two bare branches with sparklers duct taped to them. Hip Hop pulses out of the boom box, the lamp is switched off, the sparklers ignite, and River begins to dance.

The cascading streams of light dapple his narrow,

concentrated face. God's burning bush played by an angry adolescent in a disco shirt, gorgeous sparks showering from his hands.

Mother smiles big and clasps her hands in delight. She claps wildly when the kids take their bows, each one in their own awkward way, towels falling off their heads as they bend.

After the play, Mother returns with the Seder plate to find the only vacant chair next to Mateo. As she sits, Mateo tries to fit an embroidered yarmulke onto his big bare head. It is close quarters, their shoulders brush, their knees accidentally click. The windows steam over with their heat.

Michael, opposite her, wiggles a silver flask he's pulled from his jacket pocket, winks at her.

Mateo chants the blessings in his Chilean-accented Hebrew. Hebrew sounds more melodious to Mother with a Chilean inflection.

Inez asks the four questions. Everyone is sipping sweet wine, except Michael, who's chugged his glass and is already taking nips from the flask.

They're at the plagues, the wind groans and batters the windows, but Mother feels this ascending happiness. She thinks maybe periwinkle blue is a better color than yellow for our room anyway. She thinks that the feast she had to paint over is right here, in her house, right now.

Blood, frogs, gnats, when they chant hail, the kids shout, pull out the mini-marshmallows they have been hoarding on their laps and pelt everyone. Mother's mouth tastes sweet and sticky from grape juice, charoses and marshmallow.

And lately we can taste what Mother tastes. There's not as much room to float anymore, but we slide around each other, in love with the dizzying echoes of grape and apple. One of us finds a smooth cheek, the other sucks on it. We push and poke each other gently through our almost invisible sacs, like children playing on two sides of a sheer curtain at night.

When it is time to beat each other with scallions to symbolize the hardships of the Jews, it is an all out war, scallion beatings upside the head. Mother feels a brisk smack on her cheek. Turns. "It wasn't me, it was Michael." Mateo smiles huge.

She hits him in the mouth with the scallion.

Mateo puts his hand to his lips in surprise.

"I'm sorry!" she says.

Michael whips his scallion down the table and it thwacks Joan on the forehead. Her eyes bulge. She jumps up and throws her glass of Manischewitz onto Michael's sports jacket. Everyone goes quiet.

Joan stands over Michael, the empty glass raised.

Mother remembers Joan has "done time," imagines a cafeteria scene from a TV prison movie.

Mateo laughs loudly, probably fakely.

Michael grins crookedly. "You win again, little sister."

Joan lowers the glass. "I can get that stain out," she says.

Joan carries Michael's jacket into the bathroom. While everyone slurps matzah ball soup quietly, Mother excuses herself and knocks on the bathroom door.

"Come in." Joan is on her knees beside the bathtub.

"Try soaking it with salt." Mother hands Joan the box of kosher salt and sits on the edge of the tub. "What's going on?"

Joan pours salt into the water. "Somebody's stealing."

"What do you mean?" Mother says, thinking, it could be something else.

Joan shrugs, scrubs at the maroon stain with her short nails. The water has already turned pink.

"What are they stealing?"

"It doesn't matter. It's just that I'm sure it's River who's doing it. He denies it—made up this ridiculous story about a ghost. I tried to talk to Michael about it, and he said I was in denial—that Inez has always been the thief in the family. He's the one in denial."

"I'm sure it's not River."

"You don't know him. I love River, but he's sneaky, everyone knows that."

"Joan, I know it isn't him. Just let the coat soak," Mother says miserably. "Let's finish the Seder."

Mother's roast chicken is perfectly respectable, but the party has lost its festive air. Mother is determined to get it back. She puts her hands over her heart. She announces, "In Hebrew the word for Egypt is mitzrayyim, which means narrow place. Why doesn't everyone go around and tell a story about a time you were confined to a narrow place? After all, that's what Passover's about, escape from confinement."

There are general groans. "Inez," Joan says, "You go first."

"I don't get it," Inez rips into her drumstick. "A narrow place, ¿Cómo? ¿Qué es esto? Like that time I got stuck in a drawer? Estúpido."

"Oshun, can you think of a time you escaped a tight situation?" Mother says.

Oshun hunches his shoulders, shakes his head.

Michael waves his flask. "This here is what helps me out of my narrow places."

"Are we done now?" River asks.

"You have to respect other people's traditions," Joan says.

Mother doesn't look at him, but she says, "Mateo?"

Mateo stares at his plate, adjusts his yarmulke, looks up and smiles at Inez. "One time, they called a general protest against Pinochet. My neighbor and I, we creeped out after curfew. We filled a tire with the gasoline to set on fire in the middle of the calle. In this manner, when the police come, they couldn't get by, and everyone knows we are protesting for freedom. But the police come while we are still filling the tire with the gasoline."

Inez stands up on her chair: "You're so cool, Papi. Did you have hair then?"

Joan says, "Long hair and a beard. He was playing revolutionary."

Mother can picture all of it in detail, down to the noxious smell of the gasoline and his adrenaline-clumsy fingers fumbling to light the match. "Go on," she says.

Mateo smiles at her. "We ran the block to return to the house. They were chasing us in their armored truck. I lived in the end of a small alley and at the front of the alley we have a gate. We were able to lock the gate, then we ran to the end of the alley, hoping to reach to my house at the very end. The police officers pushed their guns in the bars of the gate and shoot a tear gas at the front window. We ran into the house and kick the can from the front door, but then they shoot another one in. My mother was in the house. Smoke was all over us. My neighbor and I knew tear gas, we held lemons on our noses and didn't rub our eyes, but my mother never experiences this. She wouldn't allow us to hold the lemon near her face. She rubbed her burning eyes. She thought she couldn't breathe. She was choking and coughing, but we didn't dare to leave the house. We thought we wont escape that narrow place."

Joan says, "I always wonder why he ran to his mother's."

Mateo sighs. "Try to forgive me, mi amor. I was sixteen." Mateo looks at the children. "Perhaps the moral of this story is that once you emerge from your narrow place, you should not try to go back onto it."

"Into it," Inez corrects. "But what happened, Papi?"

"The police finally left. Mama was fine."

"I've always appreciated that story, Mateo, really," Joan says, "but how about what's happening right now, today, outside our personal little circle. What about what's happening right here in this country, at this moment—the so-called war on terror? Do you know there are plans to invade Iraq?" Joan's hands make fists. Watching Joan, Mother thinks of the word burning. "Where is the anti-war movement? Everyone's just letting it happen. Margaret told me that asshole Lassiter wrote over thirty letters to the government complaining about the so-called Lonely Rincon conspirators."

Mother looks over at Christian to see if the mention of his mother upsets him, but he just nods in agreement. "And the really pathetic thing is there's no conspiracy," Joan says. She looks around at them. No one says anything. She shakes her head, takes a slug of wine.

"Aunt Joan is a straight up warrior chick like Weetamoo," River says.

"Weetamoo," Oshun says. "From the séance thingy."

River hisses, "Shut the fuck up."

"You shut up, River!" Michael says.

"What séance?" Joan says.

"Nothing, okay?" River scowls. "We were just fooling around."

Inez says, "Yeah, we were just trying to bring that Indian lady back from the dead."

"Oh my God, Inez was there?" Joan gives Michael a hate look.

"Don't stress. Jesus," River says. "And she's not some lady. She's the Wampanoag Warrior Queen Weetamoo." River looks at Mother.

"It's painfully obvious," Joan says. "River is completely obsessed with that poison little Mary Rowlandson book. That's why he broke into our house and stole things and ate things."

"It was Evie," Inez says.

Everyone laughs.

"It's true," Inez says. "She sleepwalks and eats food. She told Sondra at the birth place and she said don't tell. I heard her."

Now everyone is looking at Mother.

Mother's face steams, her hands wring each other. "It turns out I have this sleepwalking syndrome brought on by pregnancy. I'm the one that broke into your house."

"That's ridiculous," Joan rolls her eyes. "You don't need to protect River."

Mother looks at the little puddle of grape juice left in her glass. "I kept myself from doing it again once I figured it out. I tied myself in at night and put a chair at the door. But this morning I woke up and it turned out I had painted the babies' room blue in my sleep."

Inez giggles. Mateo throws his head back and laughs. Everyone starts cracking up. A cautious smile begins to flower on Mother's face.

"So, you're the ghost of Mary Rowlandson," Michael chuckles.

The basement door bursts open in a rush of cold, moldy air. It bangs hard against the wall. Several people jump up. A chair falls over. Oshun shrieks. A glass tips, spilling purple wine on the white tablecloth. Mother's heart spasms. They all crowd around the basement door.

"Did you see that?" River says in a high voice, hopping around. "Did you freakin' see that?"

"It was the wind," Michael says.

"The wind? Are you buggin'? That's the freakin' ghost," River says.

Oshun starts to whimper.

"River, zip it." Michael pats Oshun on the head.

"There's a window down there that doesn't have glass in it," Mother offers.

"I can fix that," Michael says. "No problem."

"Whoo," Mateo laughs. "What a surprise."

Joan reaches down and picks up the cardboard box from the basement landing. The baby doll with the burnt face rides on top, winking at them. "My mementos." Joan turns her sparky eyes on Mother. "Why are they stuffed away in this box?"

Everyone looks at Mother.

"I must have done it in my sleep."

THE SEVENTH REMOVE

City On A Hill:
The Community Building Blog
For Lonely Rincon Road
By Margaret Langley Gonzales

Hold onto your hats, because yours truly has done an about face! Believe it or not, we have just registered the only child we have left back at the high school! Why, you may ask? The secret lies in none other than that sweet little widow, Evy Rosen! (FYI, her husband passed tragically in a skiing accident and that is the reason she is here all on her lonesome.) Despite intimidation from a left wing radical that shall remain nameless, Evy has begun teaching the awe-inspiring story of the faith and resilience of our founding fathers, The Captivity and Restoration of Mrs. Mary Rowlandson. Score one for Evy! I also heard that (after a very shaky start!) her class has become a model of discipline. Score two for Evy! And finally, Christian came home from Evy's Passover dinner (a Jewish ritual borrowed from the Easter celebration) full of praise for the biblical teachings he'd learned and the fun he'd had learning them. Home run, Evy!! I'm entrusting my only child into her care from May through June, the final six weeks of the academic year. Public education, you get one more chance!

God Bless!

On Saturday morning they slam open her door, Oshun and Inez in the midst of an argument over who gets to hold the grocery bag, which promptly rips, four cracked eggs on the floor, bottles and cans rolling.

Everyone helps clean up, and then Mateo announces, "This

morning, food that is healthy! No more dulce de leche. Orders from la jefa." He pulls out a yellow sticky pad. "And Spanish lessons! Also very healthy! Maybe we can set you to study Spanish in your sleep, very convenient. Or maybe Mary Rowlandson will study for you." He laughs and mimics her flinching face. "I'm only teasing you Evitina, don't be so serious."

She smiles as she ties an apron around Oshun. Mateo puts one on, too. He seems unbothered that it's flowery with scalloped edges. The effect of his masculine features—that big, shiny pate, big teeth, chest hair all the way up to his neck, combined with the daisy covered apron is ridiculously charming, in our Mother's opinion. She annoys herself with her idiotic beaming.

"First, we boil the eggs," Mateo says. Inez writes *huevos* and slaps the sticky onto the egg carton. While Oshun toasts the bread, Inez smacks a *pan* sticky on the end of the loaf, *aceite* on the bottle of oil and *sal* on the package of kosher salt.

"You would love the food in Chile," Mateo says. "You can buy empanadas directly from the street. Or completos outside the National Library. Completos contain hot dogs with mayonnaise, tomato and mashed avocado. Very delicious. And my mother, she has her specialties of course, for example soup with squash, spaghetti and meat, and rosquitas. I think you tried these at the potluck? Little donuts with orange and powdered sugar? My mother kept these rosquitas warm under a towel, for when I returned from the library very late. In the morning, she woke at five a.m. to cook me breakfast while I begin to read. Soft boiled eggs and pieces of bread with oil and salt in a cup. Huevos a la copa. This is what I am making you. It's, what is the phrase, comfortable food."

Mateo sets four large glasses out on the counter. He instructs Oshun to rip up the toast into pieces, then cover it with oil and salt. "Not too much, Oshun, like this."

Inez gently strokes a yellow *Estupido!* sticky onto Oshun's back. Mateo scoops out the soft boiled eggs without breaking the yokes and lays them on top of the bread in each cup, then more toast, salt and oil, and a final egg. Inez continues her vigorous labeling.

They all sit down at the table.

Mateo makes little satisfying murmurs as he eats. "What is it about an egg?" he says.

"I've always been squeamish about eggs," Mother admits. "If they're too loose or too hard they gross me out, but this is really good." She thinks it tastes elemental—bread, oil, salt, egg—there seems to be an exact correlation between her hunger and the taste and consistency of the food. Inez and Oshun eat about half of theirs, then run off into the living room, chins smeared yellow, but she and Mateo eat until their spoons scrape the bottom of the glass. Mother remembers that Mary Rowlandson wrote, "After I was thoroughly hungry I was never again satisfied." She thinks, And that's why I'm nothing like Mary Rowlandson. I'm satisfied, right now.

Afterwards, while Mateo washes up, Mother helps Inez and Oshun start on friendship bracelets in the living room. They bicker companionably as they choose colors, then knot the embroidery thread the same way over and over.

Mother imagines us, one dark-haired, one light, our heads together, murmuring like pigeons as we braid the thread. She smiles and strokes the back of Inez's head. Inez jerks away.

When she returns, Mateo is putting out two cups of tea. Seated at the table, she can see outside the kitchen windows—the flowering trees that surround the house are in effervescent first bloom: magnolia, cherry, red bud, quince bushes, forsythia, lilacs on the verge. After a winter as constricted as pursed lips, Mother thinks, May in western New York is like a mouth opening, like carbonation, thousands of bubbles rising. A butterfly kiss.

In the mornings lately when Mother wakes, the pregnant doe is breakfasting on grape leaves out the back window. If she brings her tea to the back porch, the doe watches her, then goes back to stretching her long, graceful neck to nibble the newest leaves.

"Spring is beautiful here," Mother says.

"So, the story of your first kiss," he asks.

"You don't give up, do you? It's not a story, seriously. I practiced kissing a girl in camp once and then in eighth grade my best friend Molly's boyfriend kissed me under the mistletoe. I tried to pull away at the last minute, and he ended up kissing about half my lip."

Beso, Mateo writes on a sticky and presses it to her forehead, rubbing a little with his thumb so it will stay. That thumb-sized pressure threatens to unbalance her.

"River says you are a storyteller, but I guess it's all lies," he says.

"I can tell a story, just not about myself."

"I challenge you to tell a story about yourself."

"Fine. Let's see." She takes a sip of tea, which is more sugary than she usually likes it and without the milk she usually puts in, both of which make it strange and wonderful. "I'll tell you about how I met Steve. I warn you though, it's quite boring."

"Boring, my favorite." He puts his dimpled chin in his pudgy hand.

"The night we met Steve, I was with Molly. We have, we had, a standing margarita date every Wednesday at five p.m. at the same Mexican restaurant. We didn't even have to call each other. But, this particular night, Molly phoned and said, 'There's a new restaurant in town, a health food restaurant. Let's try it.'

"To be honest, I like routine. Molly likes to shake things up. Do you like routine?"

"Oh, no, I'm not falling for that. This is your story, not a conversation," Mateo says.

"Okay, fine, where was I then? Of course we went. When Molly wants something, she gets it. It was a little restaurant called Vida, in what used to be a diner, but now it was full of plants and wooden tables and framed close-ups of vegetables. Like a huge cauliflower. I remember Molly and I couldn't stop cracking up about the photos."

"This is hilarious?" Mateo smiles.

"Yes, a giant vegetable is very funny in California. We ordered organic wine. There weren't that many people in the restaurant. I was missing my margarita. Then this guy emerges from the kitchen in a sparkling white apron."

"Steve?"

"Yes."

"How was he?"

"He looks, looked, like Superman, old-fashioned good-looking."

"So. The night you met your Prince Charming."

"He came out in his apron and said he was the owner. He said we were drinking the wrong wine. He brought out another bottle, on the house." She wishes now she hadn't started talking about Steve. "So, that's how we met."

"What? That's it? When do you know he likes you?"

"I just assumed he was hitting on Molly. He insisted on walking us home, took off his apron, said his staff could handle it. We dropped Molly off first, and I said to him, we were still on the sidewalk in front of Molly's house, I said, 'She has a boyfriend.' And he said, 'It's you. I chose you.' I was startled. It did feel like the beginning of a fairy tale, at first."

"What did you love best from him?" Mateo says.

She drinks her tea. "He got up at five a.m. and went running before work, every day. I admired that. He was totally organized and practical and meticulous and hard working. I guess I thought I was taken care of."

"In Spanish we say lo siento mucho. It literally means I feel this deeply—I feel your sadness with you."

Mother smiles, but her chest is tight. "Tell me about Juniper." There is a rime of sugar on the empty cup and she uses her finger to finish it off.

"Juniper and I were a pair for a year, a little less. Then one day I go to her house and there is Michael in his boxers."

"Oh, no. I'm sorry."

"I remember Michael winked to me. He said, 'Bro, we were

just talking.' It's funny now, but then, I was very outraged. He is like a brother to me. But after a few months Joan comes home from prison, and the four of us were all friends together. All was well."

Mateo rinses both mugs in the sink. He starts back to the table, then rummages in a kitchen drawer. He returns with a scissors. When he leans down she feels his warm breath on her ear. "You have a loose string," he says, and snips off a tiny rose-colored thread from the arm of her pullover. He puts the thread in his pocket. He replaces the scissors.

She holds her hand over the snipped-off part of her shirt.

"I must go to work," he says.

"Thank you. For breakfast."

"More stories next time."

After Mateo leaves, Mother begins rehearsing a play with Inez and Oshun. She'd done this play about the devastation of the Brazilian rain forest with her fourth grade class the year before, but she abbreviates it now so that there are fewer parts. Oshun is the hunter and Inez is variously a deer, a monkey and a porcupine. Inez falls in love with her last line, "Señor, when you awake I hope you will look on us all with new eyes." She repeats it over and over in her gravelly porcupine voice, her soft, girlish deer voice and her nasal monkey voice. At first, Mother and Oshun laugh, and then when it starts to get really annoying, Joan arrives.

Joan barks at the kids to get going and grimaces at the scraggly bracelets they shake near her face.

"How was doula training?" Mother asks.

Joan just shrugs a shoulder. "How was breakfast?" she asks Mother, her mouth pruned. "More junk food?"

"It was good," Mother says. "Joan, you're okay about this, right?"

Joan gives her a quick, squinty-eyed look. "Okay about what?"

"You know—" Mother starts twisting her fingers. "Breakfast."

"I have to get home now." Joan has a scary, accusing look on her face. "But come over on Monday after school. We'll figure it out."

After Joan and the kids leave, Mother just stands in the kitchen. Her vision starts to shimmer, her throat starts to close. She calls Molly: "Where are you? Is Steve leaving you alone? Did you send the letter? I just want him to leave us alone." She blinks, rubs her eyes. "I'm getting that wavy eye thing I get. You know how whatever I did with Steve it was always wrong? I feel like it's starting here. I think my neighbor Joan is mad at me. I think I'm in over my—" she hears the whine in her voice and stops, clears her throat. "I know, stop trying to please everyone. Don't worry, I'm totally fine. I'm a pioneer woman. It's just pregnancy hormones. Call me. I miss you."

Monday morning when Mother arrives twenty minutes before the first bell, Christian is already front row and center, pushing his thick glasses up his nose, in a light blue Oxford buttoned all the way up and chinos with pleats and loafers. He has his pencils and pens lined up in a row, his notebook, and a glossy annotated copy of *The Captivity and Restoration of Mrs. Mary Rowlandson*.

The bell rings. As each group of students enter, Christian looks up in an expectant way, smile at the ready, but the kids smirk and whisper and only say "Welcome back" sarcastically. Christian has placed one of his books on the desktop next to him and tells a group of girls he is saving it for River. They seem to think this is hilarious. River walks in late, hood up, slides into a seat in the back. Someone says, "Your girlfriend saved you a seat, River." River doesn't acknowledge this comment, just slumps into his chair, one knee up, one leg out, hip-hop style. Christian turns all the way round in his seat and smiles. River whips a pink eraser at him, which hits him on the shoulder. Everyone laughs.

Mother writes River's name up on the board. She's pressing so hard that the yellow chalk snaps in half when she dots the i.

After class Christian stands at her desk, staring at his feet: "Mrs. Rosen, mumble Mrs. Rowlandson's spiritual hunger. Mumble internet, the Indians were savage mumble mumble believe in God, mumble not skin color. It was a religious war, not a race mumble. Her soul mumble. Mumble Christian nations and Islamo-terrorists. Mumble Bin Ladin mumble devil, mumble mumble the faithful and the mumble. That's what I want to write my final paper on."

"That sounds interesting Christian, but—"

Behind Christian, River pretends to cough, barks, "Freak!" into his fist.

"Just one minute, Christian," Mother says. "River, I need to —" But River pulls his hood down so all you can see is his sneer.

He slouch-struts out the door, whistling.

After school, Mother stands at Joan's front door in jeans with a rubber band twisted around the button and through the buttonhole to accommodate her belly; she is wearing a large navy UC Santa Cruz sweatshirt with a yellow slug on it, her hair up in a tight ponytail. She is determined to soothe Joan. She is determined to make it all right.

Before she can knock, Joan calls, "Ready!"

Mother stamps the mud off her brown clogs and slips out of them, walks into the house in her socks with pink teachers and pink blackboards printed on them. Joan is nowhere in sight.

The windows are steamed over, and there is a putrid smell in the house, like a stew of straw and manure. Mother mouth breathes. "Thanks for making time for a little talk," she calls.

Joan strides into the room carrying a down quilt, wearing a blue silk Japanese robe with a rip up one of the side seams. She shakes the quilt vigorously and spreads it over the floor. Dust motes rise up to meet the tiny feathers floating in the air. "Please remove your sweatshirt and jeans," Joan says in a deep, calm voice, perhaps channeling Sondra.

Mother looks at the quilt, which doesn't appear entirely

clean, spread out over the dusty floor.

"Lie down on your side, please."

"What are we doing?"

"Prenatal massage." Joan unties her robe and tosses it over a chair. Underneath, she wears a white Italian t-shirt and white underwear. She is super trim, and if you add to that her short cow-licked hair, you end up with Sigourney Weaver from *Aliens*.

"But, I thought you wanted to talk."

"Talk about what?" Annoyance or possibly even rage shivers through Joan's left eyebrow.

"Nothing. I just didn't know I was getting a massage today. Yay."

"Please remove your clothes and lie yourself down on the quilt," Joan repeats soothingly.

Mother hesitates, then slowly pulls off her sweatshirt, undoes the rubber band on her jeans, carefully slides her jeans down. She folds her jeans with the sweatshirt on top and slides the neat package of clothes onto a chair. She is down to a t-shirt, jog bra, and apricot-colored granny underwear up to her bulging navel.

"Lie on your side. This is going to feel great."

She lays herself out.

Behind her, Mother hears Joan squeezing some kind of lotion onto her palms and whisking her hands together. The smell of lavender blends in with the eau de barn. Joan crouches behind her. At the first warm, smeary touch, Mother flinches.

"Try to focus on letting go of tension. Breathe through your diaphragm." Joan's knuckles bare into her back. The lotiony pads of her fingers inch along until they discover a knot, then worry the knot until it loosens.

Immediately, Mother begins to fear that Joan will stop. That's how good it feels.

"Swedish massage is ideal for the pregnant woman," Joan says. "I won't massage your ankles or your wrists—those are pressure points that induce pelvic contractions." Joan's voice is still professional, but breathy with effort. Her knuckles move slowly up Mother's back. Mother feels the cool caress of the copper bracelets when Joan changes position. "This may soothe your twins, as well. I've been reading up on this— they have begun to fight over space now. One always comes out bigger than the other. One always hoards resources. Even in the womb. It's really profound."

"I never imagined it as a battle," Mother says. "It reminds me of *Charlotte's Web*—you know, how Wilbur is the runt."

"I'd love to get in there and fight for the runty one," Joan says.

How could we battle ourselves? It's this way: as children, Mother and Molly played a game. Say Molly crosses her arms in front of herself, then twists her hands to clasp her own fingers. Mother points to Molly's ring finger and instructs her to lift it, but Molly lifts her pointer finger instead—her mind can't tell which finger is which. We are those clasped hands.

"You're good," Mother says after a bit, her own breath catching as Joan starts on her shoulders.

"I think my real talent is for civil disobedience, but thanks. You're so tight in the shoulders."

"Why did you stop then? You know, civilly disobeying?"

"It's tricky to massage from the side," Joan gasps. "Because of prison. Prison totally freaked me out. I can't go back."

"I can't even imagine. I'm sorry."

"That's what's so fucked up." Joan drops the masseuse-voice for her own smoky, urgent one. "I spent my whole life with this anger issue and this anxiety thing, and I get to prison, and boom, it's gone. Not immediately, at first I didn't even notice. I was just living on federal-time. Wake up at 3:30 a.m., in the kitchen at four a.m., prepare breakfast until seven am, clean up, prep for lunch, out by 11 am when the next shift arrives. Take a shower, sleep for two hours, walk in the yard for an hour, knit and read, pray in the chapel, dinner, read and knit, asleep by nine pm. Same thing every day. I start to notice that about-to-explode feeling, kind of dizzy over-caffeinated feeling, but way worse? It's gone." Joan inches her fingers up Mother's skull.

"Wow," Mother groans, and catches herself drooling. "Doesn't your mother live in a nunnery? That's very regimented, too. Did you ever think of becoming a nun?"

"I went through a nun phase as a kid, but I have my little family. I made my choice, and now I'm going to make it work." Joan begins to whisper her fingers over Mother's back.

Mother mourns the loss of Joan kneading her scalp.

"You're so tense. Just let go."

"I thought I had let go," Mother say.

"Not at all. Stop holding back."

Mother surprises herself by tearing up. She quickly closes her eyes. "I guess I'm not capable of it. I've never been able to let go with another person."

"What are we talking about here?"

"I mean I've never had an orgasm during sex."

When Mother had confessed this to Molly, Molly told her she had to be more assertive, tell Steve exactly what she wanted, like, slowly slide your finger over the clitoris and back down inside, and don't stop or vary the rhythm. Count four Mississippi's from clitoris to vaginal opening and back. Mother tried out Molly's directions, but Father said, "You're killing it," and rolled away.

Joan stops rubbing. "That explains so much."

"It does?"

Joan starts up again, more vigorously. "You need the right partner, no offense to your husband, of course. What about Michael? Women seem to find Michael attractive."

"Oh, thanks, no. I mean, of course he's attractive, but—"

"Breathe." Joan pats her back. "Just lie there until you feel ready to get up. Slowly dress and sit in that chair. I've been brewing homemade pregnancy tea for days."

Alone, Mother slides into her clothes. She sags into the armchair. Her lotion-soft skin tingles, her head is calm. "Joan, I wanted to check in with you about something," she calls.

Joan returns with a mug. "Nettle tea is excellent for pregnant women. You should drink it every day. I made gallons of it. You can take the rest home with you." Joan hands her the mug of steaming black liquid. This is ground zero for that septic tank smell.

"You mean like *stinging* nettles?" Mother says, stalling.

"Yes, but I wore gloves to pick them, and after you boil them they don't sting anymore." Joan stands over her.

Mother puts the cup on the coffee table. "So, Joan, I just wanted to clear the air. Are you okay about Mateo making breakfast for me?"

"It was my idea."

"I know, I just want to make sure you're comfortable with it. I don't want any confusion between us."

"Wait, you mean am I jealous? Of you?" Joan laughs, but it's a laugh like glass breaking.

Mother's shoulders rise up to her ears. "Not that there is anything to be jealous about, I just want to—"

"—Don't worry," Joan cuts her off. "You're not his type—since Juniper, he only likes serious, intellectual women." Joan hands her the mug. "Drink the tea."

"The smell bothers me."

"It's just an earthy smell," Joan says. "It's good for you, not like that trash food Mateo feeds you."

Mother sets the mug back on the table. "I don't want this, sorry."

"You don't like my cooking, do you, Evie?"

"I've never even tried your cooking. This isn't cooking, anyway."

Joan grabs up the cup. Tea sloshes onto the floor. "You are not helping me help you. You're not making the slightest effort to take care of yourself."

"Okay, God! I'll try the tea."

"It's too late."

"What?"

"It's cold," Joan says.

"Just microwave it," Mother says.

"You can't microwave a natural tonic! It will kill all the nutrients. I don't even own a microwave—they cause cancer."

Mother takes a breath, tries to regain her post-massage calm. "This is silly. This isn't about the tea."

Joan doesn't smile. "You want to clear the air? Let's clear the air. I know what's going on, Evie. And I accept it. We're all flawed. But you have to accept help. I'm trying to bring you back into balance."

"What do you mean?"

"I mean kleptomania."

"What? Wait, you don't understand. That's only when I'm sleepwalking. And it was only that one time."

"Do you think anyone believes that story?"

"But. It's true. Juniper saw me sleepwalking."

"Juniper saw you?"

"Yes. She didn't know it was me, but she saw me. I didn't remember it, of course. Because I was sleeping."

"Whoa there, Evie. Juniper said she saw a woman who looked like you, and you told her it was your sister. And we both know you don't have a sister."

"No. She's the one who said it was my sister. This is crazy."

"That's why you started teaching that Mary Rowlandson book again at school, isn't it? Because she's a thief, too."

"No, that's ridiculous—"

"If it's so ridiculous, where is my little clay mother?"

"I don't know where she is. I didn't even know she was missing. I mean," Mother blushes, "I guess it's possible I took her in my sleep. I can look around."

Joan shakes her head. "I worked on this tea for days. Now I just have to throw it out." Joan walks into the kitchen. "When you're ready to accept help, I'm here," she calls.

"Joan!"

Mother hears a splash and then a great metal crash.

Back at home, Mother slams her front door so hard the knob
falls off, leaving a peep hole to the dusky front yard. She spends
a twisted minute trying to put it back in, then throws the knob
and its pin back onto the floor. She paces around, mumble sings,
There are no dinosaurs, imagines Joan joining a nunnery in Canada
or maybe New Guinea. Visitors would only be able to talk to
Joan through an ornate grille. Mother feels like she can't breathe,
decides to go out on the porch for some air. As she walks
through the back door something brushes her head. She swipes
her hand over her hair and comes up with a handful of web.
The black widow. Mother goes back in the house. Comes out
with her broom. She can see the delicate white egg sac, carefully
wrapped over and over in fine thread—the last act before the
widow died—now cradled in the right top of the web. Mother
raises the broom and hits the web. The broom comes down
covered in gauze. When she tries to pull the mess off the broom,
webbing sticks to her jeans. She growls and throws the broom
over the side of the porch, javelin-style.

That night Mother follows the smell of boiling corn and beans
into a wetu, but they will not offer her anything, so she ducks
into another, where she finds two English captives she has never
seen before. The little girls are already dressed as Wampanoag,
in deerskin smocks and bare feet, their hair pulled back with
leather thongs. A woman is boiling horse hooves. She cuts off a
small piece of hoof for Mother. Mother cracks it with her back
teeth, swallows. The younger English girl can't chew the tough,
sinewy hoof. She sucks and gnaws on it, slobber running down
her chin. When the girl sees Mother watching her she takes the
hoof out of her mouth and says, He only likes serious women,
anyways.

   Mother thinks of Gretel, pushing the evil witch into the
oven and burning her alive, so she and Hansel can make their

escape. She says, That makes no sense, and she herself isn't sure what exactly she is referring to. Then she says to the girl, You cannot bite that, and takes the piece of horse hoof out of the little girl's mouth and crunches it in her own. It's delicious, like bacon.

Then Mother is in labor: pushing, pushing, the head crowning, it is a great relief. She looks closely at the face emerging between her own legs. It's Mary Rowlandson.

Mother opens her eyes, lids aflutter in the dark.

She's standing in a room with an unfamiliar smell—a lemony detergent she doesn't use, plus a close, sweaty smell. She feels a breeze from the window—a thin curtain swells and shrinks like a jellyfish. She jerks her head to clear it. Where is she?

She's standing over Mateo and Joan's bed. They're right here—she could touch Joan's long, pale foot that hangs out from under the brightly colored Mexican wool blanket. Joan's on her back, her arm over her forehead, her snore a low buzz, like a wasp in a jar. Mateo is curled with his back to Joan on the other side of the bed, his snore punctuating hers with little grunts and whistles.

Mother presses her eyes closed. Opens them. Is this real?

Then she sees a small hand reaching out from under the blanket. A sigh. A third lump—Inez in there with them.

Weirdly, Mother does not feel horrified at her outrageous intrusion. Perhaps she's still half Mary Rowlandson. She watches.

Inez moans a little, turns over under the covers, her hand cups Joan's cheek. Mateo and Joan stir in unison. Mateo turns to hold Inez, Joan turns on her side, stops snoring.

How lovely, the way they sleep in concert with each other, Mother thinks. And then she thinks of us, the way she imagines us curled together inside her in the same way. She puts her hands on her own belly, presses in.

We re-adjust to the touch.

For the first time Mother feels us, a quick fish darting.

She pushes in another place. We startle away. She gasps.

136

Our first communion.

Inez's head appears from underneath the blanket. Her dark eyes open, maybe seeing, maybe unseeing.

Holding her belly with one hand she hurries down the stairs in her long nightgown, through the living room, bangs painfully into the table with her hip, pulls open the door, and rushes into the spindly woods. She stumble-runs for a while, then finally stops, leans against a smooth grey beech tree, trying to catch her ragged breath. She leans her head against the slim trunk. She can see a bit of moon through the trees. She presses into her belly again, and again she feels us, something that is not her inside her. She can't stop smiling and poking at us. It's a wild, satisfied animal smile. She thinks, How good not to be caught in Joan's bedroom, how good it is here in the woods. How good my babies are both alive, and they live under my ribs. She begins to walk again, hum-mumbling, *Dinosaurs, Dinosaurs, they are no more. Aren't you glad that there are no more dinosaurs.* She sings off key, and fiercely.

Students are supposed to be working in small groups to discuss the question: Would it have been possible for the Algonquin and the Puritans to have shared the land in question? Why or why not?

River approaches her desk, leans in. "So, let's hear some more about Weetamoo."

"If you do me a favor and ease up on Christian. He's your friend," Mother whispers.

"Whatever, he's a brown-noser. You know it, I know it. He's probably jealous because you and me and my pops are so tight. I might have to open up a can of whoop-ass."

"So is it a deal, Mr. Whoop-ass? You'll stop harassing Christian?" Mother whispers.

River shrugs, could be a yes. "Listen up, Ms. R, you better start educating me."

Mother looks around to make sure everyone is on task. She

notices the kids from the nearest group are listening, too.

"I'm going to finish the story of Weetamoo, for anyone who wants to hear."

Most of them listen up.

"Weetamoo heard the British shouting behind her, and she thought she heard the squeal of iron as one loaded his musket. She began to run towards the Great Taunton River."

"Not the river," River says. "She should climb up a tree or something."

"But then she'd be cornered for sure," someone says.

"Weetamoo was already winded as she pushed her way through a spindly grove of trees and burst out onto the bank. She did not stop but stumbled through the mud into thigh-high water and launched herself towards the far shore. She knew the British already stood on the bank behind her. She could hear them cursing, and one fired his musket at her. She took a breath and submerged. Underwater, she struggled out of her coat, watched it drift towards the bottom. When her lungs hurt she surfaced and breathed again. She no longer heard the voices of her enemies.

"She treaded, looking about. Bad luck had driven her into the river at one of the widest points. The other side was a long distance away, and she couldn't go back, but the water was cool and green, with only a gentle current. She opened her mouth for a drink, and could faintly taste the sea. She began to swim, found her rhythm, three pulls of her arms underwater, three kicks of her feet, a breath, and then again. When she reached the far shore she would look for mussels to eat. She would find a swamp, hide, rest. Then she would follow the Taunton to the sea, to home.

Mother's throat is closing. She clears it. "If only her body didn't feel like she was still wearing that coat. She thought of the good weight of her baby when she cradled him, nursing, his small hand tucked under her arm. Would she be too weak to carry him now? To lift his head above the water all the way to the shore? She swam that thought away. She focused on the rhythm and the shore slowly drawing nearer. She knew she could do this."

Everyone's quiet.

"But she drowned, right?" someone finally says.

"She almost made it," River says. "That's so fucked up."

"Yes. But don't swear."

"I wish I could go back there and help her out, know what I'm saying?" River says. "Like she's swimming across that river, about to go under, the British are firing their lame-ass muskets, and then bam, time warp. I'm there. With a helicopter. I come down. The water's choppy. The British are so scared they like bow down to the great bird. But I still probably spray them with an AK47. Weetamoo climbs up the rope ladder. That's it." He grins big.

"Do you know what happened to Mary Rowlandson?" Mother asks River and glances at the other kids listening.

"Nope." The others shake their heads no.

"Soon after she was ransomed, her minister husband died. She married a Harvard educated farmer in Wethersfield, Connecticut. She lived to be 73 years old."

"Makes sense," River says. "Weetamoo is like one of Aunt Joan's martyrs. Mary Rowlandson ate shit to survive."

"She mumble God's mumble," Christian says. He's standing close to River.

"Yo. Back off, Bro. You in my personal space."

"Your boyfriend is trying to get up witcha," someone snickers. The class laughs.

Christian returns to his desk, picks up his book and puts it in front of his face like a shield.

River turns to Mother. "Ms. R., I forgot my textbook. Can I borrow one?" Mother tells him he'll have to pay for it if he doesn't find it, goes into the storage room to dig out a copy of the worn, heavy book. When she returns holding a battered *Discovering Ourselves* against her chest, everyone is whispering and snickering. There is a crudely chalked drawing on the board, a face with its nose inside a woman's butt. The butt is labeled *Ms. R* and the face, *Christian*.

Just then, Christian lowers his book, notices the drawing, leaps up, knocks his chair over, trips on it, scrambles to his feet, runs to the board and rubs his palms over the drawing, chalk dust flying. Then, shockingly, he seems to choke. He stops breathing. He starts up again, but wheezing, each breath a tortured whistle. He tries to speak three times, then finally manages to say, "The nurse has my mumble."

Mother asks two girls to walk Christian to the nurse's office. She says she'll meet them there. The class is quiet, sitting in their little circles, watching her.

Mother turns to River. "Go," she says to him. "Just get out."

River shrugs, shoulders his backpack. "Whatever," he says.

When Mother returns home from school she calls Michael and asks him if he has time to talk.

"On the phone?" he says.

"Whatever you prefer."

"Okay, I'll be over after dinner."

At eight p.m. he arrives, his hair still wet from a shower, smelling of a musky aftershave. He holds out a bottle of red wine.

She points to her stomach.

"You believe that malarkey? Our mothers drank while they were pregnant, and look at us—leaders of the free world."

"We can all have a drink together in four months." She fills a glass for Michael.

He grabs the glass and the bottle. "Let's sit outside," he says. "It's a nice night."

Mother gets a sweater. They sit on the porch. The sky is an upside-down bowl of stars.

"Do you know the constellations?" Michael asks, looking up.

"No, but I recently read that before King Philip's war

someone in Wallingford saw an Indian made of stars that took up most of the sky."

"I'm guessin' they didn't consider that a good sign."

"So, Michael, I wanted to talk to you about River."

"About River? Jeez. I took a shower and shaved and everything."

"I'm just concerned because since Christian started at school River's been giving him a hard time."

Michael rolls his eyes, drinks. "Okay, here's the skinny. They've always had a what you might call dicey relationship. They've been friends since they were little. Sometimes they get along great, but you know, Christian's irritating, and River's easily irritated, he's got a temper, what you'd call a mean streak, and then he starts to tormenting Christian, and Christian's kind of a pussy, pretends he has asthma. I used to tease Joan a little when I was a kid. How about you, Evie, did you ever torment anyone besides me?" He smiles his crooked smile.

"Do you think you could talk to River? It's disrupting the class. And it's making it hard for Christian to be in school. I keep waiting to read about it in Margaret's Community News blog, but I guess he's not telling his mother because she hasn't mentioned it."

"He's not as dumb as he looks, that Christian." Michael pours himself another big glass.

"Christian is a very smart boy. I think part of the problem is that River's a little jealous because Christian is a dedicated student. But River is really smart, too, and he was just starting to open up."

"They both have crushes on you."

"Oh, no, it's not like that. They just want attention. Michael, you could help with that, with River." There is some kind of bug biting her. "God, what is that?" She slaps at her arms.

"What, you don't have no-see-ums in paradise?"

She smiles. "I never seen 'um."

"Good one."

"The point is that River is having a hard time. With his mother away, you could give him more attention. I'm doing the best I can, but you have to—"

Michael's face is in close up, his red wine breath washing over her, his eyes closed. Evie's palms press against his chest, she's not sure if she's pushing him away or just holding on, but the kiss lands anyway, a little too hard, there's a click of teeth, and his eyes open and they are staring at each other. But then he crosses his eyes, and Mother laughs, and he moves back.

"Michael." She shakes her head.

"Don't worry, that was just an exploratory mission. Mission control, the eagle almost landed. Colonization comes later." He pats her round tummy. "Get the moon metaphors?"

She laughs, stands up, and he laughs a little too, then he picks up his bottle of wine, groans and unbends himself, like the Tin Man in need of oil.

"But about River—"

"Yeah, we'll do some male bonding, we'll rassle, eat some barbecue." His face hovers wistfully around hers again, his lips stained maroon, but she gives him a little shove.

"That bottle's empty. I'll recycle it. Go on home."

He grins, nods. "One small step for man." Winks.

What's with all the winking in this place, Mother thinks, as she watches him list down her driveway. She tells herself, I bet he tries that on every woman he meets, plus he was tipsy. It doesn't mean anything.

Saturday morning again, weather softer and softer, the smell of lilacs in the air, the sun shining down on newly leafed trees, trembling leaf shadows on the barn. Small white butterflies flit around the lavender.

Six days after the nettle tea conflagration, and no word exchanged between Mother and Joan. Although she isn't sure Mateo, Inez and Oshun will show up, she hopes they will, and she dresses carefully, grey velvet stretch-pants and the rose colored pullover whose string he snipped.

They appear, right on time. After a group Post-It-fest and then breakfast, Mateo and Mother sit at the table, both sipping their sweet, sweet tea. In the other room, Inez and Oshun decorate the paper dolls she has drawn for them. They can hear Inez saying over and over, "Señor, when you awake I hope you will look on us all with new eyes.

Oshun keeps moaning, "Shut up, please, just shut up."

Mateo calls out, "Cállate, Inez."

Then there is a silence over the whole house. Mother had given Inez a close look when she first arrived, assessing if she had seen her when she sleepwalked, but Inez said only, "I dreamed about you." And mother said, "I dreamed about you, too." And that was it. Now Mother says awkwardly, "I'm sorry about the misunderstanding with Joan. It really is just a misunderstanding. I swear I'm not a klep—"

"Joan needs you. She has been better since you arrived here. Perhaps you can talk with her—she is difficult, but she has a good heart."

"Sure. But about the stealing—"

"You are not taking things away. It's the opposite. We all know this." He smiles at her, and she smiles at her tea. "You look radiant. Something special has happened, no?"

Mother allows herself to meet his full frontal smile. "I can feel the babies."

"It's something I will never experience. I think romantic love is a subconscious yearning for the original moment when two people share one body. And think for your twins. Their longing will be so much greater, yes?"

We long for a little more room. We can no longer tumble serenely. Now, our chins are so often pressed into our chests, our backs forced into C's. And if anything startles us we kick each other in the face, a sharp elbow in the back. In our struggle for more room we push against our mother, too, angling for more breathing room.

On Sunday, Hector appears with a heavy toolbox. He nails plywood over the window in the basement, then installs heavy duty locks on the front, back and basement doors. "Boss' orders," he says. When mother thanks him he says softly, "De nada. It's the man's job to keep the women and the children safe. We need to protect our homes. My daughter fell out of my hands. Be careful."

That night Mother dreams again, and not about Mary Rowlandson. This time, she's back in the avalanche, she's suffocating. She's digging her way out.

When she wakes in bed she is very cold—there's a cool wind coming up through the house. The nails on her ring fingers and pointer fingers on both hands are ripped and bleeding. On the floor by the bed is a kitchen knife. Mother immediately feels her throat closing, her eyes blurring. She picks up the knife with her pulsing fingers and walks downstairs slowly. Both doors are wide open, the locks on the doors have been pried off. The basement door is open. She takes a few steps down the basement stairs. The board has been pried off the wall. She closes the doors. At least I didn't hurt anybody, she thinks. She puts the knife in the sink. Her fingers throb, and she opens the freezer for some ice. Joan's clay mother sits on a package of frozen tater tots. Mother takes her out. She grips the little mother in her wounded fist, pulls on her winter boots and walks through the early, spring dawn.

Dewy, misty, sky just blurring to pink and grey, birds beginning to sing. She goes up to Joan and Mateo's. She tries the door. It's unlocked. She gently turns the knob, slips inside. Stuffs the clay mother behind the books where Joan had perched her before.

Turns to leave.

Joan stands in front of the door, her hands on her hips.

They stare at each other.

"Just tell me what you want," Mother says.

"I already told you." Laser-eyes from Joan.

"You want me to admit I'm a thief," Mother says.

"I know I can be judgmental, but I am trying not to judge you. I know that's not my job. In fact, here." She goes to the shelf and pulls out the clay mother, hands her to Mother. "I want you to have her."

Mother puts the clay mother on the table.

"Take her," Joan says. "I want you to."

Mother shakes her head no.

"Look," Joan says, jerking her chin towards the window. Mother turns. The white-tailed doe is grazing her way out of the woods and into the yard, followed by two spotted fawn. Mother goes to the window, and Joan stands next to her. The fawns pull up grass, raise their heads, prance sideways. One begins to nurse. The other pricks her enormous ears and raises her narrow head—she seems to be staring straight at them with her big brown Bambi eyes.

"Wow," Mother says.

"Listen," Joan says with an intensity that makes the doe skitter sideways. "I know I'm annoying. It's annoying to be me, too. Sometimes I feel like the crown of thorns is lodged inside my heart. But I just can't stand the idea of you lying to me or even worse, lying to yourself. The thing that scares me most in the world is not seeing clearly."

Mother says, "I did take your clay mother. It just doesn't feel like I did, because I did it in my sleep."

"You weren't sleepwalking just now."

"I know. But I was before."

They look at each other. "You have to admit you have a problem," Joan says.

Mother feels her face flush, but she says, "Okay. I have a problem."

"Are you going to stop?"

Mother thinks, Joan is a bully. "I'm trying."

Joan suddenly looked triumphant. "Everyone believes

you're this calm, kind angel. I'm the only one who knows your insides are as full of thorns as mine."

"That's not true—" Mother starts, but then she forces herself to say, "You're right."

Joan gives her a long once over. "I'll forgive you as long as there's no more stealing. Agreed?"

"Agreed," Mother says. When she leaves she takes the clay mother.

THE EIGHTH REMOVE

This is summer, summer! The heart says, and not even the full of it.
Mother writes this quote from William Carlos Williams on the blackboard, and so it is, hot, hotter, humid and overcast, mere days before school ends, the students can not quite believe they are almost free, and yet can not believe they are not free yet. So here they sit in her classroom, windows open, moist air billowing in and out, lulled into an expectant trance.

Mother stands in front of the class, her heart burning up to her throat. She wears a loose beige cotton top and a large peach silk skirt fastened by a safety pin to accommodate her belly. "What was the primary conflict over in King Philip's/ Metacom's war?" she asks. "Resources? Religious beliefs? What else?" Mother twists from the board to face her heavy-lidded students, yellow chalk in hand. In the midst of her twist, she feels a small flick as the safety pin opens. The peach silk skirt waterfalls down and puddles at her feet.

And there she is, standing in front of her whole class in her big girl pregnancy underwear and navy clogs.

She stares at them, her mouth a little open, heat exploding on her cheeks. They stare back, their mouths open too, perhaps wondering if they are dreaming their teacher standing before them in her underwear. The worst part of it is that no one says anything. It is as if they have all suddenly come down with locked-in syndrome. Then Mother looks at the white globe of her stomach with its brown road down the middle, her popped belly button like a tiny volcano. "Surprise," she says, and does a clumsy curtsy.

Everyone laughs themselves awake while Mother whips her skirt back up. Mother begins to laugh, too. It is a laugh no one in the class has heard, a deep, ho ho ho, fee fi fo fum kind of laugh. Surprised, they all laugh harder. Which makes Mother laugh harder, too.

Then River calls, "Ms. R, you'd do anything to get us interested in history, wouldn't you?"

Which is not funny, but Mother is belly laughing so hard now, she has to hold onto the desk, tears streaming down her cheeks. She's leaning forward, gasping and moaning.

"Stop it," Christian says in his soft, disapproving voice, as if he is just waking from a spell himself. "Stop disrespecting Mrs. Rosen!"

This just makes everyone break out into laughter again, including Mother.

"Don't worry, Christian," Mother gasps, trying to refasten the safety pin by feel.

Christian rises up from the front, center seat and walks to the back of the room, where River sprawls. "You mumble mumble of yourself. You mumble Mrs. Rosen cry." Christian's pointer finger is almost touching River's nose, which causes even more hilarity. Mother notices that River's smile has turned into a snear, but her awkwardness with the safety pin keeps her from moving forward.

River sweeps his outstretched leg into the backs of Christian's calves. Christian falls, producing a bigger explosion of laughter. There is a smack as Christian's head hits against the corner of one of the desks.

Mother walks quickly over, holding her skirt closed in her fist. Little black beads have spilled all over the grey rug. Christian lies in the fetal position between two desks. She wonders what Christian had in his pockets. Then she sees a long red smear on the side of the desk. They are not black beads but beads of blood.

City On A Hill:
The Community Building Blog
For Lonely Rincon Road
By Margaret Langley Gonzales

It is with great sadness that I write of the following event: My son was brutally attacked during his history lesson yesterday. He sustained a head wound. Rhonda Boucher, the school nurse, stopped the bleeding with direct pressure. Christian was rushed to the Emergency Room, where he received five stitches.

I have concluded that my son is not safe in our public school system. I am appalled at the culture of neglect that infects our own high school, paid for by our own tax dollars. My son was attacked after he tried to defend the teacher's honor from an angry young man that desperately needs more stability and structure. I have heard through the grapevine that the family of this disturbed adolescent has displayed a shocking lack of understanding for the gravity of the situation. This young man received in-house suspension for the rest of the year, a week and a half. That is all.

I know many in our community, including myself, feel betrayed by the school, the young man and his family, and the teacher/neighbor who allowed this to happen. And who shouldn't be teaching at all in her condition or at the very least needs to wear proper maternity clothes. Those in question might feel so ashamed that they will try to hide away, but that will only cause a larger rent in the fabric of our community. I suggest those in question reach out with explanations and apologies, so that we can all begin to heal. I cannot give more details at this time as I am in consultation with a lawyer.

God Bless!

Mother reads Margaret's blog on the second evening after the incident. She walks over to Margaret and Hector's house. Hector answers the door all scrubbed-looking as usual in his pressed khaki's, his plaid shirt buttoned to the last button, and his shining white socks rising out of brown corduroy slippers. He offers her a seat on the pale pink velour couch. He sits opposite her, awkwardly upright in a light blue recliner. Margaret can't sit still, is in and out of the room, pinching leaves off her ivy plants, spritzing them, not looking at Mother.

Mother sits with her hands folded on her knees, explains what happened, and then expresses concern about Christian's difficulty in picking up social cues. That he mistook her laughter for tears. She asks if he's had psychological testing. Hector watches her, mournfully polite and silent. Mother feels that he will never let her in, is not listening, and she finally says, "Christian needs support."

Margaret suddenly turns from her plant work. "He gets support from his family, his church and his Lord. What more support does he need?"

"I know you love him deeply, but I also believe Christian could benefit from psychological counseling," Mother answers. "Even just to talk about his sister."

Margaret says she has a headache and leaves the room.

Mother and Hector sit in silence. Finally, Mother says, "If there isn't anything else you want to discuss—"

Hector says gently, "I think my boy was right to try and protect you. My boy could sense something was wrong."

"What do you mean?" Mother asks.

"Something is possessing you."

Mother feels her face bloom with heat. "What are we talking about?"

But then Christian comes through the front door, his hair shaved over his ear with the five ugly black stitches visible, and Hector doesn't say anything more.

First Friday in June, night of the potluck. Mother leaves a message on Joan's answering machine: "I have a little heartburn, but mostly I just feel like being alone tonight, nothing to worry about, have fun!"

Mother is preparing a bowl/bol of cereal, thinking about what Hector said to her: he's obviously crazy, he's talking about spirit possession, definitely not about Mateo, Hector's as disturbed as Christian, of course they both are, pretending that their daughter is dead, but then why do I feel skinned, as if he can see inside me?

She hears someone crunching up her gravel driveway. Joan and Mateo, together, Mateo holding a loaded down paper plate and Joan clutching her glass of red wine in one hand and his beer bottle in the other. They are walking quickly and talking. Their shoulders bump against each other, and Mother notices that though Mateo is stocky and Joan tall and narrow, they are exactly the same height.

Mother only has a minute to wedge herself between the refrigerator and the wall. There is just enough space there for her to stand sideways next to the mop and the broom and the green plastic bucket, her belly bumping against the fridge. The sticky on the broom, la escoba, flutters to the floor.

A brisk double knock on the door. Mother hears them conferring, turning the knob. "It's open," Mateo says.

"Evie!" Joan calls in a stage whisper. "She probably cried herself to sleep," she says to Mateo. "She's not as easy going as she appears."

"I'll just leave the food," Mateo says in the same loud whisper.

"You know," stage whispers Joan, "sleeping half-sitting alleviates heartburn. Maybe I should just sneak up there and prop her up."

"Are you crazy?" Mateo says.

Joan smothers her laughter. "Put the food in the refrigerator."

"Then it will be cold."

"But we shouldn't leave it out all night. It will rot."

"Historically, the spice on curry was there precisely to hide the rot."

"You want to give her food poisoning? You want to kill her babies?"

"I'll put it in," Mateo says.

Mateo opens the refrigerator. Mother can see his Birkenstocks. His feet are hairy and bony—there is some kind of crazy bump on the outside of his big toes. And why does his deformed feet in his ugly Birkenstocks make her want to sob?

"Jesus, Mary and Joseph, look what she's eating—sugarcoated cereal," Joan says. "Her diet is a big reason she's out of balance. Sugar makes you crazy."

Mateo closes the refrigerator. "Vamos, Chinita."

"I'm writing her a note. I'm telling her she has no reason to avoid us. Telling her boys will be boys and all that. No one is mad at her. Margaret doesn't count."

"Enough note now. Time to go."

"I'm just telling her to drink a glass of milk when she gets heartburn. And eat small meals and sleep propped up, and avoid processed cereal—"

"—Joan!" He laughs.

"Be quiet!" She laughs, too.

"You know we have left a house full of guests," Mateo says.

"Inez will throw them out soon enough." Joan laughs a little more.

"Cállate," Mateo says. "I'm leaving."

"You shut up," Joan says mildly.

Joan eases the door shut. Mother hears them crunching over the gravel again. She doesn't move right away, just stays there, wedged in.

The next morning, Saturday, when Mateo, Inez and Oshun arrive, Mother hands each child a pirate eye patch, then ties a bandana over each head. She hands them the treasure map she has made look antique by soaking it in tea. All this pirate preparation happened the night before. After she squeezed herself out of the space beside the refrigerator, took the curry out, and slid it into the microwave/microonda, she stood in front of the white glow as the food pivoted, staring into the face of the radiated glow. She had allowed herself this small revenge-suicide by microwave, until she remembered us and moved out of the toxic light. Then she'd trashed the curry, ate three bowl/bols of sugarcoated cereal and spent the rest of the evening doing pirate prep.

Now, she and Mateo watch the children take off into the woods, Inez holding the map, Oshun calling, "Wait for me!"

Mateo and Mother turn their backs to the collapsing barn, the white and green grape vine, the overgrown garden and the woods that hide the children. They lean against the peeling porch railing. "Did you eat the food we left last night?" Mateo asks. He wears shorts and a t-shirt for the first time outside of a soccer game, a blue t-shirt with a little pocket. His forearms look muscular as he crosses them over his chest.

"Yes, thanks, it was great."

"Are you unhappy about Christian?" he asks. "Is that why you hide yourself away?"

"What do you mean?"

"I mean because you don't come to the potluck. Perhaps because you were unhappy about Christian and River?"

"It's been a rough week." Mother's voice wobbles, so she says, "Not to mention the fact that I had to explain to the principle why I was standing in front of the class in my underwear."

"Oh, yes, I heard of this." He laughs, and Mother does, too. "Is that why you decide to hide in the refrigerator?"

Mother stops mid-laugh. "What?"

"When Joan and I come over. You hid in the refrigerator."

"Not in, beside."

"Yes, beside. Why did you hide beside the refrigerator?"

"I'll tell you why." Mother looks at the pale green jungle that the garden has so quickly become. It looks like the fence is only just holding the tangle of weeds back from the slightly less scraggly yard. "Because that's what I do." She laughs, then puts her hand over her mouth. She removes her hand. "Steve isn't dead."

"So," Mateo says. "Tell me."

"We were on a skiing vacation in Colorado. I was buried in an avalanche. I thought I was going to die. Then I unburied myself. The air hurt—it hurt to breathe, the air felt thin and sharp coming in, but it was so good. To breathe.

"Then I saw Steve, about twenty yards from me on the slope. He was probing the snow with his ski pole, searching for me, calling my name. I'd lost my skis, but I struggled through the snow towards him, and I started crying, and I threw my arms around him. But he pulled away. He held onto my shoulders and he shook me, really hard, my head was jerking all around, and he was talking in this really intense low hissing voice, because I guess if you yell you can start another avalanche. And he hissed that I'd totally screwed up, why didn't I listen to him, why do I never think. He started crying then, and he hissed, 'You could have killed my baby. My baby could be dead right now because of you.' Oh, and then he said, 'I wish to God I was the one that was carrying the baby. You're just too weak to do this.'" Mother finds that if she holds her face very still, with her jaw pushed out a little, she can keep from crying.

Mateo takes her hand. Neither of them talk for a while. "You know, this is our last Saturday," Mateo says. "Joan's class is over."

"It is?" Mother says, and she is embarrassed by how high and squeaky her voice sounds.

"I thought of a last story to tell you. Do you know this story Sleeping Beauty?"

Mother nods, still working to keep back the tears.

"So, this story is very much the same one you know, except the sleeping beauty is a man, and he is not so much a beauty. And he doesn't even know that he is asleep, until the beautiful princess cuts her way through all the weeds and wakes him. And he is so full of gratitude."

"Thank you," is all she can think to say, staring at his hand holding her hand. She feels that if she looks at him, full on, in the face, she might dissolve into a puddle of salty water and drip down through the cracks between the boards of the porch, she might drag her tent dress over her head and stand naked before him.

The children break through the woods, yelling triumphantly, holding the treasure they have unburied to their chests.

Outside it's raining lightly, a warm early summer rain, inside Mother has laid out on the kitchen floor the disassembled parts of a twin rocking cradle that her mother has had sent to her from Italy, directions in Italian. It's ultra modern, blonde wood, all ovals with slots, it looks so simple but has so far proved impossible. Mother calls Molly at the time they've arranged. It is three p.m. our time, Molly's lunch break.

"I'm done teaching," Mother says. "And guess what, it's raining. And I have good news."

"Raining in June? That's crazy," Molly says. "I'm sitting on the back porch at work under the Palm tree. I can hear the seals barking. So, I've got annoying news."

"No, me first—guess what?" Phone cradled between shoulder and chin, Mother sits on the floor, turning the ovals, trying to figure out which slot goes where.

"What?"

"Despite the fact that I lost my skirt, the principal offered me a permanent job."

"So?"

"So, I don't have to start until December. I can have three months maternity leave, six weeks of it paid. Yay!"

"Alright yes, yay, you can stay in Hicklandia forever pining for that fucking guy. The married one."

"That's ridiculous. God." Mother thinks she's found the slots that fit, maybe if she pushes a little harder.

"Yeah, right. What's going on with him?"

"Nothing. We had these conversations for a while. They're over now." She puts the boards down and watches the soft rain patter over the light green world. "I'm so attracted to him I get this nineteenth century swoon feeling when I'm within ten feet of him. It's like I have some kind of reverse allergy or something. What is that? Do you think it's chemical?"

"He's going to break your heart, Evie, no joke. All the books and movies will tell you the same thing. A woman who involves herself with a married man is as doomed as the black man or the bald man in a blockbuster. Plus he is bald, right? Double whammy."

Mother rolls her eyes at Molly, at blockbusters, at the crib, wondering what *strumenti* means and why it is *no necessari*.

"I mean, Steve was a total asshole, but at least he was your asshole. Which brings me to the annoying news."

"What?" Just like that, two pieces slide into each other, lock.

"Okay, don't freak out. But he knows."

"Knows what?" Mother holds herself still, holding the two-sided cradle.

"Steve knows you're pregnant."

"What?" Mother scrambles off the floor.

"Your health insurance sent a bill for the ultrasound to his house."

"But I had my mail forwarded. I paid that bill!"

"Well, he knows. He gave me a letter to give to you."

"You didn't tell him where I am, did you?"

"Of course not."

"Okay, just read it." Mother is still standing.

"Don't you want me to send it?"

"No! Just read it to me and then throw it away."

Mother doesn't hear the rip, but Molly says, "Ready?"

"Yes."

"Okay. 'Dear Evie, looking back on our relationship, I have come to realize, with some help, I could have been more patient

156

with you.' Patient? I wonder if he's seeing a shrink or something. Maybe he's gotten on some meds finally."

Mother starts to feel dizzy, she sits down. "Just read it."

"Okay: 'The weaker you became, the more controlling I became. I admit I can be exacting and I like things done right, and I can be pushy about that. I know now that you are pregnant. I don't want to take the baby from you, but I want to be a part of it. I'm in a better place right now. The best ever. You have to admit I'm competent—and I have financial resources, too. And I'm worried about the health of the baby. What you're eating, is it organic, that kind of thing. Sometimes I can't sleep thinking about it. So, contact me. I'm the father. Our baby needs it's father and I need —'

"Oh, look at this. He crossed out my baby and wrote our baby. Ha." Mother closes her eyes, presses the heel of her hand into her belly, feels us push back.

"'Please, Evie, think, think about this.'"

Mother opens her eyes. "You're joking right? He didn't really write, think, think."

"Okay, yeah, I added an extra think."

Mother bends down, takes another piece of the crib from the floor, finds the right slot, presses it in, she's figured it all out. "Tear it up."

"Are you sure?"

"What do you mean am I sure?"

"If you work it out with Steve, you could come home. You know, co-parenting. He's right. He could help you. And he is the father. And I could help, too. It doesn't really make sense anymore—your whole hinterland incognito witness protection thing."

"Are you crazy? He broke into your apartment."

"But he sounds like he's getting his act together. And he is the father. I hope you're not staying because of that guy, because that's not real."

Mother's hands stop moving. Her voice is quiet. "He says I

woke him up. He listens to me, and he just, listens. And he cut a loose string off my sweater."

"He cut a loose string? Really? I had a boyfriend who bought me a houseboat, remember that? You deserve a man of your own."

Five days after school lets out, and Mother is still correcting final exams and calculating grades. She sits at the table working over her belly while the late morning dew steams off in the backyard. Already, her back has begun to ache and she shifts, trying to accommodate her girth. When she is still, we kick, when she moves, we grow still. It seems our little utopian experiment is running out of room.

A polite knock. Mother puts both hands on the table to raise up her doubled body. She opens the door.

"I heard the lock was broken again," Hector says. "I've come to replace it." He is, as usual, immaculately dressed and coiffed.

"Thank you so much."

He sets his toolbox carefully onto the floor, opens it, and begins working.

"Would you like tea or coffee?" she asks.

He shakes his head. "No, thank you."

Mother hesitates, then goes back to correcting papers. He takes out some kind of loud power tool, but Mother keeps working.

"There," Hector says after a little while. "See?" He turns the knob, demonstrates how the door closes. "And I've added this." He pats the hefty gold-colored metal slide bolt that he's screwed into the door and the wall. It is twice the size of the one he put on the door last time.

"Thank you."

"I screwed it in pretty tight last time."

"I know, it's kind of crazy. Maybe you've heard. I sleepwalk. I took it off in my sleep."

He nods sadly. He just stands there holding the power tool in his hand, just kind of staring around, as if he had more things to fix. Mother looks around, too. There are yellow Post-Its everywhere, making a slight flapping sound in the breeze from the open window.

"I'm learning Spanish," she explains.

"They are like a hundred fluttering hearts."

Mother blushes.

"Do you know the story of La Llorona?" he asks her.

"No," Mother says.

"The story tells of a woman who drowned her own children so that she could run off with her lover. But her lover rejects her and Llorona kills herself. At the gates of heaven the angels say, Where are your children? La Llorona is condemned to search the earth for her children, weeping, without end." Hector puts his tool back in his toolbox.

Mother's throat starts to close. "That's a terrible story."

"A mother needs to be calm, to settle and nest. For your babies' sake, you must stop." Hector holds his pointer and middle finger up and makes a scissoring motion with them across his chest.

After Hector leaves, Mother sits at the kitchen table, absently running her fingers through her now thick, glossy hair. Then she begins to dispose of the Post-Its. They flap and skitter to the floor. She sweeps them into the dustpan. Estúpido, suelo and huevos stick to her new broom. She tries to bang them off against the garbage can/basura. When she pulls them off they stick to her fingers. She notices ventana and luna are stuck to her slipper. She sits back down, panting, waiting for her breath to come even. She glances out the window. The doe and her two fawn are watching her, ready to bolt for the woods.

She goes up to our room where the egg shaped double crib is the only furniture. She kicks it with her foot and it rocks a little. The ghosts of her earlier efforts and her nighttime hieroglyphics haunt the lavender-blue walls. What kind of a room is this for babies, she thinks. I need more layers. She begins to paint.

Four hours later the walls of the small room are covered in another, thicker layer. She'll have to do a lot of coats to fully hide all this.

She leaves the walls to dry, goes downstairs and calls the garage. Mateo answers. "I have something to say," she says.

"Excellent!" Mateo sounds jolly.

"I know this might sound silly to you, but I think we should stop talking to each other." She leans against the counter for support.

"You're breaking up with me?" He still sounds jolly.

"It's not good for me or my babies. It's unbalancing me. And I just need to be patient. To wait until I get what I deserve. And I am thinking of getting back in contact with my husband. My babies need their father. I might even move back to Santa Cruz," she says, not sure if she means it.

"But we should have this conversation in person," Mateo says, not so jolly anymore. "This is too important to speak over the phone."

"I don't have anything else to say."

"Why not talk by the stream behind your house? It's private. If you leave the house at two, it takes you ten minutes to walk, you'll arrive at 2:10. Simply walk at the end of your yard and go downhill to the right, you'll see the water at the bottom of the hill. I'll leave now and be there at 1:55 and wait for you. I'm leaving now."

Mother wonders if Mary Rowlandson was ever at peace, even one time, during her captivity. There's a circle of sunshine on the pale wood floor near the door, and Mother imagines Mary Rowlandson sitting there, sucking on a bean. Maybe she lifts her face to the sun, and she doesn't chew, she just lets the bean sit there on her tongue, and maybe that one time, with the sun and the bean, it was enough.

Mother looks at her watch. 2:00. She imagines climbing out

of her extra large pregnancy suit and leaving it here on the floor while the rest of her, all that is only her, runs to the stream to meet Mateo. But she can't do that, so she pushes off the counter, we her captives stashed inside, or perhaps the other way round. She leaves the house for the woods.

As she enters the yard, the doe snorts and leaps into the trees. Her fawns follow clumsily. Mother thinks, I'm certainly not Snow White. Fawns run from me. She enters the woods after them. She walks down to the gorge, her calves tensing on the incline. Mother feels as if she is being watched. She keeps her back straight. She notices that her arms look frail next to her round stomach. Mosquitoes sail around in the still, hot air and a blue jay calls the same four notes querulously, over and over. She has a vague sense of dread—she doesn't know exactly how, but she is fairly certain she will be humiliated. She slips a little, slides down the last of the steep embankment to the gorge and stands there, sweating.

"You are covered in violet paint," he says.

"I was working on the babies' room. It's periwinkle."

"You've got huevos on your butt," he says.

"What?"

"There's a Post-It there." He grins as she pulls the sticky off her butt and crumples it up.

He says they should sit down. He cradles her arm above the elbow and puts his other hand lightly at the small of her back, helps her to sit down. She thinks, if I just had that constant small pressure, that steadying press there, maybe that would be enough.

He takes his hand away. He rolls his jeans up carefully, three more times. His ankles are brown, thin, hairy, he sits down next to her, but doesn't put his feet in the water. He rests his sneakers on a rock. She takes off her own sneakers and slides her feet into the water. They look so white, the green water sliding over them. The brown tadpoles look like a cloud of little commas around her long feet. The hem of her dress soaks through and clings to her legs, but it feels good.

He takes his pointer finger and draws a small circle on the cloth that covers her knee. They both watch him draw the wet circle on her knee. "I have grown to admire your sweet manner, your kindness, the way you listen. You are always welcoming to me. You can be silly, and you can be wise. We are both worm books. I think you are brave to go into that classroom every day and to move here alone. You are beautiful quietly and hopeful quietly. You have never had all that you deserve, and I wish I could give it to you."

Neither of them say anything. They watch his finger circle her knee.

He takes his finger away and clasps his hands together over his own knees. "I dream of staying up all night with you, simply talking. Maybe kissing, maybe a few kisses. But I have a commitment to my family, and I must to honor that commitment. That is why I ask you to meet me. So I can tell you how I feel, but that nothing can come with it. Perhaps this is impossible, but I dream that maybe we can continue to have a spiritual friendship. Maybe we can communicate through email."

"I don't have an email account."

"I don't either, but let's create them." He looks at her. She notices that his green eyes are shot with brown and gold, like agate or moss. "I see you Evie. And I am in love with what I see."

"I love you, too," Mother says, perhaps a bit too quickly.

They hug, a little awkwardly, around her belly. His rough cheek is against her forehead, his neck smells of his aftershave. His skin is very smooth and warm there. Her lips brush his neck by his ear and she feels him shiver, or maybe that is her.

"It is very hard to be spiritual," he says, and she laughs.

He stands and helps her up. "I must go back to work," he taps his watch. "I'll leave now and return up the stream. You wait ten minutes and then go home, yes?"

She watches him walk away. What about that slightly funny

gait he has, she wonders. There is something in the hips. She thinks, What just happened? She thinks, I'm so happy. I have never felt so happy in my entire life.

The next morning, very early, Mother sees Mateo rushing up her drive. She comes down the stairs, her heart thrumming, but he is already walking away. She opens the door and a piece of folded paper falls to the ground.

"Mateo!" she calls from the doorway.

He stops, turns back, stands just outside the door, bouncing on his toes. "I haven't written any poetry since I was an adolescent. It's nothing. It's almost nothing. It's in English. I checked everything with a dictionary. I couldn't sleep last night, so I write it down." Then he leans over and kisses her.

His lips create a tiny burst, almost like pain, between her legs. This kiss-clitoris connection has never happened to her before, like the two cups and a string kids use to communicate. "Come in," she gasps.

"No, I can't. I must go to work!" Then he inclines just past the doorway. He raises his eyebrows. "Where have all the Post-Its gone?"

"I hid the evidence," she says.

"But you must keep up your Spanish!" He picks up his fallen note and bustles through the doorway, whips up the little yellow pad by the phone. He writes briskly and holds it up. "Say it."

She shakes her head.

He says "enamorado" slowly, as if it is a magic incantation that will coax a golden coin from her mouth. He looks so hopeful and watches her mouth so intently it makes her laugh instead of speak Spanish.

He bounces on his toes, laughs too, but says, "Please, mi gringuita, try."

"Enamorado," the end of the word twists awkwardly in her mouth.

He bounces again. "Excellent! Perfecto! That's it! That's it!"

She says, "You know very well that's not perfecto. You remind me of Tigger in *Winnie the Pooh*. Did you ever read *Winnie the Pooh*?"

"Of course. You are Piglet."

"I'm not a pink little wimp."

"Well, you are kind of pink and round."

She grabs the sticky and writes "Bouncy Bouncy Bouncy" on a Post-It and smacks it on his butt.

He posts "The Honey Pot" between her legs.

They look at each other, smiling.

"Now you'll see," he says. He hands her the note.

"Wait, here is my new email." She writes it on a Post-It.

He grabs it. "I have to go!" And he rushes away.

Mother closes the door and unfolds the piece of lined notebook paper:

> Perhaps love has come like a disaster natural,
> A brutal, powerful accident in our lives,
> And yet the expression of the necessary nature on its
> unrepentant, unstoppable search for life.
> I live. I let us, but how could I otherwise?
> Accident our lives, make them necessary, allow us for
> some coherence.
> I think this is it. This story
> demands a meaning.
> I let you live me, and I want to live you.

That night Mother dreams she is pushing Joan into a microwave, hissing "Hush!" and Mother wakes gasping for breath, soaked in sweat, as if she herself were being cooked from the inside out.

Please, she thinks, hear Mateo's prayer. Allow for some coherence. Let there be enough love to go around. Please, help us hold this in balance, just like this.

Mother has found the old lawn mower from the barn that took eight or nine pulls of the cord to start, then burns oil and stalls out every few yards. She is attempting to create a small circle of lawn out of the tangle of Sleeping Beauty weeds and prickers that the back yard has become.

It is wet and hot and green July, dew-rising off-the-leaves-in-the-morning-green. This is a wet green never seen in Santa Cruz, and the sudden explosion of plant profusion surprises her. Seemingly overnight her backyard has become the pastoral she'd imagined on that frigid day in February when she arrived.

As she mows, we shift inside her, trying futilely to create a little more space for ourselves, but she has grown used to our inner struggle. She is used to the constant burning just above her breastbone, too. She is not used to the shock of that kiss, which also burns, heightening her senses, so that everything looks so sharp and close that the world seems hyper-real, and thus, not real at all. She feels as if the whole world has become Evie La La Land.

All she hears is the muffled cough and growl of the mower, and all she smells is burning oil, but she sees that the grapes have finally ripened on the vine. She stops pushing and wades through thigh high weeds to finally try one. The skin is sweet while the flesh is so bitter she has to spit it out. The blackberry bushes have overgrown themselves, seedy berries on every spiked whorl. She eats some of those, ignoring the branches clawing at her. A massive bed of comfrey and chives has taken over a whole swath of the backyard, and as she mows an herbal smell steams up around her.

She feels a precise burn, as if someone has put out a cigarette on her leg. Then another on her ankle. A swarm of ground bees circles the hem of her skirt in a loose tornado. She has mowed over their home. She runs into her own home, trailing bees. She puts her leg up on a chair and holds ice cubes to the stings, a sheen of sweat under her heavy breasts and between her round thighs. Her fingers are stained with blackberry and grape juice.

Her shoes give off a sharp vegetable smell.

A trapped bee vibrates nervously against the inside window.

She watches the lawn mower grumble away over the hive, exhausting bees, until it finally stalls out.

As the ice melts in her fingers, a restlessness gnaws at her. What is he doing? Where is he? How can I reach him? She looks out the window in vain, then checks her email. As if her desire has conjured him, here is the first ever email from Mateo's new Hotmail account: My Dear Gringuita, The stream, same place, eleven a.m. I will drive the road in a maroon Volvo Wagon, I will press the horn as I pass. I will park the car in the bend and go to the stream. If you are not there by 11:15 I will assume you don't get this email. I hope you get it. I am hungry for you. Love.

At 10:55, Mother avoids the ground bees and walks carefully down the incline to the gorge. He is not there yet, and she sits on a flat, bluish-grey slate rock and soaks her swollen ankles in the green water.

Then he is there, an outsized presence, Paul Bunyan lowering himself down next to her. No words, they just begin to kiss. They kiss and kiss and kiss. They seem to be really good at it.

He puts his hand under her t-shirt and into her bra. His small hand seems huge. "I love your breasts," he says.

"They're only temporary," she says.

He keeps one hand on her breast and with the other he begins to stroke her between her legs through her underwear. They continue to kiss, and she is one long, unfamiliar ache. "Let's have sex," she says.

"We can't," he says.

The kissing becomes desperate. It feels as if they are trying to eat away at their desire, and they continue to kiss and he continues to rub and suddenly, outrageously, she comes. With their foreheads touching, she sighs, "Que cosa mas linda." Then she says, "What did I just say?"

166

He smiles. "It means the prettiest thing."

"I've never done this," she says. "I don't mean never spoken Spanish. I've never come with a man."

"I know, Joan told me."

"She told you?"

"You are espactacular," he says. He slides his hand gently over her breast. "Your eyes cross when you come," he says.

"That's a lie."

He says, "Look at this," and he pulls down his shorts.

"Perhaps that's too much of a good thing," she says.

"It is crying with desire for you," he says.

She laughs, rolls her eyes, and grips his member. She expects this to be a fairly exhausting chore. Steve always said she was too slow, and he lay there while she labored on and on, switching her aching hands. It reminded her of scrubbing a pot, the kind of pot that was so impossibly dirty that in the midst of scrubbing you think it might be easier just to throw the pot out and buy a new one.

But Mateo makes little happy sounds like Winnie The Pooh with his honey, then suddenly starts speaking in tongues, and before she knows it, here he comes.

Afterwards, they clean up with Mateo's handkerchief and the gorge water.

Mother feels they have broken through something, that a new way has been forged and they can never go back. "What are we going to do now?" she says.

"Just this," he says, "no more. We have to keep all in balance, my love for you and my love for my family."

"Of course," Mother says.

She thinks of Mary and her bean.

On the way back from the gorge, Mother stumbles dreamily across the lawn, and still in her post-orgasmic fog, starts to push the mower back to the barn. She is bitten on her thumb and on the back of her neck.

Holding an ice cube to her stings, she calls Michael's apartment and River answers. She tells him she wants advice from his father about ridding herself of ground bees. River convinces her he can take care of this problem himself, tonight, for a small fee.

After lunch, she calls the garage hoping Mateo will pick up, but she gets the answering machine.

She takes a walk down the road, hoping to see Mateo as she passes the garage, but everyone is inside, the garage doors closed against the heat. By now, she is hot, swollen, her bee stings are pulsing, her heart is burning, and she feels insane, unmoored. Mother thinks of Mary Rowlandson, restlessly wandering from wetu to wetu, begging for food.

She tries and fails to take a nap. She opens her laptop on the bed beside her and starts an email:

Dear Mateo,

I don't want to take anything away from anyone. I can't even write her name. What would it call down on me? I wish you were twins, one for me and one for her. I wish there were legions of you, one for each love-starved woman on the planet, a Mateo would be handed out by the Red Cross along with that crackling metallic blanket and the bottled water.

She deletes the email. Writes instead: Dear Mateo, I adore you. Sent.

In the afternoon two things happen: first, she hears a loud, unmuffled engine. She looks out the window and sees a helmeted Christian drive by on a three-wheeled ATV. A few minutes later he drives back. Up and down the dead end he roars on his red ATV. She closes the window to blunt the noise. Back and forth, the noise scourges her brain. She puts her earplugs in. After an hour non-stop, down the road he comes with a helmeted River seated behind him.

And then after the ATV is finally put away, Mother pulls out her plugs and goes downstairs to find a phone message from Joan: "Evie! Where are you? We need to make a birth plan. Mateo, turn that burner off! Mateo says hi. Plus I was talking to Neela and she wants to do a baby shower for you. And, check out this quote from Bush: 'Our security will require all Americans to be ready for preemptive action when necessary to defend our liberty and to defend our lives.' Preemptive. You get it, right? He's going to invade Iraq. Something has to be done. We can't allow this to happen. Call me back ASAP."

Mother deletes the message, and that is the second thing.

In the evening, River and Christian arrive dressed all in black. Christian is wearing a headlamp and River has an enormous flashlight. River carries a rusty red gas can and Christian has a blowtorch. "We're here to bust a cap up their butts," River says. "Them bees."

"Good evening, Mrs. Rosen," Christian says.

"This looks a little extreme," Mother says.

"No worries, all pre-approved by my pops," River says.

"It mumble at night," Christian says, "because the mumble mumble in their hive."

"Stay in the house," River says. "You don't want to get hurt."

"I'm tougher than you think," Mother says.

River smirks, "Yeah, right. So, where are those bees anyways?"

"They're underneath that lawn mower."

"I mow lawns, mumble, Mrs. Rosen," Christian says. "I mumble access mumble ride-on."

"We'll see," Mother says. She hands them each five dollars. They pocket it.

"So, we want to build a killer fort in the woods this summer," River says. "Pops says I have to ask you 'cause you're renting all this property back here."

"Sure. Will you show me your fort?"

"When it's done, Ms. R."

River and Christian switch on their flashlights and stomp

out onto the back porch. Mother closes the door.

She watches through the window as beams of light discover the lawn mower. The lawn mower wheels into the darkness. She can't really make out what happens next until she sees the blue flame of the blowtorch and then a hiss and a three foot fiery plume erupts from the ground. She hears the boys' shouts of triumph. In the firelight she can see Christian and River high-fiving, chest bumping, their grins shining.

"Boys," Mother says. She puts her hand to her tummy, thinks, I can't believe I have one of those in here.

Two. We will dance around the fire. We will chest bump and shout into the night. As soon as we have a little room.

Mother comes back from a check-up with the doctor. She has told him she isn't sleepwalking anymore, that it's probably because she's so happy, he told her she's doing just fine, he thinks in all likelihood she'll make it to 36 weeks, and there's a message from Molly: "Okay, so get this. My neighbor told me some guy was going through my garbage today. A guy in a suit. Either the homeless have started dressing a lot better, or Steve has hired a fucking private detective or something. You were right, Evie, he's insane. It's good you decided not to contact him."

Mother doesn't call back.

Neela calls and leaves a message: "Evie, I am planning your baby shower. You will find it delightful. Call me back as soon as you receive this message."

Mother deletes this message, thinking, This is not like me at all.

Phone message from Joan, deleted: "Evie, I need to talk to you, not only about Iraq or the birth plan, either. Something's wrong with Mateo. I think he's having some kind of nervous breakdown. He's so—twitchy. He said last night that our relationship was more like brother and sister. Did he say anything to you on those

Saturday mornings, about me? Call me. Where the hell are you?"

Two days later, Mother is meandering back from the gorge. Barefoot, sneakers tied together over her shoulder, she runs her hands over the plants she passes, thinks: This is a bower. Sunlight sparkles dustily through the trees. She loves the feel of the heat on the back of her neck. She doesn't mind the drying water on her legs or the dried streaks of mud on her feet, or occasionally stepping on sticks or rocks. She looks at her hands, turns them palms up, smoothes them over the curves of her stomach and breasts. Everything is round here, she thinks absurdly. She touches her own cheek, and it is as amazingly soft as the ferns she runs her fingers over.

Never has she imagined anything close to what has just happened to her. Each dawn is now a new beginning for her. All she can think to think is, Wow. Who knew a tongue could feel rough, smooth, sharp, wide.

A branch snaps. She stiffens. Another branch snaps. She can't even get her tight throat to call hello. She thinks: Joan. She listens as carefully as she is able. She clearly hears someone walking quietly towards her down from her backyard, someone trying not to make noise, but unable to muffle the occasional soft complaint of twigs and leaves. She turns and rushes away, not back towards the gorge, but sideways, in the woods parallel to the road.

She is seven months pregnant with twins, and rushing through the woods isn't easy, ankles swollen, her lungs compressed. The incline flattens out, and she seems to have stumbled onto a deer path. She rushes past maple and birch trees, over dried leaves, the occasional rotting, moss-covered logs. It's much messier than the woods of her childhood, in which redwoods and eucalyptus killed everything underneath. She thinks, I've seen this before. This is the forest from *The Blair Witch Project* movie. Her path leads her into a clearing.

In the middle of the small meadow, surrounded by scattered

red trillium and skunk cabbage—a wetu. It's just there, bent saplings neatly tied with baling twine, a half dome covered in birch bark, its door a shadowy mouth.

"Hello?" No one emerges. That old throat squeezing closed, tunnel vision thing begins again, that prickly, dazzling, feeling faint and buried thing. Mary? she thinks to whisper, but doesn't. She walks towards the wetu, reaches out and runs her fingers down the shredding white and pink birch bark. She crouches at the opening, but before she enters she imagines herself hidden inside, the footsteps drawing near, only that one opening. Or else sitting in there, and noticing that someone else is in there too, hunched in the shadows. She doesn't enter. Instead, she turns and walks quickly towards where she thinks the road is. She moves so fast she hits the swamp before she knows it, sinks ankle deep in watery grass. Something brushes against her leg, and she thinks of Weetamoo's drowned body, lying just under the water, swaying in the weeds. She slogs back out, skirts its tangled edge, and reaches the dead end she's never seen before. Literally the end, the dirt road giving way to a green field sloping down and down for miles of rolling pasture.

A growling engine draws near, and here comes Christian on his ATV. He stops beside her, unhelmets himself. He takes in her forehead dappled in sweat, her heaving chest, her wet, bedraggled sundress and dirty, scratched feet. She has lost her sneakers. "Mrs. Rosen, are you okay?"

"I was walking. Briskly. Hiking, actually."

"Is that okay in your mumble?"

"Can you give me a ride back to my house?"

"Right now?"

"Yes."

"But I was—" River appears out of the woods from the side of the road opposite the swamp, the wetu and the gorge "—I was meeting River here, Mrs. Rosen," Christian finishes.

Mother looks carefully at River. "Were you following me?"

He snorts. "What have you been smoking, Ms. R?"

172

"Is this where your fort is?" she asks.

River jerks his head towards the side of the woods he appeared from. "Back there aways."

She watches him. "Are you telling the truth?"

He waves his hand in front of her eyes. "Ms. R, you're freaking me out. Are you having some kind of hypoglycemic fit or something? Do you need sugar?" He pulls a squished mini-chocolate bar out of his pocket and offers it to her.

"I can take you home," Christian offers.

"No, I'll walk. Thanks."

She begins to move away, then whips her head back, thinking she will catch them at something, but they are just watching her, as if they honestly think she is a freak.

It's a short way, a few hundred yards of straightaway, then a long bend, and there's her house, with Michael wedging a note into the doorjamb.

"There you are, Missy!" he says.

"I was just walking!"

"Okay."

"What does the note say?" she asks.

Michael holds his pointer finger over his lip, moustache-like. "You must pay the rent!"

"Oh my God, I'm so sorry. I forgot. Come in, I'll write you a check. I never do that. Really, I always pay on time." As she writes out the check she says, "While I was walking, I saw the weirdest thing in the woods, on your property, near the swamp. A wetu."

"A what too?"

"A wigwam, you know, the round huts that the Algonquin people lived in."

"That was most likely what the hippies hereabouts call a sweat lodge. Juniper and her boyfriends loved to perspire and then plunge themselves into the swamp. I used to hear them chanting and drumming from the back porch."

"And let me ask you something else." She hands him the check. "What do you think Christian and River are up to in the woods?"

"They're fifteen going on ten. They're playing knights of the round table or ninjas. Either that or they're building a nuclear bomb from old tires. It's hard to concentrate on this conversation. You look so beautiful."

She feels her face heat up. "That's ridiculous, I'm a mess."

"A wild, beautiful mess."

Before she moved here no one had ever called her beautiful. "It's just the glow of pregnancy."

"You're bewitched. Or maybe you're bewitching me."

"Okay, okay, turn off the auto-charm. Good-bye. Go."

He waves the check at her, winks. "At least I got one thing I wanted."

She receives an invitation from Neela with a stork rocking a baby in a yellow handkerchief. It's an invitation to her shower, next Sunday afternoon at her own house.

She wants to tell Mateo about the wetu/sweat lodge and about the person following her, so she calls the garage, but Hector answers, so she hangs up.

That night, her sleep is fitful. She wakes once bathed in sweat. She wakes twice to pee. The fourth time she wakes, she stands naked at the curtainless window, staring at the empty, moonlit road. She imagines Mateo asleep a few hundred yards away. She knows exactly how it is—Joan asleep on her back, Mateo curled on his side, Inez wedged between them, their snores and rustles weaving together. She puts her hand on the window and stares out. She thinks, He is not twins.

At nine p.m. the next night Mother drives down Lonely Rincon with the lights off, and only switches them on once she is jolting over the ruts on Mateo and Joan's long, narrow driveway. She pulls up in front of the house, cuts the engine and rolls down her window. There are fireflies in the clearing, and she can hear crickets sawing away, and bullfrogs bellowing from the swamp, all of the noise and light signaling, Pick me, pick me.

He opens the door and slides in. He says, "Joan is at her new anti-war meeting until ten. Inez is completely asleep, but I brought this baby monitor." He sets up the pink and white plastic box on the dashboard and turns it on. Inez's even breathing fills the car.

"How are my other babies today?" he asks, laying his hand on her basketball tummy. "We are able to give you this monitor, when they're born. We don't use it anymore."

"Thanks," she says. He slides his hand up her tummy onto her breast. "Something weird happened yesterday," she begins.

His eyes are unfocused, under the spell of endorphins. He strokes her hair. It's disconcerting for Mother, the way he listens less because he is paying such close attention to her body.

"I think someone was following me, when I was leaving the gorge, after you left."

His eyes focus, his hands still. "Tell me everything," he says.

She explains about the quiet footfalls, and the wetu, and River and Christian. Then she says, "But Michael said the wetu was just a sweat lodge." She can't help including Michael's "wild and beautiful" comment, she is so amazed and proud of her sudden ability to attract. She finishes with, "He said I must be bewitched. I guess I am."

Mateo has a weird look on his face, kind of unfocused again, but not in a good way, more like an animal with its leg in a trap way.

"Do you think Joan could have been following me?" she says.

"Do you like Michael?" Mateo says.

"Do you think Michael was following me?"

"Are you interested in him romantically?" Same quiet voice.

"Of course not."

"You can tell me the truth. I have no claim on you."

"Yes, you do."

Mateo looks like he's been hit in the head with a large rock. "How much time do you spend alone with Michael?"

"None!"

"You have never been alone with Michael until yesterday." His voice is flat, as if all the feathers have gone out of it.

"Once in a while, on business, but Mateo, I'm in love with you!"

"Has Michael declared himself to you?"

"I've never felt like this about anyone. I've spent hours every day dreaming about you. All I do is think about you."

"Now I can never call you beautiful again. Michael has stolen that word from me." Mateo stares through the front windshield at his house.

Mother laughs. "You can call me espactacular instead," she says.

"I should go," he says.

She cups his chin. "I didn't know you were the jealous type."

He smiles bravely. "I didn't know I was either."

She tilts his chin so he has to look at her. "I know you're thinking about Juniper and Michael in his underwear, but this is a different story. In this story, I am all yours."

Mateo nods. "I know." He rubs his face as if he is trying to scrub the jealousy off. "I don't know what's wrong with me."

The monitor crackles. A voice trailing static breaks through, a voice whispering in a language that is not English.

"My God," Mother gasps, "is someone in the room with Inez?"

"That happens sometimes," Mateo says calmly. "The monitor receives voices from walkie talkies and two-way radios. Even phone conversations."

"Can they hear us?"

"No, this is just one way. What language is that?"

They listen to the whispering male voice, coming from somewhere nearby. He speaks hesitantly, one or two words at a time, with pauses in between.

"I think that's Algonquin," Mother says.

"What?"

"You know, the language the Wampanoag speak."

"That's not possible. What is it saying?"

"I have no idea."

"That's not Algonquin," Mateo says.

They are quiet, listening. As if suddenly self-conscious, the static and the voice switch off, too, and Inez's steady breathing returns.

"It must be an Eastern European language," Mateo says. "Pobrecita, we are both going crazy."

"I'm good—I'm great."

He strokes her cheek. "You should leave. Joan will return soon."

"No, not yet."

He gives the end of her nose a soft pinch. "I believe we could both use a rest."

Sunday afternoon, the baby shower, muggy, overcast, a thunderstorm threatening. Neela has decorated the whole party in yellow, as if she has guessed what Mother has painted over in periwinkle: a string of paper ducks across the room, yellow helium balloons bob against the ceiling, a platter of turmeric-colored potato samosas, a yellow cake and lemonade. A waterfall of festively wrapped presents spills over the table, a chair, and onto the floor. And like all gatherings on Lonely Rincon, this baby shower is potluck, so there is also a bottle of New York State wine, a liter of generic orange soda, a metal bowl of potato chips and a plate of pot stickers. Mother has never figured out who actually brings those pot stickers. They just appear. Maybe it's Mary Rowlandson, she jokes to herself.

Everyone is here. River and Christian kick a soccer ball back and forth in the small circle of mowed lawn. They are using the scorched patch where the ground hive used to be as their goal. Inez and Oshun pry the buttercream roses off the cake. Neela shoos them away, so they try to break a balloon by stomping on it instead. Michael is at the counter, spiking his lemonade while Sondra shakes her head at him. Joan and Mateo are out on the porch with Margaret and Hector. Joan is drinking coffee and smoking a cigarette. Margaret talks at her while Joan blows smoke towards the soccer game. Mateo jokes in Spanish with Hector.

Mother stands at the top of the stairs, observing all this from above. When Neela arrived an hour ago, she had insisted Mother change out of her jean jumper into Neela's gift, a Salwar Kameez. Neela helped pull it down over her head, scolding her all the time for hiding herself away from everyone.

The Salwar Kameez is a loose red cotton sleeveless top with baggy pants and a wrap of the same deep color. It has patterns of white beads decorating the hem of the tunic and the wrap. It's light, comfortable, and Mother, who favors pastels, has never worn anything like this brilliant scarlet in her life. She has put her hair up to relieve the heat, and the escaping strands corkscrew around her face. She self-consciously holds the wrap across her Rubenesque chest as she descends the stairs, her stomach leading grandly.

Everyone oohs and aahhs.

Michael meets her at the bottom, raises his cup, and with his lopsided grin, begins, "You look—"

"—Don't," she says, glancing out at the porch to see if Mateo is watching.

Michael loses half his smile. "I was going to say you look like a giant tomato."

She laughs. "I like your shirt," she says, to make up for her rudeness. He's wearing a faded John Deere tractor t-shirt with a rip under the arm. He looks down at it, and she takes the opportunity to escape.

She knows she should avoid Joan, but she walks past something boiling in a pot on the stove, heads towards the back porch and Mateo. Hector and Mateo are deep in conversation. Mateo speaks so quickly in Spanish, she can't understand a thing. She wonders if he is a different person in Spanish, one she can never fully know. When Joan sees her she flips her cigarette off the porch and leaves Margaret in mid-sentence.

Mother hasn't seen Joan in a month, since she had promised to stop stealing. She feels electric with anxiety. She grimaces at Joan. "Hi!" she squeaks.

"Jesus, Mary and Joseph, return phone calls much? I need to talk to you, as in now. Let's go—"

"—Christian mows lawns." Margaret is beside them, and for once, Mother is relieved. "Your lawn is a little bit of a disaster. You need to act fast." Margaret says to Mother. And to Joan, she says, "I can't imagine what your mother would think."

"How much does he charge?" Mother asks brightly.

"My mother wouldn't give a shit about the lawn." Joan blows smoke in Margaret's face.

Margaret bats at the smoke. "Of course she would. She always kept everything in good order."

Mother uses the moment to turn to Mateo and Hector.

"Your new pajamas are very nice," Hector tells her.

"You look espactacular," Mateo says quietly, his smile like a tanning booth.

Mother blushes like a giant tomato.

"It's true," Joan says, turning, too. "We used to be two scrawny chicks, but now look at you. Even your hair. What are you eating?"

Suddenly Inez is there, leaning on Mateo. "She ate Papi's food," Inez says. "He made her fat."

Everyone laughs, except Joan. Joan smiles vaguely, and watches Mother, her head tilted a little.

"She's Winnie the Pooh and she ate all the honey," Oshun giggles.

Mother blushes again.

"That's a good game," Mateo says, smiling at Mother. "If you were a character in Winnie the Pooh, who would you be?" He lifts Inez and rubs his nose in her hair. "You are Tigger," he says to Inez.

"No! I'm Roo!" Inez says.

"Evie is Piglet on the outside," Mateo says, "but on the inside—"

"You're wrong, buddy," Michael says, suddenly there beside Mother, throwing his arm around her scarlet shoulders. "She's one of those goddesses that lures men to their deaths, inside and out." Mateo's face closes down. Michael continues, "Joan, you're Rabbit. Margaret, you're Rabbit, too. Hector, you're kind of a cross between Piglet and Owl."

"This is a Disney film?" Hector asks.

"Come in for the cake!" Neela calls.

They all move towards the kitchen. Mother tries to catch Mateo's eye, but he is all about Inez, refusing to look at her. Mother feels a jab of hostility towards Inez, the slightly revolting way she coos and baby talks and nuzzles Mateo.

Joan stands next to Mother as Neela passes out the cake. "Let's just go into the living room for a minute, okay?" Joan stalks into the other room and Mother follows, holding her plate of yellow cake against her chest.

"Why haven't you answered my phone calls?" Joan's eyes glitter.

"It's the pregnancy. I feel like nesting. I've been hibernating."

Joan nods, her face softening. She leans closer to Mother, her breath smoky, her whisper urgent: "Mateo and I had a breakthrough."

"What do you mean?"

"Didn't you get my message? He'd just peck me on the cheek and turn over every night, and finally, I couldn't stand it anymore."

Mother presses a piece of cake into her mouth.

"So, I just started screaming and throwing things. I actually turned over the dining room table, but it really worked, it shook us up. We both ended up crying. We realized there was nothing wrong with our relationship."

"I don't feel well, Joan."

"I'm so unfulfilled, even with the doula training. I have to take a stand against this impending war, no matter what the consequences. And Mateo is so cautious and careful, always trying to keep everything in balance. He doesn't want me to take any risks. He's totally freaked out about this FBI agent that Lassiter siced on us."

"What FBI agent?"

"There was this guy in dark glasses at the garage on Friday, asking questions about everyone. Anyway, the point is, Mateo cried when he realized how he had held me back without even realizing it."

Mother stuffs the entire piece of cake in her mouth.

"It was beautiful. Afterwards, we made love—"

"—I think I'm going to throw up."

"What do you expect? You inhaled that cake. Your stomach is squished. You have to eat tiny portions. You have frosting on your cheek."

Mother wipes at her cheek with the back of her hand. "I'm going to go lie down."

"Sure, I'll tell everyone. Prop yourself up in bed."

Mother sits on the edge of her bed and stares at the wall without seeing it, her breathing shallow, voices bubbling up from below. Her throat starts to close, so she tries to put her head between her legs, but her stomach gets in the way. She thinks, I give up. She can feel the tears pulsing at the edge of her eyes. Her shoulders begin to sag, but this posture crushes her lungs between her chest and her womb, and she can't breathe. She has to straighten her spine. She thinks of Mary Rowlandson and Weetamoo, the bravest, strongest women she knows. Her tears recede.

She walks back downstairs. The kitchen smells like stewing meat. She glances at the stove, that pot. Through the window she sees Mateo and Hector kicking the soccer ball in her backyard. Neela is wiping down the counter and Margaret is saran wrapping everything. She walks right by the women, across the porch, down the stairs and up to Mateo. "Are you giving up?"

"Not now," he whispers, looking over her shoulder at the porch and then at Hector, who waits to kick the ball to Mateo. "We can talk later."

"I need to know now. Joan says there is nothing wrong with your relationship. She says you had sex."

Hector flips the ball onto his knee and begins counting the bounces, "uno, dos, tres..."

"It was simply sad. Neither of us has the life we want. We both compromised too much, and we comfort each other, that's all. It's sad. Please, Evie, go, Joan is watching from the porch."

Mother goes back inside. Sondra, Neela and Margaret are gathered around the pot on the stove. They all look worried.

"Someone brought this," Neela says. "I don't know who."

"Let me see," Mother bellies her way in. She puts on an oven mitt and lifts off the lid. In the white bubbling froth there is some kind of small skinned animal, bones and all.

"Christian has hunted squirrels and birds," Margaret says. "But we always roast them on a stick."

"Where did those boys get to, anyway?" Sondra asks.

"Christian didn't do that."

Mother turns. It's Hector. He makes that same scissoring motion across his chest.

Mother puts the lid back on. "Delicious," she says and laughs.

Then Mateo is beside her, too. "Are you going to eat that?" he asks.

The day after the shower Mother receives an email: You are the love of my life, but I need to speak with you, today. I will come over at noon. You do not need to respond to my email because I am closing this account. In love forever, Mateo

Don't panic, Mother tells herself. She showers. Towel dried, steaming pink and enormous, she pulls her espactacular vermillion Salwar Kameez over her head. She hears the knock on the door, thinks, I can do this.

When she opens the door, Mateo smiles at her in a damaged way, and she knows she was right to gird herself. "Why are you dressed like that?" he asks. "You don't look like yourself."

"It's just me," she says, refusing to lose her balance. "Come in."

Once inside, he collapses into a kitchen chair and covers his face with his hands, which doesn't work that well because his head is so big and his hands are so small.

"Don't worry," she says. "It's going to be okay."

He takes his hands away from his face. Shockingly, he has tears on his cheeks. She thinks of him crying with Joan, but blinks that thought away. You can do this, she reminds herself. "What's wrong?"

"I despise my guts. I am making no one happy."

"That's not true. I am more fulfilled than I've ever been," she says firmly.

He shakes his head. "You are full of nerves. It's not good for you nor the babies. I myself am nervously wrecked. And I am making Joan crazy, too, or let us say, crazier. And Inez, I could never bare to be away from my baby." Tears float around his mossy eyes.

"It's okay." She stands over him, strokes his head. "We'll figure this out."

"If only I had met you sooner." His hands cover his face again.

"But anything's possible. If we love each other enough, we can make this work."

Mateo smoothes his thumb on her cheek. "I have lived two places in my life—a dead end alley in Santiago and this dead end dirt road. Only two. I am a creature of habit, of small comforts. I like my tea with many sugars. I like to help Inez with her studies, and to tease back and forth with the people. I like to coax Joan down when she is in a fury. I like our futbol games, and our potlucks with the terrible food and all the crazy children running about. I like to read. I am a secret reader, in the car, in the office when I am needed to be balancing accounts, in the bathroom when Joan thinks I have stomach problems. That has been my small, secret passion. But my passion for you is too much for a man like me. It's like a thing that grows on its own, swallowing me. Did you ever see this old American film, The Blob? A creature arrives from outer space and consumes the whole town and grows bigger and bigger." Mateo's arms show how alarmingly big, and it is alarmingly like the size she has become.

Then the yelling begins.

Mother hears someone bellowing somewhere outside her house. She looks out all the windows, sees nothing but green. She cracks open the front door, steps onto the front step. At first there is silence, but then there it is again, almost like growling, then moving into a high screech, like a cartoon witch, coming from the woods. Mother remembers the end of Snow White, when the defeated stepmother is made to dance in red hot iron shoes. She imagines the stepmother would sound like this as she danced. She feels a hand on her shoulder, and startles away.

Mateo's behind her.

"Do you hear that?" she asks him.

"That's a so," he says. When she looks uncomprehending, he says, "You know, a motosierra, a chainso, to cut down trees, at a distance of several kilometers, perhaps off Leeman road."

She listens again. She can hear it now—the high whine of the chainsaw's motor and then the growl as it bites into wood. Mateo is watching her with great pity.

Mother says, "When Mary Rowlandson was finally released, it was nothing. A man she didn't know, a Mr. John Hoar, arrived on a donkey with food and tobacco and cloth worth twenty pounds. A bottle of liquor sealed the deal. He led her away on the donkey. She must have thought, This is it? She must have thought, This can't be over."

THE NINTH REMOVE

The end of August, 34 weeks pregnant. Blue morning glories twist up the dead end sign, high chill blue sky with a mottled moon visible, leaves bone to gold. Mother's eyes are very dry, so she blinks often. She thinks it must be a result of pregnancy. The burden of us aches her pelvis. It feels too loose down there. She wouldn't be surprised if a hand or a leg just slipped out. Her belly is so enormous she can barely clasp her own hands together over it. Her ankles are swollen, so are her fingers. She has nightly sweats and sleeps on a towel; she has to pee hourly, day and night. She breathes shallowly, from the neck up.

We don't feel loose. The walls of our pulsing room grow smaller each day. A hand presses into a face from the force of a knee pressing into a hand. Every action, a foot twitch, a shoulder shrug, requires multiple reactions, until the whole complicated machine is in motion, struggling to make space.

For mother this pregnancy now seems like an extended dream, a reverse fairytale in which the princess wakes to find herself prince-less in a cottage in the woods, about to give birth. She thinks, This is not my house, my land, my people, but here I am. Mother eats little bits, some crackers, toast, applesauce, a poached egg, yogurt, several times a day, but if she eats more her heart begins to burn. She reads, she goes to the bathroom and showers, sleeps, wills herself to lumber through the day.

It's like this. Say she's washing her hands at the sink, the warm water rushing over her fingers, and she remembers Mateo's small wide hands, and she caresses her own hands, remembering. But then she has a vision of herself as a scarlet giantess, consuming everything in her path. She thinks of Mary Rowlandson crunching the bones of the fetal fawn. She turns off the water, begins to shuffle into the kitchen. An ugly sob disgorges itself. She grabs onto the wall. Sometimes another one comes, sometimes not. She makes her way into the kitchen.

This interminable moment, after Mateo, before birth, draws itself out, a breath held underwater. And in this intermission, we must confess that though we pledged to tell all we never confessed our last visit to the midwife. At first it was the usual, the midwife mistakenly claiming we are a boy and a girl, but then in the waiting room on the way out, we passed a woman and her newborn baby. Mother stopped to admire the flushed creature, face still squashed from birth. It was an ugly thing, a mouse baby, barely sentient, barely more than a loaf of bread or a log, eyes blinking and unseeing.

Our future.

Though there's no breathing room within, there's that wilderness without, and so what should we hope for?

Although we feel all is still, this held breath, to others Mother is a coiled spring, a jack in the box, an accident waiting to happen. When she hobbles into the supermarket in unlaced sneakers to accommodate her swollen feet, the formerly silent cashier jokes, "Not on my shift!" Her teaching substitute stops by to go over lesson plans for the upcoming school year, and when Mother opens the door, he takes a step back, says, "I'll make this quick."

And then Margaret shows up one evening after dinner. She's carrying a shopping bag and stands next to the woodstove, looking around the kitchen with her lips peeled back.

"What do you have there," Mother finally says, reaching for the shopping bag.

Margaret grips it closer, smiles bigger. "It's to help you."

"Oh, thanks." They stand there in silence. "Margaret, what is it? What's wrong?" Thinking, did Hector send her?

Her bright pink smile shivers. She takes a seat at the table, hugging her bag.

"I've been talking to my daughter, Deandra," Margaret whispers.

"That's wonderful!" Mother says, relieved.

"I can show you how, too. I can help you."

"What do you mean?"

She's still clutching her grocery bag tight against her chest. "I can help you to communicate with the dead."

"What?"

"I've been watching you, Evy. You're like me, cheerful on the outside, but on the inside all torn up with grief and anger and shame."

"That's not true—"

"Deandra doesn't talk, but I see her in the mirror, just for a minute. She looks good. She's smiling. I think she wants to tell me something, but we haven't been able to share words, yet. It will happen though."

Mother touches Margaret's hand, the one that grips the handle of the shopping bag. "Are you sure that Deandra is dead?"

"She fell out of the towers." Margaret's still smiling, but her cheeks are blotched and burning. "Hector says she's gone to the devil, but he's wrong. She's an angel that fell from the towers. That's why I search the photos. To show him. So he'll know."

Mother pushes her chair back a little. "Margaret, I promise I won't tell anyone about this, but I don't need your help. I'm sorry, I just don't want to contact the dead. Thank you, though."

Margaret's smile twists off her face. She curls over her shopping bag. "You judge me," she whispers into the shopping bag.

"No, of course not." Mother touches Margaret's hair, but Margaret remains curled, as if she were about to empty herself into the bag. "Okay, sure, I'll do it."

"It's your husband isn't it? The one you need to reach." Margaret says.

"No, definitely not."

"Then who?"

Mother looks at the small gold cross on Margaret's neck, says quietly, "How about Mary Rowlandson?"

"Yes." Margaret pops up and walks into the living room. "No

curtains," she says. She hangs bath towels over the windows. She turns off the lights in the living room. She positions the rocker in front of the long dusty mirror. She turns the mirror around so that it's reflective side out. She tells our mother to sit there.

Mother sits in the rocker.

Margaret takes a fat pink candle in a plastic wrapper out of the shopping bag, lights it, and places it underneath Mother. The smell of coconut insinuates itself into Mother's nose.

Margaret tells Mother to gaze into the mirror: "Unfocus your eyes, you know what I mean? Just sort of look but don't look."

Margaret sits on the futon couch, squeezes her hands between her thighs.

Mother looks into the mirror, remembering that moment when she thought she saw Mary Rowlandson. The candlelight makes her face strange, all dark hollows and chin. Patterns shiver over the mirror. Despite her unbelief, goose pimples shiver up and down her arms.

"Do you see anything?" Margaret whispers.

Mother shakes her head. Margaret says, "Sometimes it helps if I sing. I'll sing one of Deandra's favorite songs. It might help. Margaret begins to sing in a shaky, high voice. "Good-bye Norma Jean…" It's Elton John's song. "And it seems to me you lived your life like a candle in the wind, never knowing who to cling to…"

Mother is afraid she's going to laugh, because it's ridiculous and because she's suddenly afraid. She glances up from the mirror. "Margaret, I don't—" In the dark space between the towel and the window frame there's a face.

Mother screams.

"What. What." Margaret twists up from the couch.

Mother stands, the chair rocks wildly. "There was a face."

"Was it her?"

"I don't know. There was definitely a face."

In the kitchen they hear the front doorknob turn, the door

189

begins to open. Margaret and Mother reach for each other's hands. Margaret's fingers are thin and cold. They watch the door.

Hector's head appears around the edge. "What are you doing?"

"I—" Margaret starts but doesn't continue.

Hector turns on the light. Margaret and Mother still hold hands. He gazes sadly at the towels, the candle burning coconut into the air, the overturned chair and the mirror. He sits down on the futon couch. He says, "In my country, they say that when a woman dies in childbirth her angry spirit waits at a crossroads to snatch children."

"What an awful thing to say," Mother says.

Hector pats the couch next to him. Margaret squeezes Mother's hand.

"I say this because what you and Margaret are doing endangers your life and your children's lives. When you traffic with the dead, you invite the devil into your home. Now we must perform an exorcism."

"No," Margaret and Mother say at the same time.

Hector says, "My dear, that's the devil talking. Can't you hear him?"

"It's not the devil," Mother says. "She needs to see Deandra."

Hector rises. He wraps both his warm, calloused hands over Margaret and Mother's linked hands. He says quietly, "Evil Spirit, I command you in the name of Jesus Christ to leave this house. Thank you Lord for your sanctification, in Jesus's name, I command—"

"Stop." Mother pulls her hand away. "This is too much. You can't just come in here like this." Her voice is only shaking a little. "I need to ask you to leave."

"He's trying to help," Margaret says. "We should let him perform the exorcism. You said she was keeping you from peace."

"I never said that." Mother looks at Margaret. "I don't want you to take Mary Rowlandson away. Please, just go, both of you."

Margaret takes Hector's arm. Hector starts to cry. He says, "I am crying for you because you are so lost." Margaret begins to cry, too. They hug each other.

"I'm sorry," Mother says. "But could you two do this somewhere else?"

That night Mother wakes to find Mary Rowlandson lying in bed beside her. Mother edges out of bed, takes her bone comb out of its velvet case, and walks heavily and barefoot downstairs. She can hear Mary's light tread behind her. She doesn't look back. In the bathroom Mother fills the tub with hot water. She turns to Mary in the doorway. She walks over to Mary. They are the same height. Mary smells of urine and body odor, a homeless smell. Let me help you out of those clothes.

Mary starts to unbutton her blue jacket from the top, and Mother unbuttons the jacket from the bottom. The jacket is thick, a heavy weave. When Mother pulls on one of the sleeves, it rips at the shoulder seam.

Underneath the jacket, Mary wears a stained corset that has wooden ribs sewn into the bodice. Mother unties that from the back and cracks it open like the husk of a dried seed. The next layer is a loose, torn shift. It is sweat-stained under the arms and blood stained where she's been shot. Mother unties the ripped apron with its large pocket. The pocket sags with hoarded things, damp and stinking. When Mother unbuttons the skirt, the wooden button comes off in her hand. She pulls the skirt down, and Mary steps out of it. Under that is a heavy petticoat, smelling of wet wool. With that off, Mary stands in her yellowed shift, her stockings and boots. Mary lifts her shift and unties her stockings, which may have once been white but are now grey, and peels them down until they sit in dirty rolls above her boots. Mother holds onto the side of the tub and eases herself into a kneeling position. She unbuckles Mary's ankle high round-toed boots. The left flaps open at the toe. Mary raises her feet one at a time, holding onto Mother's shoulder, and Mother eases off the boots. The stockings are ripped open at the toes. Mother rolls them off. She can hardly look at Mary's feet. They are a ruin, swollen, blue white and soggy-looking, covered in blisters and rubbed raw. Some of her nails are black, two nails are missing on her left foot.

The clothes lie in a heavy heap on the floor. Mary stands by the tub and slowly pulls off her shift, as if it hurts to raise her arms. Her ribs, her collar bones, her hip bones, it's as if her skeleton is insisting on itself. The bullet hole in her side has healed over into a purple, puckered kiss. White fuzz covers her face, neck and arms, and runs in a V down her back. There is something heron-like about her, still and as if her bones are hollow, also as if she could suddenly dart for a fish.

She holds onto the wall and slowly lifts one leg, then the other into the tub. She stands there.

Then Mother pulls her own white nightgown over her head. She holds onto the tiled wall to step into the tub.

They slowly lower themselves into the steaming water, concave against convex, both their bodies aching from wear, stretched or shrunk beyond recognition, in need of ease.

Mother sits behind, her bulging stomach pressed against Mary's ribs, her legs cupping Mary, her feet resting on Mary's thighs. Steam rises.

Mother takes up her bone comb, opens it, and begins to inch it through Mary's matted hair. She hums as snarls like little tornadoes come off in the teeth.

Mother thinks of the word restore. She leans close to Mary's neck and whispers, "I forgive you for what you ate."

Or perhaps it's the other way round.

Two days later, on September first in the morning, Molly calls and asks Mother how she's been.

"It's a long story but the short of the long is that I'm a giant, no other way around it. I accept it."

"You sound different," Molly says. "Like your voice isn't

going up at the end of your sentences or it's deeper or something. Anyway, where do you think I am?"

"Under a palm tree?"

"Nope. I am talking on my new cell phone at JFK waiting for my connection to Syracuse, where I will then board an Airport shuttle. I took a week off of work so you better pop soon. I believe I will be seeing you in approximately four hours."

"I'm so happy," Mother says.

"No, you're not."

"Okay, I'm not so happy, but I'm okay. I'm a big girl now."

That first night of her visit, Molly sits at the kitchen table and listens to Mother talk about Mateo and the rest of Lonely Rincon for hours while they slug black tea. Late afternoon September light comes through the windows and describes shifting leaf patterns on the floor. When Mother laughs or cries she has to literally hold herself together. Molly can't cook, but that evening she orders take-out and drives a half hour to get it.

In the days that follow they hole up. Molly is good at exercising before Mother even wakes up. She is good at answering the phone and the door and telling people Mother is sleeping. She is good at chatting with Neela when she brings over lamb curry in a clay pot. She is good at hunting through the three aisles at the local video store, finding the period dramas and romantic comedies they watch on the tiny television/video player Molly bought at the Goodwill.

On the second afternoon they go to a used furniture store and buy a changing table. They go to a box store and buy onesies and blue curtains for all the windows. While Mother assists, Molly assembles the changing table. Molly looks up at the walls of our room, deep lavender-blue with ghostly images underneath, and says, "Gorgeous. You were always so talented."

For some reason when Mother looks at the walls she thinks of Peter Pan and his lost shadow. She says, "Do you believe in ghosts?"

Molly is efficiently wielding the screwdriver.

"Molly. Do you believe in ghosts," Mother repeats.

"That would be a no," Molly says. "What? Do you?"

Mother runs her finger over the faint lines of a snowflake still visible under the paint. "No, but I believe in being haunted."

"What's the difference?" Molly says. "And hand me that little bag of black screws and washers."

"It's like, our skin isn't the barrier we think it is."

"La La Land," Molly snorts, and consults the directions again.

"I've got at least two people stuffed inside me right now," Mother says, tossing her the plastic bag. "So go fuck yourself."

In the middle of tea drinking on the third day of Molly's visit, there is a knock. Molly cracks open the door.

Mother hears Molly say, "Hi, I'm Evie's best friend. She's resting now. Can I help you?"

"I'm Evie's best friend, too."

Joan.

When Molly looks over at her from the door, Mother shakes her head violently, but Joan is already opening the screen and coming in. It is her house, after all.

Joan does not appear well. It looks as if her eyes have grown and her short hair is matted down. She wears layers of things, jeans, then a sundress, then a big blue sweatshirt with the hood up, rubber boots.

Joan looks at Molly who is still standing by the door, then says to Mother, "I'm here to get my mementos."

"Okay."

Joan returns with her arms filled with a burnt baby doll, a rock and rum bottles. The old fedora is on her head. "Will you come out on the porch for a minute while I smoke a cigarette?"

Molly and Mother share frantic eye signals. Mother says, "Sure." She heaves herself out of her chair.

Mother uses Joan's shoulder to lower herself and they sit

side by side on the top step. There is a lot of wind, there has been for more than a week, on and off, but Mother has hardly noticed since she's been hibernating. Mother's hair whips into her face, and all of Joan's layers flap about. The ramshackle barn groans.

Mother crosses her arms on her stomach, and Joan cradles her bundle of relics.

Joan cups her hand around a cigarette, takes a long drag, rests her chin on the doll's tufted head. "He's leaving me," she says.

"What?"

"This morning he told me our accounts are overdrawn. He's moving into the office at the garage."

"What do you mean?"

"That's what our relationship is to him. A bank account. I figure this might be temporary, some mid-life stupidity. Or maybe he's gay."

"I'm shocked," Mother says. "I'm sorry, this is—totally unexpected."

"He's so selfish," Joan says. "I could kill him. A bank account—he's never made a decision for love in his life. And you know what's really fucked up? He's my best friend. I've always had really bad taste in friends." Joan begins to cry, choking on cigarette smoke. Mother cries, too, and they just sit there like that, staring at the groaning mouth of the barn, crying about the same and different things.

Then Joan stands up and opens her arms. The rock tumbles off the edge of the porch into the grass. One of the bottles bumps down three steps and doesn't break. The doll lies at her feet. She nudges it off the porch with her toe. She tips her head and the hat slips off, somersaults away. Joan stretches her skinny, braceleted arms out into the big wind. "Look Ma," she says, "no hands."

That night after Joan leaves, it's around midnight, just becoming

September fourth, there is a tap-tapping on the door downstairs. Mother listens. Then pebbles ping onto her bedroom window. Mother just lies there. Then a rock smacks against her window.

Mother edges out of bed trying not to wake Molly, tiptoes down in her giant t-shirt.

Mateo peers into the heart-shaped window, grinning. For the first time, Mother thinks, What a big smile you have, Mr. Wolf.

She opens the door. He is wearing jean shorts, a jean jacket and his standard white socks and Birkenstocks. He has on a backpack. She whispers, "What did you do?"

"You know?"

"Joan told me. What are you doing here?"

"You look unbelievably sexy in that pajama."

She doesn't let him in. She hiss-whispers, "Are you sure I don't look like the Blob? Maybe taking up a bit too much of your personal space?"

"Yes, you take up too much space in my heart. But I accept it. I am not familiar with big love—I sit in my usual chair with a book, but I can't read. All I can think of is you. I realize I am looking at Joan. She is reading a political article. And I hate the way she hunches over this newspaper, the way she sniffs in a little and absently runs her tongue over her teeth and mumbles angrily when she reads. Joan is my family. I only hate her because she is keeping me from you. Joan is not stupid, she looks up and knows how I feel. She puts away the paper. She wants to talk. And I just say it. I just tell her I have to leave. I felt I had no choice."

"Joan is really upset," Mother says, and she laughs. She puts her hand over her mouth.

"Why are you laughing?" Mateo asks.

"Because I'm so freaked out." They look at each other, one still inside the house, the other one out.

"I told her I will always help her," Mateo says. "We will make this work. We'll take it step by step. First, I will move into the garage. I will focus on ending my relations with Joan. Then finally, after, we will be together. We did the order a little crazy, no? But now we will correct and make the order right. Can you give me another chance?"

She turns sideways but she is so large he still has to hug her to get into the house.

"And now I will cook for you." He pulls a package of matzah ball soup mix from his backpack. He opens the packets, boils the water, mixes the egg and oil and matzah meal. He says to her apologetically, "I can never get my matzah balls as hard as Mama used to make." While the mix is in the refrigerator for the required fifteen minutes, he takes out his Walkman from the backpack and sticks one white earplug in her ear and one in his. He places the Walkman in his breast jacket pocket. He tells her that this is a compilation of love songs from around the world that he has made for her.

A Hawaiian love song comes on and he begins to hula. Mother watches him move his hairy arms in two little waves and frisk his hips. She thinks, Is this really happening? Just like this, everything changes?

The next track begins. A gravelly male voice moaning *Quiero Bailar Slow With You Tonight,* fingers aching over a steel string guitar.

He presses her against the kitchen counter and breathes into her neck. "This is it, this is it. I want to dance slow with you tonight."

She says, "I'm 35 weeks pregnant with twins."

"It's okay," he says. "We have soup."

Then there is Molly in men's plaid pajamas at the top of the stairs. "Finally decided to grow a pair?" she says.

Mateo pulls out of his backpack a sweet Chilean wine that tastes like blackberries. Molly and Mateo drink, and Mother takes a few sips from their glasses. It is one a.m., but they all eat soup and say ridiculous things. With the taste of wine in her mouth for the first time in months, she watches Mateo and Molly cracking up together and realizes she must have some kind of predilection for big headed, shiny toothed, belly laughers with M names. Near dawn, they dance together, Molly, Mother, and Joan's best friend.

September seventh, Mother's beginning her 36th week, dark clouds, an occasional grumble of thunder.

Molly is waiting for the airporter to pick her up. "Your children are already turning out badly," Molly says. "Tardy. Rude."

"You're early, they're not late. Now my doctor wants me to try for 37 weeks."

The phone rings. When Mother picks it up she hears Mateo whisper: "Remember the woods? Remember you thought you were being followed? It's in the blog."

"What?" Mother says.

"I don't know if Joan knows yet, puta! Here she comes. I have to go. Read the blog."

"What was that about?" Molly asks.

"I don't know," Mother says. "It was Mateo, he said I need to read the blog—he must mean Margaret's blog."

"Let's look at it—maybe it's funny." Molly leaves her bag by the door and opens up the laptop.

"Now?" Mother has a feeling it isn't going to be funny.

"The airporter's not here yet. We'll keep an eye out."

Mother clicks to the site, but doesn't look. She watches Molly's smile slip down her face.

"What?" Mother says, but she knows.

"Shit."

"What?"

There are two sharp beeps from outside the house.

"Maybe I should stay," Molly says.

"What are you talking about? You'll miss your flight."

"But they know."

Another two sharp beeps.

"Just go," Mother says.

"They know!" Molly says.

"It's okay." They stare at each other. "Call me tonight," Mother says.

"I'll call you from JFK," Molly says.

Another long beep from out front.

"I can come back," Molly says.

"You have work."

The driver revs his engine. Molly begins crying, then rubs her nose fiercely and says, "Fuck." Mother doesn't cry.

They walk outside the house, Molly dragging her rollie suitcase. While the driver puts the bag in the trunk, Molly says, "Come with me—just leave. Listen to me."

Mother shakes her head.

They hug, Molly climbs into the airporter. Mother walks into the house and closes the door. Slides the heavy gold bolt closed. Too late for that, she thinks, and slides the bolt open again.

City On A Hill:
The Community Building Blog
For Lonely Rincon Road
By Margaret Langley Gonzales

URGENT URGENT URGENT

Recent revelations have forced me to write this open letter.

Dear Evy and Mateo:

I must express the shock and sadness that many in our community will soon feel when they hear the news.

Yesterday, while cleaning my son Christian's room I came upon a notebook between his mattress and the box spring.

Written on it were the words: PRIVATE KEEP OUT.
Concerned, I read this notebook and found that he and a
disturbed neighbor boy have been witness to a terrible secret,
the kind of secret young boys should not be responsible for, a
burden that you both have given them.

We now know that you, Evy, the teacher who allowed my
child to be physically brutalized, befriended by Joan (who
was taking a birth assistant class for YOU!), living in
Joan's family home, a woman haunted by a tragic past, you
have formed some kind of inappropriate relationship, be it
transitory, with Mateo. And Mateo: long trusted member
of the community, taken in and fostered by Joan's family in
your youth, given a life long job by her brother, father of a
young, troubled girl, you two have betrayed Joan (Joan—I
left a message on your machine).

The fabric of a community is woven by trust, each thread a
potsticker, a friendly hello, a soccer game, an exorcism, a good
deed done. With one or more acts you two have rent the fabric
of our little quilt, the patchwork quilt that covers us all.

You have not just betrayed Joan, you have betrayed us all.

Perhaps you will hide away in shame, but we suggest you
will need our community even more in this painful period.
If not for yourselves, for the sake of poor little Inez and for
Evy's innocent unborn children, we urge you to reach out.
We have questions. Understanding is needed. Besides seeking
psychological counseling and answers through prayer, we
strongly suggest that you each post letters of explanation to
the community. You can email them to me and I'll upload
them.

Perhaps this letter, along with yours, can serve as a re-

stitching of the community we all treasure.

God Bless.

It is quiet in the farmhouse on Lonely Rincon. Mother tries to busy herself with chores, but can't stop herself from re-reading Margaret's blog again and again. Where is Mateo? She doesn't dare call him at Joan's or at the garage. What about Joan? What now? At one point she goes upstairs and begins to pack, but stops in the middle of folding onesies into the suitcase. Who would even let her on an airplane?

She decides to try baking bread.

When she arrives in the kitchen she realizes she has no yeast. Since she has baking powder she switches over to muffins, takes out a cookbook and pulls down the package of flour. She unfolds the top and finds a moth, delicate, brown, all folded wing, nestled in the flour. She picks it out and puts it on the counter. She shakes the bag, peers in—the flour is woven through with dead moths. White webbing, evidence of their larval feasts, festoon the sides of the bag. Goose pimples shiver up the back of her arms. Defeated, she eases her swollen self down the side of the cabinet and sits on the floor. She thinks she may never be able to get up from this position. Which is where Michael finds her.

He doesn't say anything, just creaks himself down to the floor beside her, jostles her shoulder with his shoulder. Mother tries to breathe normally, but it leads to shuddering. He hands over the silver flask from his back pocket. She takes a slug, chokes.

"Would this be a bad time to ask for the rent?" Michael asks.

"Oh, I'm sorry." Mother hands back the flask and grabs onto the counter.

"That was a joke." He takes a long drink from the flask. "So, I guess this makes us some kind of relatives once removed. Plus

I'm almost famous, kind of related to a web celeb. There's got to be a way to make money off of this. Maybe rename the garage The Scarlet Letter." He elbows her. "Huh? Impressed by that literary illusion? Didn't actually read the book in high school, but I remember copying off Mateo's essay." He takes another long drink, passes it back to her.

Mother absently takes the flask, doesn't drink. "I'm so sorry that River had to be involved in this. How is he?"

Michael shrugs. "Doesn't want to talk about it. He's worked up, has been for a while. I think he was kind of hoping you were going to be his stepmother." Michael winks. "He's never home, when he's home he can't sit still, paces, fiddles with things till he breaks them. Tortures Oshun."

"I'm sorry," Mother says again. "I should talk to him."

"So, what would you say my chances are at this point?"

She barks out a laugh, passes the flask back, and Mateo walks in. He is carrying a bright red futbol bag, stuffed so full it won't zip. He stares down at them, shoulder to shoulder on the floor, drinking and laughing. His face takes on that look, like all systems have powered down, just a red emergency light blinking in his eyes.

"Mateo." Mother reaches her hand out to him for help in rising.

Mateo turns and leaves, carrying the futbol bag with him.

Michael tries heaving mother up from the floor. Mateo returns and puts his futbol bag down beside them. "You leave," he says to Michael.

Michael settles back down on the floor beside Mother. "Hey, I'm the landlord, Bro."

"Then we'll leave. Evie, pack your bags."

Mother laughs, because she is nervous and because it is a little funny.

Mateo doesn't smile, glaring down at them both.

Michael smiles up at him. "Brother, calm down." He puts his hand on Mateo's ankle. Mateo kicks his hand off.

Michael raises his palms. "Hey, I'm not the enemy."

"Just leave." Mateo turns sideways so Michael can pass him on the way out the door.

Michael still doesn't get up.

Mateo takes a step closer. "Do you know how many people have told me they no understand why I never beated you?"

"You never beated me because you no beat people. That's not your style. And I really like Evie. How was I supposed to know?"

"Now you know."

"Okay, I know. But you got to remain calm. I could fire your ass."

"Ha. I'm the only one who knows the accounts. You will never find your money without me."

Michael looks at Evie and up at Mateo. Each one gets a big, crooked smile. "I have to admit to being slightly psyched," he says. "Ever since he arrived Mateo was the straight A student, the brain, the jock, the responsible one, a one glass of red wine on the weekend kind of guy. Just kind of gracing us with his presence. He was slumming, know what I mean? He couldn't even speak English, and he was the valedictorian of our class! I was so psyched when he started prematurely balding, thought that would even things up, but the girls still fell for that big ass toothpaste smile!

"Meanwhile, I was the boozer, had to take geometry twice, drove Ma's car up onto Neela's lawn, ran over Neela's puppy—yep, she used to have the regular amount of legs. Just what you'd call a generally fun-loving loser type guy, which as we all know ended in me stealing his girlfriend, which has made him the better man for the rest of our frickin' lives. But now, yeah, you got the girl, but at what price, man? We're even! We're on the same level—just two regular fuck-ups."

"We're not on the—"

"—Uh uh uh," Michael flips his hand up. "You cheated on my sister. You lose, man. You're lucky I haven't beated you."

Mother reaches her arms up towards Mateo to help her rise. Mateo pulls, they're both groaning, but her butt hovers a few inches off the floor. Michael tries to make a seat with his arms and heave up from below, but mother gives up. They slide back down to the floor together. Everyone's breathing heavily.

"You know what's funny?" Michael gasps. "We all love Joan. Am I right?"

"She set fire to our bedding." Mateo sighs big and joins them on the floor.

"God," Mother says.

Michael laughs. "That sends a message."

"She grabbed the sheets and blankets and poured gasoline in them and burned them on the fire pit."

"I'm afraid of her," Mother says.

"Crazy not to be," Michael says.

That night, Mateo and Mother lie together in a bed for the first time. They lie face to face in the dark, Mateo in boxers, Mother in a long t-shirt, under the covers. It is a good sleeping night, the beginning of September, quiet and cool.

"So, are you ready to fight for our love?" Mateo says.

Mother smiles, rolls her grey eyes, whispers, "I think I'm ready to retreat from the battlefield. We should go. You know, as soon as the babies are born. Just pack and leave."

"Where would we go?" Mateo whispers, running his thumb down her cheek.

"Anywhere that is not Santa Cruz and not here. What about Portland, Oregon or maybe Portland, Maine?"

"I can't leave Inez, and Joan needs me, too."

"Michael can take care of them," Mother says.

"Michael?" Mateo laughs. "Michael needs me most of all. Don't worry. I have good feelings about the future."

"You do?"

"Yes," Mateo whispers. "We will all live happily ever after. Now tell me why you are wearing this giant shirt?" he says, reaching for her.

September Eighth, Mateo walks to work in the morning. Molly calls while Mother is in the shower: "Are you okay? I'm so mad I had to leave you there. Jesus."

After Mother catches Molly up, she washes Neela's clay pot, walks down the dirt road with it. Hector drives by in a Volvo station wagon, shifting gears experimentally. Mother waves. Hector does not wave back. Defeated, Mother begins to turn back to the house, but then she continues to the trailer. Neela's three-legged dog watches her warily as she walks up to the front door and knocks. Neela opens the door with a big smile that immediately wilts when she sees who it is.

"I brought back your dish. Thank you so much," Mother says.

Neela takes it from her. "I've known Joan since she was a little girl. She's very sensitive. Mateo was her anchor. Yesterday, I knocked on her door. There are cigarette butts all around the doorstep, she has taken up her nasty habit worse than before. She wouldn't answer, but I could hear her sobbing. You can't imagine how loudly she cries."

Mother tries not to cry, takes a step down from the door.

"You were her friend," Neela says. "Why do you want to steal her life? You must make your own life."

"I don't want her life," Mother says. "And I didn't steal her over-the-top, once-in-a-lifetime love. I couldn't because she never had it."

Neela's eyes suddenly grow moist. "Sondra told me this must be a question of true love..." Neela reaches her soft hand out to her. "Come in, come in, we need to talk. We have so much in common."

September 9th. Mother back from a doctor's appointment. The doctor has decided to try for 37 weeks, just a few days now.

But we are more than ready. We are impacted, two teeth in

205

need of extraction. No matter the wilderness we will encounter, pull us out now.

The doctor says he will induce if she hasn't given birth by then. He told her to keep off her feet and stay hydrated.

Now, Mother stares at the phone. Finally, she dials. When Joan picks up, Mother's heart starts banging as if it wanted out, too. "Joan, it's me."

"Ah, the phone. Coward's way out as usual," Joan says.

"I know sorry isn't going to cut it. But I am. So sorry."

"So, your kleptomania raises its ugly head once again. Are you going to stop stealing my husband?"

Mother closes her eyes. "He's a grown man."

"Are you going to stop?"

"No," Mother says.

"Then I hope you die. I hope you both die." Joan hangs up.

September 10th. That evening, dusk, Mateo and Mother are reading Neruda's love sonnets, a bilingual edition, aloud to each other on the couch, their fingers lacing and re-lacing as they read. The radio is tuned to the classical music station. Something clangs against the window in the kitchen. "What was that?" Mother says.

"A bird?" Mateo tries.

There is another tiny thud, like a stone thrown against the house.

Mother heaves herself up and into the kitchen. She parts the curtains over the stove.

Joan stands in the driveway. Her face twists as she wrenches off one of her bracelets and flings it at the house like a frisbee. It ricochets off and lands in the grass. There is spit on her lip. She pulls off another. Copper bracelets litter the lawn.

"Take that," Joan yells. Her skinny green arms are almost bare now. "Take everything! I refuse you!"

September 13th. Mother is resting on the couch with her feet up when she hears Joan's Volvo coughing down the rode and up her driveway. Here it is, she thinks, and winches herself off the couch. She peers through the heart in the door. The car jerks to a stop. Mother thinks about calling Mateo or even 911, she even thinks about hiding in the fall-out shelter, but instead she picks up the poker behind the stove. Joan climbs out of the car. She is wearing white drawstring pants and a white t-shirt. The back door opens, and she helps Inez and then Oshun out.

Mother can't believe Joan is involving the kids. She puts the poker back down by the door.

Joan opens the trunk and pulls out two green garbage bags. She hands one to Inez and one to Oshun. She kisses Oshun on the top of his head, pats his arm twice. She kneels down and looks at Inez. Their faces are very close together. She says something. Inez nods. Joan kisses Inez's closed eyes. Joan stands and scans the yard, as if she were looking for her bracelets, but those have mysteriously disappeared. She still has the clasped hands bracelet around her wrist, the original, God's gift.

She looks at the house, sees Mother watching through the window, and there it is—just one glance—but it is the kind of stare that causes milk to sour, chickens to stop laying eggs, the kind of look that gives babies' colic, that sends bad luck nipping at the heels for years, not because it is so furious, but because it is so full of seeing.

Then Joan gets back in the car, drives to the end of Lonely Rincon and turns right onto the county road.

Inez drags her garbage bag towards the house. Oshun follows, clutching his. They stop on the top step and stand looking up at Mother's face through the window. She opens the door. It is chilly out there, and the cold wind snakes in with Inez and Oshun. There are two folded pieces of yellow lined paper safety-pinned to Inez's sweater with Mother's name on it. Mother unpins it. Inez and Oshun watch her unfold it.

September 13, 2002

These two will be your responsibility. If nothing else, you seem to be able to entertain children.

You can choose to follow your animal desires or you can choose a higher path. They seat you at the table, but you don't have to eat. You can spit it out.

But don't flatter yourself. Your trivial story is not the center here. Our president declared war on Iraq yesterday in a speech to the UN general assembly. Missed it?

I have explained everything to Inez, and I believe she understands what is at stake and why I do what I do.

I am driving to the army recruitment office outside of Binghamton, New York. The recruitment office is in a small shopping center with a Mexican restaurant on one side and a copy center on the other. Like the Mexican restaurant and the copy center, it has a beige cement front. In blue painted letters over the door it says Armed Forces Career Center with a plastic American flag next to the words.

I will enter the recruitment center wearing a maroon backpack. I will walk down a short hallway with public restrooms on either side and into a small lobby with red plastic chairs, recruitment posters and a flag in the corner. From noon to one each day the officer in charge eats his take-out burrito from the Mexican restaurant on a vinyl lawn chair out back, listening to the local hip hop station on a battery operated Army-issued radio. The chair faces a washed-out, scraggly line of Poplar trees and a dumpster.

I will walk lightly on bare-feet through the linoleum-tiled lobby, across the small office with its grey desk and grey file cabinet to the back door. I'll lock that back door. Then I'll return to the lobby. I will ease off the backpack and unzip it. Take out a coffee thermos filled with my own still warm blood. Unscrew the lid, dip in two fingers and begin to paint. My brushstrokes will be careful double lines. The blood won't drip, I've tested it. I'll paint NO MORE UNJUST WARS on the flag, NO WAR on the window, PEACE on the door. The knob on the back office door will begin to twist. I'm not bringing tissues, so I will wipe the blood on my fingers down both cheeks.

The officer will now bang on the back door. I'll slide handcuffs through both front door handles, turn and click the silver cuffs over my wrists so that my handcuffed hands are behind me. I'll kneel. The officer will appear at the side window. He will peer in, under the words NO WAR. He will rap on the window. Maybe the radio will be playing Eminem. I will bow my head and begin to pray silently: Lord, make me an instrument of your peace. The officer will try to pry open the window, will call, "Hey. Lady." I'll pray, Lord make me an instrument of your peace. The officer will kick the wall of the recruitment center. "Hey! This is government property!" he'll yell. I will pay no attention to the officer swearing on the other side of the window or to the pulsing in my raised arms. I will not have a thought for you or Mateo. I will think of Inez, because I am doing this also for her, for her future, and then I will let her, even her, go. There will just be the prayer, filling me: Lord make me an instrument of your peace. My teeth will press together to make a jagged white wall that will let nothing more out and nothing more in.

—Joan

It is still September 13th, evening now. After the police called the garage, Michael and Mateo drove over to the Binghamton county jail, but they hadn't been allowed to see Joan. Joan would be transferred tomorrow morning, but they wouldn't say where. Joan has refused a phone call, refused a lawyer. She made a statement that she wanted to wake people up to the bloody costs of the impending war. She said that she was not acting alone. That there were those that would soon join her. There would be other acts of protest. "My bank account is full," she said.

The various local evening news programs have led from their reports on Bush's speech, one quoting Bush—"In cells, in camps, terrorists are plotting further destruction and building new bases for their war against civilization"—to Joan's story. They reported that she was planning a hunger strike, that she belonged to a radical fundamentalist cult, that she may have been part of a terrorist cell, that she might be brought up on felony conspiracy charges that carried a sentence of up to eight years, that she might be brought up on domestic terrorism charges that carried a life sentence. A news van has already stopped at every house on Lonely Rincon, and Channel 34, News at 11, promised to air a clip of an interview with neighbor Margaret Langley Gonzales who would tell them about a former teacher who claimed to have uncovered this left wing conspiracy almost a year ago and been fired for it.

Mother spent the afternoon with Oshun and Inez. She helped the two unpack their bags and made up their air mattress bed, passed out cookies and milk, played a long, tedious game of Monopoly. The kids had been glum, but they finally cheered up when she brought out fabric pens and let them decorate their pillowcases.

Now, dinnertime, the phone off the hook, the television unplugged, the curtains drawn, Neela and Sondra bring over curry for seven. Sondra says she'll stop by tomorrow and give Mother techniques to go into labor naturally, so she doesn't have to be induced. Mother tells Sondra that Hector isn't speaking to her. Sondra promises to go over to the garage the next day, talk to Hector for her, and then come see her.

Mother looks around the table, says to Michael, "Where's River?"

Michael doesn't look up from eating. "He already boiled himself up a hotdog. Plus, he's got homework."

"He told me he never—" Oshun begins, but Michael cuts him off, says, "Did anyone hear a hippy bought the diner? There goes my Salisbury steak with mashed potatoes."

Mateo puts his fork down. He beckons for Inez and she climbs into his lap and rests her head on his shoulder. Oshun jumps into Michael's lap. Mateo says, "Permit me to say that though we know she is quite safe, we're all thinking of Inez's mommy. And Inez, I want you to know we are all extremely proud of your mother. La mama es muy valiente."

"To Joan," Michael says, raising his beer. Everyone raises

various juice glasses.

"And also the dinner is damn good, as usual," Sondra says, raising her own beer.

Neela takes Sondra's hand, brushes it against her cheek, kisses it. "To love," Neela says, raising her own glass.

"Hear, hear. To love."

That night, around 3 a.m., Mother opens her eyes in the dark bedroom. Someone is in the room. Her first thought is Mary, but it is Inez, standing by the bed. Inez nudges Mateo.

"Chinita, gordita, ¿que pasa ?" Mateo says to Inez.

"Tuve un bad dream," Inez says.

Mateo lifts Inez up and tucks her in between them. He turns over and returns to snoring.

Inez's eyes stay open, watching Mother.

Mother watches Inez.

"Go back to sleep," Mother says. She runs her hand over Inez's eyes so they close.

The next morning, September 14th, week 37, Mateo is on the phone with a lawyer. Upstairs, Mother is making a fort with Oshun and Inez. They have hung two lime-colored sheets over chairs and dressers in the guest room. Mother sits on one of the chairs, her head under a sheet, the children below her, all three hidden there in the greenish light. "It's like we're under the leaves," Inez says. When Mother sits she compresses us even more. We kick and push, hoping she'll stand. As if Oshun can hear us, he says, "I can't breathe," and scrambles out, knocking the other chair over, and the fort collapses onto Mother and Inez. Inez swears in Spanish.

"Something is happening over to the garage," Oshun says.

Mother pulls the sheet off. Her hair sticks to her hot cheeks, and she stands beside Oshun at the window and looks out. A dark blue van with tinted windows is parked in front of the garage. At first Mother thinks it is another news van, but then three men in navy suits and two men in police uniforms usher Michael, Hector and Sondra into the van. Michael is handcuffed.

"Mateo!" Mother eases herself down the stairs as quickly as she can, the kids crowding behind her. Mateo is still on the phone with the lawyer. "Get off," Mother says.

"In a minute, mi amor."

"Now."

"Sorry, can I call you back?" After he hangs up, he says, "That was important."

"They're arresting everyone at the garage." Mother tries to keep her voice even.

Oshun starts to cry.

Mateo walks over to the window, parts the curtains. "A van comes here," he says.

Inez and Mother start to cry. "Papi, hide, por favor," Inez says, pulling at his hand. "They'll steal you like they stole Mama."

"Why will they arrest me?" Mateo says, hugging her to his side. "Ridiculo."

"It's about Joan, don't you get it?" Mother says. "It's what they said on the news—they think you're all part of a terrorist cell."

"They're coming!" Oshun squeals. He hides himself between the refrigerator and the wall.

"Papi, hide in the fall out shelter. Please hide down there." Inez pulls on his hairy wrist so hard his watch comes off in her hands.

Mateo puts his glasses back in his breast pocket. "It's not possible to hide."

Mother finds herself saying, "Inez is right. You could hide, then we could leave the country, all of us."

Mateo runs his thumb over Mother's wet cheek. "Don't worry, we will fix this. I didn't do anything."

There is a crisp double knock on the door. A man's face in dark glasses fills the window.

Inez screams, "Papi," and presses herself into Oshun's

hiding place, clutching Mateo's watch.

"All will be fine," Mateo says. He opens the door.

Late afternoon, the kids have finally calmed down enough to watch a video. Mother tells them she is going over to Neela's.

Inez jumps up, pulls the bottle she's returned to out of her mouth. "I'm coming."

Oshun turns off the television. "Me, too."

The weather has gone bad, trees whipping around, flinging leaves, rain. They huddle together under Inez's small red umbrella. As the three of them head up Neela's drive they see her Volvo sedan pulled up on her lawn near the door. She comes out in an ankle length yellow raincoat and rain hat, balancing a pyramid of Tupperware.

"Neela!" Mother calls when she is still a few feet away.

Neela looks up, her face mottled and swollen with weeping, her mascara bleeding. "Please leave my property," she says.

Mother stops, her little gaggle crowded round her. "But Neela, we can do this together. You can use the lawyer we've already hired for Joan."

"No, no, no. I am taking this food to Albany. I know Sondra is hungry. I've booked a room at a hotel with a kitchen nearby. I won't leave until she's free."

"We'll go with you," Mother offers absurdly.

"No. Go home. This is all your fault. She was there at the garage to speak to Hector for you. Everything is all crooked because of you." Neela begins to weep. She sinks into the wet grass and the Tupperware tumbles down around her. "I haven't seen my daughter in eight years. I've never laid eyes on my own grandchildren. I am a monster to them. I gave up everything for Sondra. She's all I have."

Mother wants to rush forward to help, but Inez is squeezing her hand, and Oshun hangs onto her coat. "Neela—" Mother says. "Just wait."

"No! I should have realized when you wanted to add

problems to my children's book." This burst of anger seems to rally her, and she gathers up her Tupperware, heads towards the car and unloads it all into the back seat.

Neela walks over to the doghouse, her raincoat making a harsh, vinyl shriek, and unties the dog's lead. The rope is so long the dog doesn't have to move as Neela hands the wet end of it to Mother. "Her name is Gloria," Neela says. "She's been diagnosed with post-traumatic stress disorder."

September 15th. Mother is scheduled to deliver herself to the Montour Falls hospital tomorrow to be induced. She thinks about the pink room at the birth center, about Sondra's voice and hands, and then she thinks, Let it go. Let us go, too. We have already begun to shrink to fit, we're almost as bony as Mary Rowlandson, and like Mary, our only thought now is of release.

The lawyer calls. They're all being held in Albany, Joan without bail under the Patriot Act provision for conspiracy to commit an act of domestic terrorism, activities that are intended to intimidate or coerce a civilian population and influence the policy of a government by intimidation or coercion. They claim that Joan's blood could be defined as a biological agent or toxin, the use of which carries a mandatory prison sentence of ten years. Joan has refused everything but water, and he might be able to get her transferred to a hospital.

"What about Mateo?" Mother asks. "And the others?"

"I think we should know within 72 hours what they are going to do with them. They're threatening to charge Mateo, Sondra, Hector and Michael as co-conspirators. Even if they don't go forward with the co-conspiracy charges, they claim they might continue to hold Mateo as a material witness. They say they are looking into his immigration record. They claim he participated in terrorist activities in Chile. They say they are exploring deportation. They're making a lot of threats right now, playing hardball. Fishing for information."

"How is he?" Mother asks, her voice trembling annoyingly.

214

"Fine," he coughs. "Under the circumstances."

"But when will he come home?"

The lawyer coughs again. "Look, Miss Rosen, normally, he would have been out already. He would have been home for dinner. But these are not normal times. Also, lest I forget, Michael and Hector are worried about their sons. They ask that you locate the teenaged boys."

"Isn't Christian with his mother?"

"I believe Hector's wife is having a difficult time. She's with her mother in Utica, and her son's whereabouts are unknown. They have all requested that you take care of the boys in their absence."

Mother waddles over to Michael's apartment, Inez and Oshun attached to her as always, and now Gloria limping nervously beside her, too, and knocks. She tries the loose door, pushes it open. They stand in the tiny, neat kitchen/dining room. No sign of anyone.

She knocks on Margaret and Hector's door, peers in the windows. No one.

Later, as twilight falls, Mother drives up and down the dead end, windows down, all three of them calling, "River, Christian." Nothing.

Back home, Mother takes out a jar of tomato sauce and some pasta, puts on the water to boil. The phone rings.

Mateo. It's Mateo.

After hello, they don't say anything, just listen to each other's breathing. Mother holds the receiver so hard against her ear it hurts.

"Let me talk to the children for a minute," he says.

Inez and Oshun share the phone, only tugging back and forth a little. Their eyes are wide, and they nod and say "Yes," and then they both laugh once, and then Inez says, "Chau, Papa" and Oshun says, "Bye, Mateo," and they slide down the counter and start trying to open the tomato sauce jar.

Mother takes up the phone. "How are you?" she asks.

"Fine." His voice and breath right in her ear, so close.

"I'm going to come see you, after the babies are born, if you're not out. Will they let me see you?" she says.

"I'm sure I'll be home before that."

This is a new Mateo voice, not his usual Tigger voice or his zombie jealous voice either. She can't read it. "How are you?" she asks again.

"Fine. But maybe I can give the lawyer a list of books for you to send. If we don't get out soon."

"Okay."

"Is everything fine there, Evie?"

"I'm hungry," Oshun says.

Mother nods to Oshun.

"Starving," Inez says.

"Yes, we're fine. Just, I'm going to have the babies tomorrow." She takes the jar from Oshun and tries to unscrew the lid.

"How can you know this?"

"I'm going to the hospital to be induced tomorrow morning at nine." She gets out a knife and bangs the lid with the dull side.

"Can't they wait? I should be home any day."

"No, it's all scheduled at the hospital."

Mateo sighs. "I'm very sorry I'm not there. I'm sorry you have to do this alone. I promise I will be there, soon. Thank you for taking care of the kids."

Mother doesn't answer. She checks to see if the water is boiling, slides the pasta into the pot. Sets the timer. Pours the sauce into another pot. Mouths nine minutes to the kids.

"You're not," Mateo says. "I mean, I know this is so much to ask, but please don't leave. Please don't leave us. Please wait for me."

She takes out the dishes. "The kids are taking good care of me. When I go to the bathroom, Oshun and Inez stand outside the door waiting for me. I sleep in between them. And these ones inside—I have this burning all the way up to my collarbone. The only part of my body that's still mine is maybe the top of my neck." She gets out the forks.

"Ah, mi amor, I also feel that my body is no longer my own."

"Of course you do." She squeezes the forks. "But I'm a whiner and you're not. Did you know River and Christian are missing? I've looked everywhere."

"Mi amor, you are in no place to look for the boys. You are doing enough. I'm sure they are fine."

"But it's worrisome. Where are they?" Mother takes out the napkins.

"Someone else will find them."

"Okay." She stirs the sauce, thinking, But who?

"I love you, Evie. This will all work out. It's just a set-back, a difficult moment. We will all come home in the next few weeks or perhaps a month, and Joan might have to serve some time, maybe a year or two, but then she will be back with us, all together, and it will work out! We'll have potlucks and futbol games again soon enough. Don't worry."

"Okay." Her lower back hurts.

"And tomorrow you will meet your children. I love you, forever, yes?"

"Yes." The pain subsides. Dinner's almost ready, she mouths to the kids.

"My time is up. I must go," Mateo says.

"Wait!"

"Yes?"

"It's just—"

"Are you trying to explain that you are leaving?"

"My god. I'm giving birth tomorrow. Anyway, I'm planted. I'll never get out."

"But on Lonely Rincon you have grown. And now you will flower."

"Just keep extending those metaphors—my roots are deep,

I'm definitely fertile, my field is plowed."

And there's Mateo's delighted laugh. "I love you, Evetina. I cannot wait to meet our babies and reunite with you. We are a big family now!"

Mother says they can watch a video while they eat. She spreads out a towel on the floor in the living room for the kids. Mother sits in the rocker behind them. Since they aren't allowed to watch television, and have neer eaten in front of one before, Oshun and Inez don't care that all Mother has is a documentary she has shown her class called *A Midwife's Tale*. They happily slurp their spaghetti, spraying sauce over the towel. There is a voice-over of a midwife in Massachusetts in the eighteenth century. The images are of daily life on the farm. It looks like hard work.

The phone rings.

"Inez, can you get that? But wipe your hands on the towel first."

"It's Karin!" Inez yells from the kitchen.

"Who?" Mother sighs. "Oshun, pull me up from this chair."

"Who are you?" she hears Inez ask. "Your sister-in-law," Inez yells.

Inez drops the phone on the counter and runs back to the television. Mother picks up the receiver and watches it. Then she puts it close to her ear, but not touching.

"How did you get this number?" she says.

Back in the living room the kids are still working on the spaghetti, watching the midwife canoe across a lake to attend a birth.

Mother stands between them and the television. "Guys, I'm going out for just a very little while."

They crane around her so they can see, nod vacantly. Her lower back spasms again. The pliant walls of our world stiffen.

Mother drives down the hill to the diner, her seat all the way back to accommodate the belly she can barely stretch her seatbelt around, her arms reaching for the steering wheel.

It looks like the diner is being renovated—the carved wooden bear is on its side next to the door, the gingham curtains piled on top of his head. A hand-written sign reads, "Under new management! Opening soon!" but the lights are all on and there's a person at one of the tables. Mother would have recognized Steve's twin anyway—it's as if Steve were sitting there at the wooden table, if Steve had grown two blond braids and pinned them up on his head, and then dressed himself in black yoga pants and purpled fleece.

Karin stands up when she sees Mother walk through the door. She's been coloring with the crayons the diner provides. Mother holds onto the table to ease herself into one of the wooden chairs. "How did you find me?" she asks.

"We just want to be involved. But we don't want to infringe on your space." Mother notices that Karin has neatly outlined all the farm animals on the placemat before filling them in. "We just want to be part of the miracle. You're in charge." Karen's shivering leg vibrates the table, her sparkly blue eyes are widened, blond eyebrows raised, on high alert.

"Where is Steve?" Mother asks.

"He wanted to give you some space." Mother imagines a Karin doll: when you pull the string on her back she says, 'more space, more space.' "I know Steve can be bossy," Karin says.

"Bossy?" Mother snorts. A bell dings in the kitchen. "I think your order's up," Mother says.

"We want to be here for you, financially, to use the trust fund to help the kids—"

The bell dings again, twice. "It's for you," Karin says, standing.

"I don't want anything," Mother says, but Karin is already putting a full plate and full glass in front of Mother. Mother looks at the food in front of her—a tempeh scramble and kale smoothie.

"What the—" Mother braces herself on the table to stand. The table starts to tip, the food begins to slide towards the edge.

Karin grabs the table to steady it from her side.

"This is what you call giving me space?"

"He promised he'd stay out of the way."

"Steve!" Mother yells.

Our father appears, aproned, in the doorway to the kitchen. He's grown a neat, blond beard.

He charges over to fuss with the table setting—brings the plate and glass back to order. "You didn't even try my food."

Mother reaches down and grabs some scramble in her fist, shoves too much of it into her mouth, lets half of it drop onto the table, gnashes it in her teeth. It's tough, still hot.

Two bright pink spots blossom on Father's cheeks. They blossom on Karin's cheeks, too. Father grabs the dishtowel at his waist and begins furiously wiping the table. "You're hysterical—"

Karin circles her hand around Father's wrist, like a bracelet. He stops cleaning, takes a breath. He moves next to Karin on the other side of the table. "When you wouldn't respond to my reasonable and repeated requests for a dialogue, I got resourceful with my resources." He taps his head. Mother squeezes tempeh in her fist. "I hired someone to find you. I bought this diner. I've set up shop here—I'm going to bring healthful cuisine to this impoverished region. And raise my children." Mother's heart gnarls.

Karin squeezes Father's arm. "He wants to help you raise your children, but he wants to give you space. That's why he's never ever gone to your house."

Mother grabs a napkin and fiercely wipes her tempeh-smeared mouth and hand. "Did you sign the divorce papers?"

"I have conditions —" Father begins.

"—Yes, he did," Karin interrupts. "We brought them with us."

They're burning with energy, like they could run a marathon, do 250 push-ups, colonize something. Mother feels burning behind her own breastbone, but we see their mirror faces, the way Karin finishes our father's sentences, the way her hand squeezes his wrist like she is squeezing her own wrist, the way their cheeks pink in unison, and something pink and hopeful double blossoms in us. We think: maybe, yes. Even if one of us has a knob, maybe we can imagine ourselves together out there, together.

Mother thinks about picking up her chair and heaving it through the plate glass window, but she says, "I'm going to be induced tomorrow. So I do need your help. I need you to take care of the kids while I'm having the babies. And stay with us for a while afterwards."

"Induction isn't natural childbirth," Father says. "Pain medication will—"

"Not you," Mother says. She juts her chin towards Karin. "Her."

"What kids are we talking about?" Karin asks.

"Two kids I'm taking care of, maybe four, I hope two more will show up."

"Are you a nanny?" Karin asks.

"Do you want to help or not?"

"I want to help, I'll do it, of course. Steve would love to help, too."

"He can cook for the kids. Here, at the diner, not at my house." Mother looks at Father. "I know you've done it before, and I'll get a restraining order if you do it again," she says. "No trespassing."

In front of her car in the dark, Mother has another back spasm. She arches, presses her lower back with her hand, and sees Father giving her the stink eye through the plate glass window of the diner. He taps his head twice and raises his eyebrows, then smiles. So maybe it's a joke, but maybe not. Mother gives him the finger, maybe jokingly, maybe not, but it feels good to hold it up there until he turns away.

As Mother drives back down the dead end, all the houses are dark, except her own, which is warm with light from all the

221

downstairs windows. The slam of the Volvo door sounds lonely on the empty road. But then she hears the comforting voice-over from the video. She walks in, calls, "Turn that down, it's going to ruin your hearing."

The back door is open. The pot of spaghetti that was on the stove is gone. She feels a thrill of unease. No one in the living room. The towel they'd been sitting on is bunched in the corner, one of the bowls of spaghetti is on its side, spaghetti and sauce smeared on the floor. "Inez? Oshun?" Mother calls up the dark stairs.

She hears whining from the living room, goes back. Gloria slinks her head out from behind the futon couch. "Where are they?" Mother asks her.

Head low, Gloria hops to the back door, and for the first time ever, Mother hears Gloria growl. Then Mother notices the wavering glow from a flashlight entering the woods.

She grabs the rail, eases herself down the porch steps as fast as she can, which is pretty slow. "Wait," she shouts. "Stop." Mother follows the Tinker Bell light into the forest.

Gloria hops so close that Mother keeps stumbling over her. There's a wet coolness on the wind from the rain yesterday that plays at the back of her neck. She wishes for a scarf. She inches along on her swollen ankles. She can almost imagine frost again. The moon is in its first quarter, shining now and then through the damp leaves, but the woods are very dark, quiet, with sudden secret rustlings and scurrying. There's a burst of wings.

Mother has lost sight of the light, but she stumbles forward, hands out in front of her, following the smell of smoke. She holds back a moan. Her lower back keeps spasming, a sizzling florescence, on off, on off, like a broken light. Everything aches—her back, her joints, her chest still burning from her encounter with Father.

In Mother's peripheral vision something crouches beneath a canopy of ferns, eyes glowing. It crashes away.

Finally, breathing in little gasps, she reaches the edge of a moonlit clearing.

River and Christian sprawl around a smoky fire in front of the wetu. Their faces are painted red and they have no shirts on. Both of their brown felt loincloths are held up by black leather belts. Their bodies, Christian's pudgy, River's sinewy, are bright with what looks like lard or Vaseline. They seem to have graffitied their hands and arms with black magic marker. River passes a bottle to Christian. The ground is littered with crushed beer cans, there's the empty spaghetti pot, a dirt smeared pillow, walkie-talkies. There's a stick with the blackened remains of a small, bony creature on it. They don't seem to be talking. There's no sign of Inez and Oshun.

Gloria lowers her grey muzzle and growls softly again.

As Mother enters the clearing, both boys startle into crouches.

There is something bawdy about them, their greased adolescent bodies, their sullen, red faces, the smell of alcohol and their adrenalin-heavy sweat, the hiss and snap of the fire.

Mother says, "Where's Inez and Oshun?"

The boys look at each other and laugh. Mother suddenly wonders if Inez and Oshun might have been hiding somewhere back at the house—the fall-out shelter? "Have you seen the kids?" she asks again.

Christian mumbles something into his upper arm.

Mother realizes that Christian's wearing Joan's bracelets all up and down his arms. "What did you say?" she asks.

River nods encouragingly. Christian looks at the writing on the back of his hand. "Cowesass."

River glances at the underside of his wrist, "Amaumuwau paudsha."

Christian reads, "Kunnish" off his arm.

Christian and River look at each other and crack up. It sounds false, like cartoon laughing: "Ha Ha Ha."

Gloria is sniffing at the dark entrance to the wetu. She goes

223

over to peer in. Two small, hunched shadows. She ducks down, crushing us, and enters. Oshun sits wrapped around himself. When he sees Mother he leaps up and grabs her around the tummy. They have stolen Mother's duct tape to cocoon Inez, her mouth, wrists, ankles. Even in the dark Mother can tell her eyes are burning with fury. Mother manages to half drag and half carry Inez out of the wetu. At the entrance she rips the tape off Inez's mouth, both of them gasping.

"I'll get you back, chorrero, conchetumadre, asopado, mariposa," Inez spits. Oshun begins to cry at Mother's waist.

"This is not funny," Mother says sternly to the boys, "not at all."

"You're not funny at all," River says, standing.

"Hey, you said you were never speaking English again," Christian says in an outraged stage whisper.

"You never know what I'm going to do," River says. He raises his switchblade up by his face, which he must have been holding the whole time. Mother flinches at the small clicking sound as it pops open. He clicks it closed, clicks it open. She imagines that's what's stabbing her in the back.

She holds her hand out for it. "Give me that," she says. I need it to free Inez."

He just keeps clicking it open and closed.

"Look, you did an amazing job on the wetu, but this is not okay. This playing Indian thing has gone way too far. You're terrorizing Inez and Oshun. And it's disrespectful. This is not your culture. You have your own lives with serious things happening. Your parents are worried about you, and they have enough to worry about. This is really irresponsible. I'm disappointed in both of you."

"Irresponsible?" River sputters. "Seriously? You dare to lecture us about responsibility? You—" He's searching for the word.

"Fornicator?" Christian supplies helpfully. "Harlot?"

"Home-wrecker," River says.

Mother's face flames. She shakes her head.

"Tell the real story of what happened to Weetamoo," River says suddenly.

"Oh my god, let it go," Mother says. "And put that knife away."

"So I have to say it? You can't even say it. The colonists found Weetamoo's drowned body in the river. They cut her head off. They put it on a stick in the middle of the British village of Tauntaun. Her head stayed on that stick for thirty years. And Quinnipin was hung. That's the real story, right Ms. R?"

"It's not the only story," Mother says.

"But it's the truth. Just like the truth that you came here and took over and ruined our lives. Weetamoo would have hated you, just like Joan hates you."

"True," Inez says. "My mother doesn't like you very, very much."

"Mrs. Rosen, you're not a mumble mumble," Christian says.

"What?" Mother says.

"You're not a nice person," Christian says clearly.

Mother tries not to cry. Her back burns.

"Yes, she is!" Oshun yells from behind mother's back. "She's so nice. You guys are the mean ones!"

"True," Inez says. "You guys suck."

Mother imagines what Inez and Oshun will think later, when they are River's age. Her back pulses more. The wind changes, the smoke from the fire finds her, stings her eyes and throat. She's tearing up now. "You're right," Mother says, "I'm not nice." When she twists away from the smoke, warm liquid gushes down her legs. It smells strangely sweet, her legs drenched in her own perfume.

"You made Evie pee herself," Oshun says, letting go of her tummy, stepping away.

"My water broke," Mother says. As if the amniotic fluid had been muting it, the pain intensifies now, boils down Mother's lower back. A fist squeezes and squeezes us. Her legs begin to shake. "Help me down," she says to Oshun. He holds her arm as she eases herself onto the ground in front of the fire. The heat feels good on her legs and face. Oshun sits down, too, very close to her, his hands and arms in her lap. Inez scooches over on her butt, leans against her. Gloria stands near, shivering. Finally, the back pain simmers down, lets us all go.

"What's wrong?" River says suspiciously.

"Will you just please untie Inez?" Mother says. River stands there. "She's just a little girl. Please." River clicks the knife closed, tosses it to Christian. "Untie her," he says.

Christian saws through the duct tape at her ankles. When he's barely finished with her hands, Inez attacks him. She is a wild thing, a hydra with ribbons of duct tape whirling around her, wrestling her mother's bracelets off Christian's wrists, growling, "Give them to me!"

"Inez," Mother says sharply.

Christian squeals and smacks Inez hard on the side of the head. Her head makes a dusty huffing sound when it hits the ground. She scuttles behind Mother, slipping on the one bracelet she's managed to save.

"Jeezum," Christian whines, moving close to Mother to show her the bite marks on his wrist. "I'm mumble mumble Joan. And she mumble away, anyway. Jeez."

River crouches down opposite Mother. "What's wrong with you?" he asks, his breath hot and sweet from alcohol.

Sitting with her legs splayed out, covered in children, Mother realizes she has turned into the clay mother. She makes her mouth into an O, to see what comes out of it. "Big love," she says, and then the pain begins to twist again, it's pressing us down, forcing us somewhere we don't know if we can go. Mother sucks in her breath sharply, tenses her legs, grabs River's wrist. River doesn't pull away.

When it lets us go, she says, "Go call an ambulance."

"Except we cut your telephone cord," Christian says.

"River, I need your help. Use the phone at the garage.

You're in charge"

River pops up then, face all stern and ecstatic, like he's been waiting to hear those words all his life, like finally, finally a mission. "A'ite, time to bust a move. We got a job to do."

"And take the kids," Mother says.

"No," Inez says.

"We want to stay with you," Oshun says.

"Go with River," Mother says. She hugs Inez and Oshun together. Kisses Christian on his greasy forehead. "Go," she says.

River drops a walkie-talkie on Mother's lap. When Inez tries to stand her duct tape tentacles stick to Mother, and she has to unpeel herself. River gives the other walkie-talkie to Inez, grabs up the flashlight, and hustles the whole bundle of them off into the night, everyone grumbling, whining, urging each other on.

Gloria raises her head, watches them go, then drops her muzzle onto Mother's thigh. Mother switches on the walkie-talkie, there's static, then Inez, all breathy from effort, "Almost at the house. What are you doing? Over."

"Nothing," Mother says. The pain returns. Mother is only half by the fire now. The other half is here inside the slow motion avalanche that's overtaking us. In and out, holding onto Gloria's fur, and at some point the clenching twists around to the front, unmistakable. "At the garage," Inez says, and then later, "River called. We're coming back."

"No," Mother says. "Stay there, show the ambulance where I am." And then just static.

"They'll be here soon," Mother says to Gloria.

We are gripped again and it's so much stronger than before, stronger than we thought possible. Mother opens her throat and unclenches her hands. The grip insists on itself more forcefully. She keens, and Gloria hops into the wetu.

Mother leaves everything behind now, goes under where only we can follow.

Each contraction loosens our muscles, molds us into denser objects, rattles our bones. Our lungs cinch until we spit up fluid, our soft heads narrow into arrows. Mother keens as her insides shift. We are forcing each other through the narrowest of places, we are forcing each other to open wide.

Inch by inch the first of us is swallowed, inch by crushing inch the first one presses down a throat.

And then explodes into a chaos of noise, impossibly loud, Mother crying, the growl of the fire, far away slide whistle of an ambulance, up and down and growing louder, Inez's voice through the static, "They're here!"

Then the first rip of breath, the wail that erupts after it.

Mother feels a flowering of feral joy. She thinks, Look at my changeling baby, forest-born, a blessing given to me, the furry ears and twisting face, the blue-green liquid eyes, pulsing out this yellow light.

The first is assaulted by smells, tang of sweat, bite of smoke, and then the sweet, sweet whiff of Mother's leaking milk. All consciousness condenses into a single yeasty need.

Mother thinks, Look what we just did, my good luck Pucks. True, we're not done yet. True, the hem of the world has ripped open. The seam has broken and things I cannot fathom have fallen through. But together we will stitch it up.

But the second one's still inside, half-swallowed, half spit out, riding out the last comet's tail of bright blue doubled consciousness. To emerge, captured forever in a single skin, or to struggle and fail. Either way it hurts so much, this business between we and I.

Acknowledgments

Heartfelt gratitude to the organizations that have supported me during the writing of this book: University of California, Santa Cruz, including our Faculty Research Grant program, The Humanities Division and The Literature Department; The Blue Mountain Center; The National Endowment for the Arts; and The New Guard Literary Review.

I owe a debt to the books and articles I've read about seventeenth century American history and culture. This research was pure pleasure. Books that were particularly influential include *The Birth Mark*, Susan Howe; *Good Wives*, Laurel Thatcher Ulrich; *The Name of War*, Jill Lepore; *The Terror Dream*, Susan Faludi; Neal Salisbury's edition of *The Sovereignty and Goodness of God*; and *A Key Into The Language of America*, Roger Williams. There were many more. I also thank The Thayer Memorial Library in Lancaster, Massachusetts; The Wethersfield Historical Society, and The Plimoth Plantation's Wampanoag Homesite.

So many talented people gave their smart, generous, patient, abiding attention to this book in its many, many revisions: my writing group—Elizabeth McKenzie, Melissa Sanders-Self, Karen Joy Fowler, and Jill Wolfson; my sister in crime, Karen Yamashita; my beloved, Juan Poblete; Kathy Chetkovich, Joanna Scott, Lisa Michaels, Kim Lau, Samson Stilwell, Bekah Perks, Naomi Tannen, Joe Mahay, Deborah Tannen, Susan McCloskey, Kate Schatz, Masie Cochran, Polly Wagner; Esther Stilwell and Tessa Bolsover helped with design expertise; although my teachers never read drafts of this book, I thank Stephanie Vaughn and Alison Lurie, always; huge thanks to my talented publicist, Zoë Ruiz, and forever gratitude to my visionary and dynamic publisher, Jon Roemer and all the other passionate book people at Outpost19; and to Orkida, Bob, Raphael, Verónica, Samson, Miguel, Esther, Natalia, and Juan, for making it work, together—you have my gratitude and my love.

photo credit: Tessa Bolsover

About the author

Micah Perks grew up in a log cabin on a commune in the Adirondack wilderness. She is the author of a novel, *We Are Gathered Here*, a memoir, *Pagan Time*, and a long personal essay, *Alone In The Woods: Cheryl Strayed, My Daughter and Me*. Her short stories and essays have won five Pushcart Prize nominations and appeared in *Epoch, Zyzzyva, Tin House, The Toast, OZY* and *The Rumpus*, amongst many journals and anthologies. Excerpts of *What Becomes Us* won a National Endowment for the Arts grant and *The New Guard* Machigonne 2014 Fiction Prize. She received her BA and MFA from Cornell University and now lives with her family in Santa Cruz where she co-directs the creative writing program at UCSC. More info and work at micahperks.com.

CPSIA information can be obtained
at www.ICGtesting.com
Printed in the USA
LVOW11s2332011216
515431LV00001B/149/P